STOP ROMMEL!

Book four of the Sword series

STOP ROMMEL!

Alan Savage

The first world edition published in Great Britain 1998 by
SEVERN HOUSE PUBLISHERS LTD of
9–15 High Street, Sutton, Surrey SM1 1DF.
First published in the USA 1998 by
SEVERN HOUSE PUBLISHERS INC., of
595 Madison Avenue, New York, NY 10022.

British Library Cataloguing in Publication Data

Savage, Alan
     Stop Rommel !
     1.   Intelligence officers – Fiction
     2.   World War, 1939-1945 – Campaigns – Africa, North - Fiction
     3.   War stories
     1.   Title
     823.9'14 [F]

     ISBN 0-7278-5367-8

Typeset by Hewer Text Composition Services Limited,
Edinburgh, Scotland.
Printed and bound in Great Britain by
MPG Books Ltd, Bodmin, Cornwall.

Contents

'Or were I in the wildest waste,
Sae black and bare, sae black and bare.
The desert were a paradise,
If thou wert there, if thou wert there.'

Robert Burns

PART ONE

Learning

'Men, some to business, some to pleasure take;
But every woman is at heart a rake:
Men, some to quiet, some to public strife;
But every lady would be a queen for life.'

Alexander Pope

Chapter One

The Desert

The explosion was almost like a rifle shot, echoing across the desert; the truck swung to and fro before coming to rest, one wheel over the edge of a small wadi. "My God!" shouted Margo Cartwright. "What *happened?*" She held her forehead where it had bumped the windscreen, fortunately without breaking the glass.

"Blow out," John Warrey said at her shoulder; he had been seated in the back and had escaped the worst of the sudden shock.

"Damn and blast and—" Graham Poultrie commented. He had been behind the wheel.

"Save your breath," Margo suggested, using her right to command. "Sufyan!" The Nigerian obligingly got down from the back of the truck, where he had been enjoying a siesta during the long heat of the middle of the day. Margo also got out, stretching as she did so. She was a tall, raunchy women, with narrow hips and a small bust, and flowing auburn hair which she invariably wore loose, even in the desert; it framed her somewhat gaunt but undeniably handsome features. She wore khaki pants under a bush shirt, a flat hat, canvas boots and dark glasses. She looked what she was – a woman who did things. But also a woman who could be impatient if frustrated. "Well?" she demanded.

Sufyan was bending beside the front wheel. "It is flat, Miss Cartwright."

"I can see that," Margo said. The tyre was shredded. "But what

3

about the truck?" Sufyan pushed up his tarboosh to scratch his head; the entire wheel hung over the edge of the wadi, which was not more than a foot deep – but the axel was resting on the lip.

"Heck." Graham stood beside Margo, and followed Sufyan's example in pushing his topee forward to scratch the back of his head. He was a somewhat plump little man, but there had been nothing wrong with his driving, till this moment. "I'm sorry, Margo. I lost control."

"Yes," Margo said grimly. "Where are we, Johnnie?"

John Warrey had also got down, and was looking around him with some disquiet. They had been following the stony ground to avoid entering the sand seas which lay to either side south of the Egyptian-Libyan border. But the track was relatively narrow and there was a lot of sand in the low hills with which they were surrounded. Above them the afternoon sun scorched down from a cloudless sky and the heat seemed to rise from the desert floor in waves, leaving one breathless. He reached into the back of the truck and pulled out his map case. He was a tall, powerfully built man in his late twenties, with somewhat aquiline features but strong mouth and chin. Like Poultrie, or indeed Margo herself, he wore a bush jacket and loose trousers, canvas ankle boots and a flat hat. He hadn't known Margo Cartwright very well before this trip, had been hired as her navigator in this particular photographic expedition, feeling very much the new boy in the group; Graham had apparently been driving her for years, and Sufyan had also accompanied her on more than one Saharan expedition.

He had wondered what one actually photographed in the Sahara, and who paid her to do it? Just as he had wondered just what happened on long and utterly intimate trips like this one. In this spring of 1939, while women were claiming more freedom with every day, they still did not, as a rule, drive off into the desert in the company of three men, not one of whom was either husband or fiancé . . . or even boyfriend, so far as he knew.

4

He had very rapidly been enlightened. Margo Cartwright, internationally known photographer, famous for going where no man, much less woman, had ever been before to obtain her pictures, dazzling in evening dress when the occasion required it, or in sports gear at the appropriate time, could equally become almost a man when necessary, and expected to be treated as one, when necessary. In any event, when the expedition had left Chad it had consisted of four trucks and sixteen people, and there had been less sense of intimacy. John Warrey, a rugby-playing extrovert who enjoyed ocean yachting when not applying himself to his desk in his father's architectural office – hence his navigational skills – liked his women to be women. And yet had been forced into fashion, soon overcoming the temptation to glance after her as she wandered behind bush or rock to perform her necessaries. The trouble was that if she lived like a man and spoke like a man she looked like a woman and smelt like one too.

But that had been several weeks ago, in Chad. Since then, in the lake-dotted mountains rising to the Tibesti Plateau, he had watched her photographing Bedouin mating habits and Bedouin births, together with Bedouin feasts and even a Bedouin blood feud, at which she had watched blood fly without turning a hair. She was one of the guys, all right. He wondered how old she was? Presumably he could look her up in *Who's Who* when he got home; it hadn't occured to him to do this before joining the expedition.

Now he suddenly wondered if they were going to *get* home. It had been Margo's decision, after they left Tibesti, to divide the expedition, send three of the trucks north on the pre-selected route for Tunis, while with the remaining vehicle and only three companions, she had turned north-east for Egypt. That had required a good deal of logistical preparation, to make sure they would not run out of petrol. And in addition, 'Judging by the map, if we're to avoid the sand, we'll have to swing up into Cyrenaica before we can reach the Egyptian border,' he had told her.

'So? I like Italians.' As always, her decision had been final. And they had had a trouble free-trip – until now.

John spread the map on the front seat. "I reckon we are here." He made a little cross on the stiff paper with his pencil.

Margo leaned against his shoulder to look. "And that is the track?"

"Right. It doesn't exist, map-wise, right here, but when we join it, you'll see it leads between the Great Sand Sea and the Calanscio Sand Sea, and eventually joins the cross track to Siwa Oasis. Which is where we are heading for. Were," he added.

Margo continued to study the map. "How far is it from here to where the track begins?"

John opened his dividers. "Roughly fifty miles."

"But presumably, if there is a track, there must be traffic."

"Sometimes. Trouble is, as far as I can see, that track doesn't lead anywhere. It just comes out of the desert, but this is not a normal trans-Saharan route."

"So that we are in a shitting awful mess," she remarked, and returned to the front of the truck.

Graham was now sitting on the ground, his head in his arms. "I really am most terribly sorry," he said. "I was taken by surprise."

"If you say you're sorry again," Margo told him, "I will kick you in the balls. Well?" she asked Sufyan.

"What we need, Miss Cartwright, is a very big jack or a lot of men."

"How many men?"

"Enough to lift the truck. Maybe a dozen. If they are strong."

Margo gave him a look that would have shrivelled a lesser man. "I think we could do with some tea." Sufyan hurried to the back of the truck and began setting up his primus. Margo returned to where John had taken off his topee to wipe sweat from his brow; the map remained spread on the seat. "You say it's about fifty miles to the beginning of the track, then another

6

fifty miles to the cross track, all without any guarantee we'll run into traffic. How far is it to Siwa as the crow flies?"

John did some more work with his dividers. "Just about seventy. But—"

"Then that's our best choice."

"It isn't, Margo. Believe me. That seventy miles is all across sand. It'll seem more like four hundred and seventy. Following the track will be much easier going."

"For a hundred miles," she mused.

"If we travel as light as possible, just food and water, we could do it in eight days," John said.

"You mean leave all my gear behind? All my negatives?"

"Well . . . no one's likely to touch them out here. We could come back for them when we get some replacement transport."

She gazed at him, lips twisting in indecision. "Do we have eight days' water left?"

"Not really. But if we were very careful . . ."

"As I said, a shitting awful mess," she remarked, and then Graham stood up. "Holy Christ," he muttered.

All of their head turned to look in the same direction. Topping the ridge to the west, not half a mile away, was a line of camels, each with its rider, and each rider with a rifle resting on his thigh.

Margot reached into the truck for her binoculars, levelled them. "Senussi."

"Is that good or bad?"

"I don't think it's good."

"Just who are these people. Are they Bedouins?"

"Actually, yes. But the Senussi, more properly the Sanusiyah, are a religious fundamentalist movement founded just on a hundred years ago by Sidi Muhammad ibn Ali as-Sanusi. They've been resisting the Italians for years."

"I thought the Italians had pacified all Libya?"

"So they say. The war with the Senussi officially ended ten

years ago, But I'm not sure all of the Senussi know that. At least where they can make a killing."

"Twenty-five men, Miss Cartwright." Sufyan had been counting.

Graham was swabbing his neck again. "What do you think they want?"

Margo looked at him, and he gulped.

"They can't be sure you're a woman, at that distance," John said. "Get into the truck." She hesitated, unused to taking orders, then obeyed. "Rifles," John said. He had done his stint in the territorials, been commissioned, and found taking military command a simple matter – although he had never actually shot at another human being.

"Four against twenty-five?" Margo asked, from shelter.

"We have a strong position," John asserted. "And hopefully, if they see we are determined, they'll not attack us." The men now also got into the truck, rifles at the ready.

"I suspect they may have been tracking us for some time," Margo said. The truck had been travelling hardly faster than a camel over the past few days.

"In which case they'll know what they're after," Graham muttered.

"You are being racistly absurd," John told him. "Do you really suppose a party of Senussi warriors are going to track and attack us just to get their hands on Margo? What are they really after, Sufyan?"

"I cannot say, effendi. Our arms, certainly. But anything else of value that we may have."

"Here comes of one them," Margo said. If she was afraid she didn't show it; that her shirt was soaked in sweat could at least partly be heat – they were all sweating profusely.

A single camel made its way down the slope towards the truck. "You or me?" John asked.

Margo shrugged. "You seem to have taken command."

"I'll need an interpreter."

"Sufyan speaks Arabic," Margo said.

"Sufyan." John opened the door and stepped down, rifle resting on his shoulder.

The Senussi gazed at him. He was wrapped in his burnous and only his eyes were visible. But he carried a sword as well as his rifle, and a great curved dagger in his belt, while his camel accoutrements were of best leather. He spoke in a rather high voice, but resonant enough.

"He asks, do we need help, effendi," Sufyan said.

"What do you reckon?"

"It is better his people do not come down here, effendi. If they come down, they will see how few we are."

"Agreed. Tell him that while we have broken down, we are expecting assistance to arrive by truck at any moment, and we will wait for that."

"He will know that is not true, effendi."

"Tell him."

Sufyan spoke for several seconds. The Senussi warrior listened, then turned his camel and walked it back up the slope.

"Now they will wait, and watch," Sufyan said.

"So will we."

They got back into the truck. Graham sat in front, beside his useless wheel. Margo and John sat in the next row. Sufyan took the back, peering through the flap, rifle thrust forward. "Have we achieved anything?" Margo asked.

"We've given them something to think about. They're going to have to make sure there isn't help coming before they do anything else."

"They'll know that by morning."

"So we must get out of here tonight. That's how we'd have to make the walk anyway, by night, resting during the heat of the day. I reckon we could have that tea now. And grub?"

Sufyan got busy. "I couldn't eat a thing," Margo peered out of the window at the ridge. "They've gone."

9

"I shouldn't think they've gone too far." She opened the other door. "Where are you going?" he asked.

"Into that little gully. Do you mind?"

"Well, keep your head down."

He watched her crawl across the track and disappear from sight, then looked back up at the ridge. For all his apparently calm handling of the situation, he had not been been in a position like this before, actually in danger of his life from other human beings as opposed to the sea and the wind. His mind kept filling with all the horrendous things he had read of what desert tribesmen, or their women, did to their captured enemies. Then he tried to reason. Even if the Senussi had been tracking them, why should they attack? They were bound to lose several of their people if they did so, with what possible gain? Of course, if they were clued up, they might reckon that a woman as famous as Margo Cartwright would fetch a handsome ransom – in which case her life, as well as her chastity, were probably safe. But that did not go for her male companions.

Margo crawled back into the truck beside him, and Sufyan served tea and biscuits. Graham appeared to be asleep. "Are we going to die, Johnnie?" she asked.

"I sincerely hope not. You ever been in this position before?"

"Not really. We're so near . . ." there was a catch in her voice, and he squeezed her hand.

"We'll make it."

"But once we leave the truck . . . they'll follow us, easily enough, and tomorrow they'll have us in the open."

"We can't stay here, Margo. We have only a few days' water left."

The afternoon drifted by. There was no sign of the Senussi. John guessed that they had sent some of their people to the north, to see if there *was* any help coming for the Europeans. "I think they've gone," Graham said, suddenly waking up.

"I wouldn't count on it," John said. "What do you reckon, Sufyan?"

"I think they are still there, effendi."

"Rubbish," Graham said. "I'm going to have a look."

"I wouldn't recommend it, old boy," John said.

Graham opened the door and stepped down. He looked at the ridge, then took a few steps away from the truck. "See? Nobody there." He turned back to them – and spun round and crashed to the ground. They had hardly heard the shot.

Margo stared at the stricken man, her mouth sagging open. John had to shake her shoulder to wake her up. "Cover me," he snapped.

Sufyan was already firing from the rear of the truck. John leapt out, reached Graham in two strides. Behind him he heard the explosion of Margo's rifle, and again, and at the same time saw a burst of sand only a few feet away. There was no time to be lost, and it took only a look to see that Graham was dying; he had been hit in the chest and blood was frothing out of his mouth. John grasped him by the armpits, half dragged him up and retreated as fast as he could, pulling Graham behind him. Graham's tunic was a mass of blood, but blood was now only dribbling from his open mouth. He made not a sound and John reckoned he might be already dead, even before his body jerked under the impact of another bullet.

He reached the door, and Margo helped drag Graham in. The door was slammed shut. The firing ceased. "Is he . . .?"

Graham's blood seemed to be everywhere, on John's clothes, on the seat, pooling on the truck floor. There was no heartbeat, and close to, John could see the terrible extent of the wound in his back. He was surprised, but secretly pleased, at his lack of emotion; he had never held a dead body in his arms before. "Open that other door," he said.

"You can't just push him out."

"He can't stay here in this heat. There's another couple of hours to darkness."

She bit her lip, but opened the door. John pushed Graham's body out onto the sand. "Are we all going to look like that by tomorrow?" she asked.

"Not if we keep out of sight. You okay, Sufyan?" he called.

"They are many men, effendi."

"Yeah." John gave Margo a drink of water from his canteen, then crawled through the truck to give Sufyan a swig before drinking himself, and then changing his bloodstained shirt and pants. "What are our chances if we surrender?"

"Now, effendi? Now it is not good. They have – how do you say? – tasted blood. They will kill us, and they will rape Miss Cartwright. Maybe afterwards they will kill her as well. But it would not be good."

John returned to the front. "I heard that," Margo said.

"You don't like that idea, then."

She stuck out her tongue at him. Suddenly she was an extremely vulnerable, and extremely young, woman. Someone he could like, rather than respect and accept as a superior.

The Senussi fired occasionally, but as the sun disappeared the shooting stopped.

"They will come in the night," Sufyan suggested.

Margo shuddered. "I really am sorry I got you into this mess," she said to John.

"I volunteered, remember?"

"That cocktail party." She sighed. "I really wasn't sure whether I should take you on or not. Oh, I never doubted your credentials, but a new man often causes trouble. And when one is big and strong and sporty, and likes his pint, the trouble often comes sooner than later."

"And in my case?"

She gave a little shrug. "You have been no trouble at all. You know, every new man feels obliged to make a pass. I'm not sure whether it's simply to do with his being masculine, and trying to prove it, or the feeling that I wouldn't have had him along in the first place if I didn't want to sleep with him, or maybe just the feeling that I'd be insulted if he didn't try, if you follow me. They all have to be slapped down. But you never made a pass."

"Don't think I didn't want to. I suppose sailing on small boats teaches you to keep your libido under control."

"I'm glad. That you wanted to."

"What would you have done if I had?"

"God, what a conversation, at such a time. I just like to be myself. I suppose basically I'm a chaste person."

"You know something? If – I beg your pardon – *when* we get out of here, I'd like to take you to dinner. Shepheard's. How about that?"

"I'd like that." Her head jerked as a shot whanged into the body of the truck. It was just on dusk.

Margo raised her rifle, but John shook his head. "They can't harm us in here, with that long-range stuff. Save our bullets for when they decide to get closer. See anything, Sufyan?" he called.

"Only the flash, effendi. But it came from the east. They have us surrounded."

"Jesus," Margo said. "So much for walking out tonight,"

John chewed his lip. Attempting to walk to Siwa had been a pretty impossible dream anyway. But to stay here meant they were going to die even more quickly. The Senussi obviously had all the water they wanted. Even if they decided against rushing the truck in the dark, they could just sit there and wait for their victims to die of thirst. He began to wish they *would* attack.

Several more shots were fired but the people in the truck did not reply. Now it was growing very dark; the moon would not rise until after midnight. It was very hot in the truck – they had to keep the windows closed both to repel the odour of Graham's body, and the flies feeding on it.

"I'd like a bath," Margo said. "A huge, hot tub. One should always be clean when one is about to die."

13

"And one very seldom is," John pointed out.

"Tell me about yourself."

"I think you know everything relevant."

"You never married. Do you have a girlfriend?"

He thought of Aileen Southern. "Perhaps."

"Aha! I was married, you know. But we split. Maybe that's why I'm cautious about men."

"Children?"

"No, thank God. Don't get me wrong. I'd like children. But by the right man."

"How'd you get into this business?"

"Began as a hobby. Then I was in Berlin in thirty-three, got some shots of the Reichstag going up, and what followed. I sold those at a profit to a British paper, and they gave me an assignment. Fashion and the huntin', shootin', fishin' brigade first. But it seems I have the knack of catching people just at the right moment. So I became popular. Then I started photographing faraway places. Simple as that."

"Seems like you had a pretty lucky ride."

"I won't argue with that."

John peered into the darkness. The whole Senussi nation could be out there, crawling towards them, and he wouldn't know it. "Anything moving, Sufyan?"

"I do not think so, effendi."

"Well . . ." he peered at his watch. "They must be planning something, because they haven't fired a shot for a good hour."

Nor did they for the next hour. "Maybe they're like Red Indians, and never fight at night," Margo suggested.

"I wouldn't count on that," John said.

"I really need to go," Margo said. They all did, so they covered each other as in turn they left the truck as quietly as possible. The darkness was now utter, and they clearly were not seen. But Graham's body reminded them that this was no nightmare. Margo eventually slept. John nodded off several times, but jerked himself back into wakefulness. Sufyan seemed indestructible. And suddenly it began to grow light.

John stretched, peered out of the windows. The sand and the stones remained exactly as they had been last night. There was no movement. "I think they have gone away, effendi," Sufyan said.

"Just like that? Why should they do that? After having attacked us in the first place?"

"I think— Listen!"

Margo sat up. "An engine!"

"More than one."

She reached for the door.

"Hold on," he said. "We don't *know* our friends have gone."

She bit her lip and stared to the north, where the track wound between the dunes. "There," she said. "Oh, glory be! I think I'm going to cry."

There were four trucks, and each flew the Italian flag on its bonnet.

"How did you know we were here?" John asked Captain Umberto, sipping a reasonably cold glass of white wine – the captain had an icebox in his truck – and inhaling the delicious scent of cooking spaghetti.

The Italians had acted with a great deal of military nous. On hearing there were warlike Senussi about, they had set up a perimeter, manned on each side by machine-guns, while a burial squad had immediately been detailed to inter poor Graham. "I suppose there are worse places to lie forever," Margo had said. Obviously it was out of the question to attempt to take him back to civilisation. Now she had retired into the interior of the truck to change her clothes; the Italian soldiers were clearly interested.

"We did not know you were here," Captain Umberto said; he wore the uniform of the military police. He was an extremely affable young man, handsome, with a little moustache, and energetic eyes. John had liked him immediately, quite apart

15

from acknowledging him and his men as their saviours. But now he suddenly had a feeling that the officer was lying. Whatever for? "This is a routine patrol," Umberto explained. "We make them regularly, to keep the Senussi in order. You agree this is necessary, eh?

"Oh, absolutely."

"But we do not often come across foreign travellers being attacked," Umberto said. "It is very sad about your driver. But this is a strange route for you to take. From Tibesti, you say? That is a very long way away. To the west. From Tibesti you should have gone north, into Benghazi or Tripoli."

"Miss Cartwright wanted to go to Egypt," John explained.

Umberto regarded him for several seconds, and John had another odd feeling, that the Italian thought *he* was lying. Then he grinned and refilled their glasses. "Who can follow the reasoning of a woman, eh? Now, my men will lift your truck back onto the track, eh? And then we will escort you to a position where you will have no trouble in driving to Egypt."

"We will be very grateful. But we need petrol, food, water and a whole lot of things. We had planned to obtain supplies at Siwa."

"Siwa," Umberto said. "Yes, of course. There are those things in Siwa. Ah, Signorina Cartwright." He stood up as Margo emerged. She had done wonders, considering the complete lack of facilities, wore a dress, had her hair tied up in a bandanna, and even looked clean – the Italians had provided her with a bucket of water. "You are a sight for sore eyes, eh?"

"What about those Senussi?" Margo enquired.

"They are far away by now. They must have heard us coming."

"They murdered my driver," Margo pointed out.

"I know. I was saying to Signor Warrey, it is a great tragedy."

"Aren't you going to arrest them?"

"Sadly, signorina, I doubt that will be possible. They will be

16

many miles away by now, in the desert. And there were twenty-five of them, you say. Who can tell who fired the fatal shot?"

"They were all guilty," Margo snapped.

"I agree. And should we ever find them, we will treat them as all being guilty. But at least you are safe. The famous Miss Cartwright. Are your photographs also safe?"

"So far as I know."

"It would give me great pleasure to be able to look at them."

"I'm afraid you can't, right now. They are all in negative. But I will send you a copy of the book when it is published."

"How nice," Umberto said. "And will you sign it for me, signorina?"

"Of course. I owe you my life. All of our lives."

"One does one's best," Umberto said modestly.

John had an uncanny feeling that he was a spectator at a play, that the two were communicating, or conversely, attempting not to communicate, on a subject of which he knew nothing. But in any event, he reminded himself, his part in this adventure was virtually over, now that they were in the care of the Italians.

They left as soon as they had finished their meal. No food had ever tasted so good, especially as it was accompanied by some more wine, red this time. "You people certainly know how to live, even in the desert," John told Umberto, who had decided to travel in their truck, once it had been dragged out of the wadi by the concerted efforts of nearly the entire Italian force, and the wheel had been changed. An Italian soldier took over the driving, and Umberto sat in the back with Margo and John; Sufyan preferred to remain by the tailgate; John got the impression he didn't trust the Italians any more than the Senussi.

"Why should a man do without his creature comforts, signor?" Umberto asked. "But alas, out here one has to do without *some* comforts." He smiled at Margo, but she remained in a brown study, no doubt brooding on Graham's death, John supposed. Perhaps he should be doing the same. It would hit him eventually, he knew. But for the moment he was too happy to be utterly secure, events, good or bad, taken utterly out of his hands. Perhaps he was not really the stuff military commanders were made of, he thought.

"What's that?" Margo suddenly seemed to wake up. They had been driving for over an hour, and to their left, half submerged in a low hill, was a gate and armed soldiers. "It looks like a fort."

"It is a fort," Umberto agreed. "They are necessary, from time to time, to control the Senussi."

John peered at the hill. The fort, if it was a fort, didn't look much like anything out of *Beau Geste*. There were no towers, no crenellated walls. No walls at all, that he could make out. Just the fence. But within the fence there were a lot of men and vehicles. He suspected it was more probably a fuel and munitions dump. To deal with the Senussi?

"It looks very impressive," Margo asked. "Where exactly are we?"

Umberto smiled graciously. "Close to the border, eh?"

"Do you think I could photograph it? It would go very well with my book, as a finale, if you like."

"Alas, signorina, photographs of military establishments are not permitted."

"Oh." Margo gave him a bright smile, and relapsed back into her brood.

"There is the cross track," Umberto said, about half an hour later.

"And traffic," John said, watching the column of trucks heading east.

"Slow down," Umberto told his driver. "We will be following them, and we do not want to eat their dust, eh?"

"What would they be carrying?"

Umberto shrugged. "Various supplies for the garrison in Al-Jaghbub. It is an administrative centre. We will reach there tonight."

*   *   *

Al-Jaghbub was an oasis brimming with date palms. A walled town, the houses were dominated by the tomb of Sidi Muhammad, but it also contained an Islamic university. John had had no idea such an intellectual flowering existed in the desert.

Umberto was as good as his word, and they rumbled to a halt in the forecourt of a rather splendid looking hotel just on dusk. "May I take photographs here?" Margo asked.

"Of course. What do you wish to photograph?"

"Why, you and your men, Captain. Our saviours."

"Ah. That is very kind." He bellowed orders, and his men assembled round him, rather like some vast cricket team, John thought.

"Is there enough light?" he asked.

"Just about," Margo said, and closed the shutter. "Hold it," she said. "I want another." This done, the Italians broke ranks, chattering happily to each other. "Now I'm ready for a hot bath," Margo declared.

"It is all arranged," Umberto said. "And for you, eh, Signor Warrey?"

"Not forgetting Sufyan," John reminded him.

"Ah, yes. The African." Umberto was condescending. "It is all arranged."

White-jacketed stewards were waiting to escort them through the hotel lobby, where both civilians and officers, all men, turned their heads to look at Margo, and then up the stairs to the first floor, which had large bedrooms opening on to deep verandahs, separated one from the other by high walls. Once again it was nearly impossible to reconcile this amount of civilisation with the stark reality of the desert only a few hours ago, the dead body, the flies . . . the awareness that one too might soon be dead.

John sank into the hot tub with a deep sigh of relief. Well, now, he thought, that particular adventure was over. It was not one he wanted to repeat. In a couple of days' time he would be on a steamship cruising up the Mediterranean. He would be sipping cocktails, straightening his tie, and perhaps ogling the odd pretty girl, supposing there were any. Would Margo be with him? He rather doubted that. But perhaps they could arrange to meet up in London. And before then there was the arranged dinner at Shepheard's. Now that was promising.

There was a knock on the door, which he had locked. He got out of the tub, wrapped himself in a towel, and dripping water, padded through the bedroom to turn the key.

"I have come at a bad time," Umberto said.

"Not your fault. I was lingering. It's been quite a while since last I sat in a hot tub."

"In Nigeria, eh?"

"In Chad, actually. But come in. Make yourself at home." He returned to the bathroom, dressed himself. He had no really clean clothes, but some were cleaner than others.

"Will you join me in a drink?" Umberto asked.

"Good idea. What do we have?"

"Some wine." Umberto poured. "Yes, it must have been a long trip. And an adventurous one. Tell me, signor, have you known Miss Cartwright long?"

"Sadly, no."

"But you accompanied her on so rigorous a journey?"

John came back into the bedroom, knotting his tie. "She required a stand-in navigator; her regular had been taken ill. I happen to be a navigator of sorts. At least on ships, and the desert isn't all that different to the sea; one still needs to take a noon sight from time to time. So I volunteered."

"But you knew where you were going?"

John drank some wine. "Well, I did, up to a point. Margo was planning a cross-Sahara expedition, Chad, Tibesti, Tunis, photographing the Bedouin at work and play."

"So you travelled from Chad to Tibesti. This is all French territory. And you were going on to Tunis. That is also French."

"So they say. We didn't see a lot of Frenchmen."

20

"But after Tibesti, Signorina Cartwright changed her mind and her plans."

Fully dressed now, John lay on the bed. He thought it might be considered a hard bed, by some more used to such comforts, but after spending some weeks sleeping either in the truck or on the desert sand it felt like heaven. "I don't know if she changed her mind or her plans, captain. Because I don't know what had been in her mind before."

"But when you left Tibesti, with presumably all the photographs and the information one could wish about the Bedouin, she divided her caravan, is that not so? She sent the three main supply trucks to the north-west, and Tunis, her announced destination, but she elected to take the remaining truck and travel across the desert to Egypt. Did this not strike you as strange, even dangerous?"

"Miss Cartwright is her own boss, Umberto."

"Absolutely. When she told you what she wanted to do, and you laid a course, as you must have done, did you not realise that it would take you into and through the lower half of Cyrenaica? Italian territory?"

"I did point this out to Miss Cartright. But she did not object. You're not going to tell me we needed visas to come out of the desert?"

"No, no," Umberto said.

"Then I'm not sure I follow your problem? Why this great interest in our movements. Oh, I realise it was a foohardy thing to do, but you see we were under the impression that the Senussi had been pacified. Signor Mussolini has said this."

"Pacifying natives always takes longer than those at home appreciate," Umberto said. "Yes, it was a foolhardy journey to make. Quite apart from the Senussi. There are so many other imponderables. Breakdowns. Such as you had. How would you have got your truck back on the road, had we not come along?"

"We were going to walk it."

"A hundred miles, in the desert? You would not have survived."

John began to feel just a little bit nettled. He sat up. "Frankly, old man, there didn't seem any alternative."

"Quite so. And the British never give up, eh? But Miss Cartwright must have known all of these things. She is an experienced traveller, is she not? She knows the desert. Yet, with a woman's whim, she suddenly determines to up and take the chance, eh?"

"Yes. So we took a risk. But here we are. Safe and sound. Believe me, Umberto, we are, and will remain, eternally grateful to you and your men for digging us out of that mess. But it's over and done with, right?"

"Unless, perhaps, it was not a woman's whim that determined Miss Cartwright to take that extraordinary route across the desert. Into Cyrenaica."

John frowned at him. "Do you know, I have not the slightest idea what you are talking about?"

"I should have thought it is fairly obvious," Umberto said. "Your employer is a British spy."

Chapter Two

Decision

"Would you mind repeating that?" John asked.

"It is very simple, and very obvious," Umberto said. "We have a dossier on Miss Cartwright. Did she not come from nowhere, as one might say, about four years ago, suddenly travelling around the world, taking photographs and writing travel books? Have you read any of her books?"

"I'm afraid not."

"But you have seen her photographs, surely?"

"Some of them."

"How would you rate them?"

"Well . . ." John bit his lip. He would have to say that they weren't all that good. But he had supposed that was his uninformed opinion.

"Quite. I do not think you will find her books on any bestseller lists. Yet she receives a lot of publicity, and constant employment. Now why should that be so? This question intrigued some of my superiors from the start. Then they began to piece together a map, a mosaic, if you like, of the places where she has been, and photographed. We can take them in a clockwise order, if you like.

"There was her celebrated journey through the delights of Denmark, down as far as the Kiel Canal. The Germans weren't very bright about that. Then there was her celebrated Alps adventure, where she went up and down hills, snapping away, but most of the shots were of the valleys and the various military installations to be found there. Then there was her exploration of the delights of southern Italy. It is amazing how attracted she was to the seaports, and especially places like Taranto and Messina. These are naval ports, as you may know, Signor Warrey. She did not actually visit Ethiopia. Perhaps because that was already a *fait accompli*.

"But now we have her trekking across the desert, for the second time. On the first occasion, she was travelling from Nigeria to Tunis, photographing the people of the Hoggar, but she managed to lose her way, and so found herself in Ghadames, which as I am sure you know is just across the Tunis-Libya border, in Libya, and where we have certain fortifications, as there is a road and therefore the obvious place for the French to invade, should they ever have that notion. Of course, as a professional photographer, she was snapping away. Such a quaint place. Ideal for her book.

"Now, on this occasion, she breaks up her caravan on a quite unreasonable whim to reach Egypt by a direct route. But one that takes her through Cyrenaica, which abuts Egypt, and in which she is again anxious to snap away at any military installations that may turn up. Do you not find this very interesting?"

John scratched his head. "Great Britain and Italy are not at war, Umberto."

"Not as yet. But we very nearly came to war only three years ago over your absurd objections to us taking our rightful place in Ethiopia. And you British are well aware that our Duce has signed a pact with Signor Hitler, which may one day involve us in war. It is certainly in British interests to know as much as possible about our military installations."

"So, you mean your coming to our rescue was not, after all, a stroke of fortune?"

Umberto grinned. "We have an agent in Tibesti who radioed us of this change in plans. So we came looking for her."

"And was it you sent the Senussi?"

Umberto shook his head. "We find the Senussi difficult to

24

work with. No, that was a genuine attack. But I am sure you will agree that we turned up in the nick of time."

"Absolutely. So, do you propose to arrest Miss Cartwright? And me? I would say your evidence is a little circumstantial."

"Of course we do not intend to arrest you, Signor Warrey. You are clearly an innocent party. Nor do we intend to arrest Miss Cartright, certainly at this time."

"But you intend to confiscate her photographs."

"Now, why should we do that? She has not had the opportunity to photograph anything of importance on this trip, thanks to our rescue. She may have some idea where that fuel store is, but she will find it very difficult to pinpoint on a map. No, no, you will be escorted to the Egyptian frontier tomorrow, with our best wishes. But I think it would be a good idea for you to have a chat with her and convey to her that she is no longer welcome in Italy or in any territory controlled by Italy. I am sure you can do this without causing offence. Now, as soon as you are dressed, shall we not entertain the lovely lady to dinner?"

Could the man possibly be telling the truth? John would have said that the least likely person in the world to be a spy was Margo Cartwright. But then, was it not the business of a spy *not* to look like one, talk like one, behave like one? And there was that very strange decision to drive across the desert the wrong way, as it were. Which had damn near cost them their lives.

He studied her throughout dinner, at which she and Umberto both engaged in lively conversation. But Umberto left them early, to enjoy their brandies in peace.

"Do you know," Margo said. "I thought that fellow was going to begin flirting with me. And I had no idea how to deal with it. Italians are inclined to come on rather heavy when they get worked up."

"I think he has other things on his mind," John suggested, uncertain whether to tell her Umberto's opinion then, or to wait until after they had reached Egyptian, and therefore

British-protected, soil. He was inclined to do it as soon as possible, but it could not be in a public place – he had no idea what her reactions might be.

"Is that so?" she remarked. "I would never have thought it. You don't mean he's had a go at you?"

"No, he hasn't. I suppose, now that our adventure is over, I am no longer in your employ."

"True. But you'll be paid until you regain England. That was the deal."

"I look forward to it. What I was wondering was, as I am no longer your employee, if we could have a little get together?"

"We're going to do that, in Shepheard's, tomorrow night. Remember?"

"And you'd rather not before, is that it?"

"Johnnie, getting together with you is going to be a lot of fun. I know it. And good things can wait. Besides, I don't know you very well, and just about twenty-four hours ago someone I did know very well was shot dead before my eyes. I'm sure you'll understand that at this moment I'm not in the mood for a bit of fun."

"I do understand that. It's just that I have some things to say to you, and I'd like to say them in private."

"Oh, God," she said. "You're not going to profess undying love for me, or propose marriage, I hope? I don't believe in either." She stood up. "I think I'll go to bed. I am very tired."

"But you do believe in getting together," he said. "When you are in the mood."

"Doesn't everyone?" she asked.

Oddly, he found himself at least as much turned on as irritated by her insouciance, her suggestion that if she chose to sleep with him it would be in the nature of a reward for his good behaviour over the past three months rather than any special interest in him as a person.

He found himself inclining towards the belief that Umberto

might have been telling the truth about her. In that case he needed to keep himself on her wavelength, remind himself that he was going to have an affair with a beautiful woman who was also both famous and a spy. He hoped he wouldn't disappoint her.

It was not to be so easily accomplished, however, as Margo had no doubt known all along. They duly crossed the border at dawn, to be greeted by a half-asleep Egyptian customs officer who had to go and wake his English superior. "Margo Cartwright?" asked that individual, peering suspiciously at Margo's passport. "My word. We were not informed."

"We had some trouble," Margo explained.

"With the Italians?" The official looked at Umberto even more suspiciously.

"Good lord, no. With the Senussi. These gentlemen got us out, and have now delivered us safely."

"Well ..." he scratched his head. "Where is it you wish to go?"

"Cairo," Margo said.

"Oh, quite. Well ... your best bet is to go into Siwa. There's quite a good road from there to the coast."

"Isn't there a desert road from Siwa to Cairo?"

"Yes, there is. But it isn't very good for most of the way. You'll do better by the coast, believe me."

"We'll take your word for it. Have we enough petrol to get us to Siwa, Sufyan? How far is it, anyway?"

"Oh, not far," the official said. "A matter of thirty miles."

"Thank you. Well, Captain Umberto, again, we shall forever be in your debt."

"I was but doing my duty," Umberto said gallantly, but he held her close for a kiss on each cheek, and allowed his hand to drift down and give her bottom a gentle squeeze. "Perhaps we shall meet again."

"Not if I can help it," Margo declared, after Umberto had kissed John on each cheek as well, but had refrained from squeezing *his* bottom, and they were seated together in the truck while Sufyan negotiated the bumpy track.

"Didn't you like him?" John asked innocently. "What would you have done if he *had* made a pass last night?"

"Oh, lain back and tried to enjoy it, I suppose. Only resist when the odds are on your side, is my motto."

He could not resist asking, "Is that part of your training? But you resisted the Senussi."

"No, no," she said. "*You* resisted the Senussi, remember? I was just obeying your orders. As for training, I suppose one could call it experience."

"Meaning you have been raped before?"

"Oh, often. Goes with the job."

"Sometimes I have an overwhelming urge to put you across my knee and spank you," he said.

"We're not at Shepheard's yet," she reminded him.

Nor did they get there that day. They did obtain petrol and some fresh food in Siwa, where their appearance aroused a great deal of interest, which meant it was well into the morning before they managed to leave. John would indeed have liked to explore, because Siwa had once been the site of the temple of Ammon, which Alexander the Great had visited in 332 BC, to be hailed as a god by the priests. There were Roman ruins as well as ancient Egyptian, but to his surprise Margo never snapped a lens, was only in a hurry to get on.

From Siwa, it was a hundred-mile drive to the coast, which they reached at a village called Mersa Matruh. The road was quite good, but also crowded, and that took them up to a late lunch. Then it was a drive of over a hundred and fifty miles to Alexandria. This was extremely pleasant, as the surface was good, the Mediterranean surfed gently onto the beach on their left, the overloaded trains rumbled by on the railway to the right, and they passed through villages with evocative names, such as Abul Haggay, Fuka and El Alamein. But this road was even more crowded than the one up from Siwa, and it was dusk when they reached the city.

"How far is it to Cairo?" Margo asked.

John studied the map. "Another hundred miles, I'd say."

"Then I propose we spend the night here. Find us an hotel, Sufyan!"

This took another hour and the establishment at which they were finally accepted was certainly not the Cecil. But it did have rooms, even if none were with bath. John presumed that Margo could have obtained somewhere much more up-market by making herself known, but she seemed to wish to keep a low profile. No sooner had they checked in, however, than she announced she was going out. "Alone?" John inquired.

"There is someone I promised to visit next time I was in Alexandria," she explained.

He raised his eyebrows. "I got the impression that you had never been in Alexandria before."

"You are always getting the wrong impression," she pointed out, and departed.

John joined Sufyan in the bar; Sufyan was a Christian, and enjoyed his beer at the end of a long day.

"How long have you worked with Miss Cartwright?" John asked.

"I was with her the last time."

"I see. How did you get the job?"

"I was recommended by the Commissioner in Kano," Sufyan explained.

"I see. The Commissioner? What exactly was his role?"

"He was the Police Commissioner."

"You mean you're a Nigerian policeman?"

"You did not know this?"

"No. No one told me."

"Well, it would not have been good for the Italians to know, I think. I am seconded, eh? Now I will go home."

"Miss Cartwright knew you were a policeman, of course?"

"Of course."

"And you were seconded as her servant?"

Sufyan grinned. "I am her bodyguard, Mr Warrey. Oh, I can also cook and drive the truck. These things I was trained to do."

"I see," John said thoughtfully. It occurred to him that he had been taken, quite literally, for the longest ride in history.

Margo did not come in for dinner. "You don't suppose it is time for you to do some bodyguarding?" John asked Sufyan.

The policeman grinned. "Miss Cartwright can take care of herself, I think. Certainly in Alexandria."

John presumed he was right, had a brandy, and went to bed. He was awakened around midnight by the sound of her door opening; her room was next to his. He got up. It was a stiflingly hot night, and he had been sleeping nude. He put on his dressing gown and stepped into the empty hallway; only a single naked bulb glowed at the head of the stairs. He tapped on her door. "Who is it?"

"John." The lock turned, and the door swung in. She had been in the process of undressing, wore only a pair of knickers. He stepped inside and closed the door behind himself. "You had me sort of worried, when you didn't come in."

"There's no need to feel responsible for me," she pointed out, turning away from him and brushing her hair. But she was watching him in the mirror. Gauging his reactions? Those were pretty obvious. She was one of those women who were far more compelling naked than when dressed; there was not a blemish on her body and no fat either; the fact that she was almost boyishly slender, at both breast and thigh, did nothing to lessen her attractiveness.

"I just thought what a pity it would be if after all our adventures you were to wind up dead in a ditch."

"Raped first, of course. You have a one-track mind." She

stood up, put on a dressing gown. "I really am grateful that you should have been worrying about me. Now I would like to get some sleep."

He had to resist being treated as a casual stud. "And we're not at Shepheard's yet," he agreed.

She took him in her arms and kissed him on the nose. "Why are all men so impatient? Everything comes to he who waits, Johnnie. And it's better for a good night's sleep." To her, no doubt, he was nothing more than a child, he reflected sadly.

"You had something you wanted to say to me in private," she remarked at breakfast. "Or was that the lot?"

They were alone in one corner of a not very clean dining room; Sufyan had gone out, perhaps dispatched by his employer. And now John remembered that he did indeed have a good deal to say to her. "Who did you have dinner with?"

"Are you one of those male chauvinists who presumes that having forced his way into a woman's bedroom he then has the right to control her private life?"

"Not in the least. But I am interested. You see, if it happened to be an officer in the British Army, or more likely, in British Intelligence, I think I'm entitled to know. Because I would say that you risked my life, and cost the life of Graham Poultrie, in order to obtain certain information. Which you then didn't succeed in obtaining."

Margo studied him while she drank her coffee. "Just who the hell are you?"

"Me? In your context I am a total nobody who you happened carelessly to involve in your plans. I suppose it's being the nobody that bothers me."

She continued to study him for several seconds. Then she said, "Umberto?"

"He seemed to know a lot about you."

"Shit!" She ate some rather hard bread.

He drank coffee in turn. "On the other hand, he is, like most

31

Italian officers, a perfect gentlemen. So he did not arrest you, or confiscate your photos. He merely asked me to warn you off. The Italians are on to you, and that probably means the Germans are too. I'm sure you'll agree there are less gentlemen in the Gestapo than in the Italian Army?"

She gazed at him. "I'm sorry."

"Thank you." He discouraged several flies and buttered some bread of his own. "Have you really been a British spy for several years?"

"Is that what he said? How the hell did they decide that?"

"I don't think you really want to know that."

"I do."

"Well . . ." he shrugged and attempted to swat another inquisitive fly, without success. "The Italians are artists at heart. Someone at their intelligence headquarters had a thought: how did such a second-rate – forgive me, but you did ask and these are his words – photographer and writer, get so many back-to-back assignments. Then he had the bright idea of tracing those assignments. And bingo, all of them covered areas of Europe or Africa in which British Intelligence might conceivably be interested."

"Second-rate?"

"His words."

"Bloody Eyetie twit," she growled. "Just what do you propose to do with your knowledge?"

"You mean you could have me knocked over?"

"I could. But it would be rather pointless, if it's the Italians who told you. I mean, what have you got to tell *them*? No, I think the best thing is for us to part company, never to meet again. There's a ship leaving Alexandria for Marseilles this morning. I think you should be on it."

"Rather short notice, don't you think? Or do I sleep on deck?"

Margo opened her handbag. "I have arranged your passage. The tickets are waiting for you on the dock. They are all paid for." She threw a wallet on the table. "There are sufficient funds to get you across France and home. As promised, your final fee will be paid into your bank account next week. I hope these arrangements suit you."

"Then Shepheard's always was just pie in the sky."

She smiled. "Not at all. Should we ever be in Shepheard's Hotel, together, I give you my word that I shall sleep with you. Now, I think you need to finish your breakfast, pack your bag and get down to the dock."

He got up. "Have you ever felt like a used rag?"

"Please don't take on." She got up as well. "You have been a great success as a navigator, as a friend, and I am sure you would have been as a lover. If it hadn't been for those Senussi, this would have been a splendid trip. Now it's over. Never look back. I never do. And by the way, this conversation never happened. I do hope you remember that."

European politics had seemed remote in the centre of the Sahara. John was quite taken aback by the atmosphere of crisis which pervaded in England, with buildings being sandbagged and gas masks much in evidence. Czechoslovakia!

"Oh, Johnnie!" His mother held him close; he was her only son. "We were so worried. When we got your cable we opened a bottle of champagne. My God, you're burned black! What on earth were you doing in Alexandria?"

"It's a long story." He shook hands with his father.

"You were supposed to be in Algiers a month ago," Harry Warrey admonished.

"I wasn't in charge of the party. The famous Margo suddenly decided there was something else she wanted to photograph, and there it was. Now, what's been happening? Are we about to go to war?"

"Over Czechoslovakia? No chance. Chamberlain will sort it out. But you're supposed to register."

"For what?"

33

"Just register. So they can call you up, I suppose."

"But you said there wasn't going to be a war?"

"Hopefully there won't be. But we need to be prepared."

John considered. "If there were to be a war, would the Italians be in it?"

"I would imagine so. They're allied to the Germans."

Now that would be a pity, John thought; he had rather taken to Umberto.

"Aileen inquired after you," Judith Warrey said, archly, at breakfast the next morning; Harry Warrey had already left for the office, but he had given John a week's rest and recuperation leave. To register? "I think she was as worried as we were," Judith went on. "She really is very fond of you. You know, Johnnie, your father and I were wondering if you shouldn't be thinking of settling down, and . . . well, you could do a lot worse."

They really had been scared, John thought. The darlings. But to marry . . . ! He had devoted very little of his life to women, up to this moment. Being fit enough both to play good class rugby and spend a lot of time in the cramped and damp berths of a racing yacht had required a good deal of sexual discipline, and perhaps he had practised that too hard. Women didn't belong on small boats. Even less did they belong on the rugby field. That was perhaps why he had fallen so hard for Margo Cartright, who would not have been out of place on either. Her slap in the face had left him in a deep bout of misogynism.

While Aileen . . . Aileen Southern was both a neighbour and an old friend. They had played together as children, had drifted apart as teenagers. As adults, they had dated from time to time, when it was necessary to have a female on one's arm at a social function or dance. She wore her black hair unfashionably long, and was attractively slinky in appearance, certainly in an evening gown, with a slender figure and long legs. He didn't know much more about her than that, save that she was pretty enough. It was the hair and the legs that one looked at twice. But could any woman, pre-Margo, measure up, post-Margo? Either for attractiveness or active dislike. He supposed he really needed to find out.

"I think she's quite keen on you," Judith said slyly. "Oh, and by the way, George Brand telephoned yesterday. He said he'd very much like to see you once you were settled in."

"Not that old soldier fellow?"

"He is a brigadier," Judith pointed out, a trifle stiffly. She was a great traditionalist.

"I wonder what he can want?" The Brands were also neighbours, although they lived on a somewhat grander scale than the Warreys. They were a soldiering family. There had been a Brand at Blenheim and one in most of all the major battles fought by the British Army since. John didn't know them well although he had a nodding acquaintance with the Brand son, a young man named Harry, who, he had gathered, was a break in the family tradition in that he did not want to be a soldier, but a doctor. Having failed his medical finals, however, he had taken himself off to . . . John stroked his chin. Ethiopia, to help the Abyssinians fight the Italians. Now, was that coincidence? In any event, Harry Brand had come home, no doubt a wiser and sadder man. Did his father wish to compare notes?

Aileen Southern called immediately after breakfast, just as John was preparing to leave for the Brand residence. "Gosh," she said, "it's good to see you back."

John felt he was in an utterly unreal world. Could this young woman ever possibly exist in the middle of a desert, surrounded by Senussi tribesmen? Or had that been the unreal world? "You've cut your hair," he accused.

"It's up," she explained, and took off her hat so that he could see it. "But I will probably have to cut it." She was looking very county in twin-set and pearls.

"Why?" he asked.

"They're calling for volunteers to form a sort of women's army. I'm going to volunteer."

"You're joking."

"I am not." She bridled.

"I meant, you're joking about a woman's army. That's not on."

"Oh, we're not going to fight," Aileen explained. "We'll be secretaries and orderlies and drive cars, things like that, which will release more men for the fighting services."

"You're quoting."

"It was on the wireless. Don't you approve?"

"Who am I to approve or disapprove?"

"Aren't *you* going to join up?"

"For what? They say there isn't going to be a war."

"I think everyone should do his bit."

"When I find out that my bit is worth something, I'll let you know."

She considered this. "I never did ask you about the desert. Was it exciting?"

"From time to time."

"There are girls I know who would kill to get a suntan like that."

"It's probably injurious to the health. How would you like to have dinner?"

"I could make it on Saturday."

He thought that perhaps she would have been a success in the desert after all; she was every bit as definite as Margo.

George Brand was tall and spare. He was a much decorated officer, having served with both gallantry and success in the Great War, in which he had become one of the youngest regimental commanders in the British Army. His wife Juliet was a soft person, while their daughter Louise was a large, bouncy young woman. 'I think Daddy means to recruit you," she confided, having presented her cheek for a kiss.

"To do what?"

"Join the Army, of course. I'm joining the Army. The ATS. The Auxiliary Territorial Service. It's a new service being formed."

"So I've heard. Aileen Southern told me. She's going to join up too."

"I know. We're going to join up together."

"Cold baths, short haircuts, running five miles before breakfast, no men . . . Are you sure you can do it?"

She stuck out her tongue at him.

"Come and sit down and have a chat, John." George Brand held open the door of the huge book-lined study, from which french doors opened onto the back garden, in the early summer a place of peace and roses. He gestured the young man to a chair. "That was some adventure you had."

John frowned. "What adventure?"

"The scrap with the Senussi."

"I didn't know anyone knew about that."

"Oh, indeed, you should read the papers. Miss Cartwright gave an interview to the Cairo newspapers, and the Italians reported it as well. Sensational stuff."

"I was scared stiff."

"Not according to Miss Cartwright. She suggests you took complete control. Saved all their lives, bar one, until the Italians got to you. Isn't that true?"

"Well . . . territorial training, don't you know."

"Absolutely. What did you think of the Italians?"

"They seemed a very decent bunch."

"Those aren't the reports which came out of Ethiopia."

"This lot saved our lives. How is Harry, by the way?"

"Harry is in the Army." George Brand paused, significantly.

"Is there going to be a war, sir?"

"Almost certainly. By occupying what's left of Czechoslovakia, Hitler has proved that he can't be trusted. He has also proved that he doesn't give a fig for the rest of the world's opinion. We are going to have to stop him some time."

37

"Can we?"

"Oh, yes. France has the most powerful army in the world, we have the most powerful navy. And there is some talk of the Russians coming in."

"We'd ally ourselves with the Commies?"

"Politics is a matter of the here and now, John. What needs to be done, can be accomplished to have it done. Our first priority is to end Hitlerism. To do that, we need all the allies we can muster."

"Doesn't Hitler know all of this?"

"I'm sure his general staff do. But the man himself has got away with murder, quite literally, so often in the past he seems to believe he can get away with it indefinitely in the future."

"So you think I should join up." John grinned. "I didn't know brigadiers were in the recruiting business. I thought that was left to sergeants and men with drums."

George Brand smiled in return. "Nowadays it's left to somewhat drab little offices. But there are special cases."

"I'm sorry, you'll have to say that again. Me?"

"After your recent adventure."

"Believe me, sir, I had no idea I was going to have a shooting-type adventure."

"We none of us know what is just around the corner, John. The point is that you have been there and done that, and rubbed shoulders with the Italians into the bargain. Thus you have what might be termed special knowledge."

"I don't really, sir."

"Let us be the judge of that. What I am saying is that were you to join up, with your territorial background, your academic qualifications – Cambridge, was it? – and your knowledge of North Africa, you could find yourself on the staff, possibly in Intelligence, in very short order. Does that idea interest you at all?"

Oddly enough, it did interest John. If only because of the implications. Obviously no one at the War Office would be stupid enough to suppose that one journey through the desert qualified him as an expert. But someone had decided that he might be useful material for intelligence work. That could only be Margo. After the way she had brushed him off? But almost everything Margo did was odd. George Brand had been studying him. "You do understand that if there is a war, you are going to have to serve somewhere, John? If you're not careful you'll wind up a subaltern in an infantry battalion."

"Where is Harry going to wind up?" John could not resist the question.

George Brand grinned. "As a subaltern in an infantry battalion. It really is up to you. But it makes sense to pick your spot while you can." He got up, went to the sideboard, poured them each a scotch and water. "Your name was given to me and I was invited to have this chat. Now, as I say, it's up to you. If you do decide to volunteer now, give me a ring and I will tell you where to do it."

"Thank you, sir." John sipped his drink. "May I ask a question?"

"Certainly."

"Have you ever met Miss Cartwright?"

"Who? Oh, the photographer. Your partner in the desert. No, I haven't, more's the pity. She sounds like quite a girl. On whom you seem to have made quite an impression."

"He wants me to join up," John told his father. "Says that with my university and territorial background I'll get a commission right off."

"I should think you will," Harold Warrey agreed.

"But, what about you? The business? I know I went swanning off to Africa, but I knew I was coming back in a couple of months. Joining up seems rather open-ended. And if there *were* to be a war . . ."

"Like I said, Johnnie, I don't believe there will be a war. And I think a spell in the Army would do you good. Does everybody good. I can manage. I'm in the pink of health. And your desk will be waiting for you when you come back. But, –" he winked, "I know it would please your mother if you were to sort Aileen out first."

John borrowed his father's car to drive Aileen to a neat little restaurant on the London road. "How did you get on with the Brigadier?" she asked as they sipped an aperitif.

"For God's sake, is it possible to sneeze in this village without everyone knowing about it?"

"Keep your wool on. I just happened to be speaking with Lou this afternoon."

"Of course. Well, we got on very well."

"He wants you to join up."

"Is that what Lou said?"

"She surmised."

"That her father personally selects itinerant young men and invites them to join the Army. It's a great world."

"Now I've annoyed you. I really didn't mean to do that." They ordered, and she sipped wine. "Tell me about the desert. It sounds awfully romantic."

He obliged, and she listened with wide eyes while they ate. "This Cartwright woman sounds quite a character."

"She is."

She digested that. "Is she very old?"

"She's about thirty, I would say."

"Oh." Some more digestion. "And I suppose she's outrageously beautiful."

"You don't mean you've never seen her photo?"

"Yes, I have, as a matter of fact."

"Then you'll know that she isn't really beautiful at all. Sort of . . . compelling."

"I'm sure she is." Conversation lagged after that.

"We join up tomorrow," Aileen said, as he helped her into her coat. "Lou and I."

"Bravo. Does that mean you'll be carted off to camp somewhere?"

"I'm afraid it does." She stared at the empty road as they drove back to the village. "So I suppose it's goodbye for a while."

"You'll be given leave."

"Yes, but by then you'll have joined up yourself."

"Hm." The car slid to a stop outside her parents' house. At just on midnight, the village was somnolent; even the pub was long closed.

"I did enjoy this evening," Aileen said. He held her face in both hands to kiss her lips. She seemed taken by surprise, remained absolutely motionless. But as she didn't draw away, he allowed his hands to slip down her shoulders and on to the bodice of her dress. "Please," she said.

He released her. "I had the vague idea you wanted that. I'm always making mistakes like that about women."

"Such as Margo Cartwright?"

"Jesus. I'm sorry. She was the boss. That's all." How to begin a relationship, he thought, by lying. But was he beginning a relationship?

"I did want you to kiss me," she confessed. "But, you know . . . What with everything that's going on . . ."

"You'd like a commitment."

"I never said that. And anyway, how could we possibly commit ourselves now?"

"Why not? You've just indicated that if we don't do something now, it may be a hell of a long time before we can."

She shivered. "It all seems so . . . terminal. Can you understand that?"

He grinned, and kissed her again. "Be positive. The word to use is seminal. Will you marry me?"

Why am I doing this? he asked himself. So they had been childhood friends, adult playmates. Did he love her? He wasn't at all sure about that. For all their superficial intimacy, he knew so little about her. His own fault. If he had expected her to stand on a touchline and jump up and down while he cavorted about a rugby field, or be on the dock to wave at him when he came in from a race, it had never occurred to him to follow any of her sports; he did not even know if she had any. She had just always been there. Was that why he wanted her there, always? A sort of security blanket? Or did he just want to possess a woman, any woman, and thus eliminate the memory of Margo? As for passion, he thought he had felt just a little, just now. He had now a flash of it himself. And instead of tearing at each other's clothes they were having a serious discussion.

Or was it really that he was afraid of what he was sliding into, willy-nilly, not the world of uniforms and guns and perhaps even at the end of the day killing or being killed – a world he had never actually contemplated until today; the Senussi had been a one-off – but the world of Margo Cartwright, where nothing was quite as it seemed? Aileen Southern was definitely everything she seemed, a well-bred young Englishwoman, whom even a spell in the ATS would not change.

"You're not just asking me," Aileen said, half to herself, "so that if I say yes, you can . . . well . . ."

"Get my hands on your body? You'll be a virgin on your wedding night, Aileen. I'm old-fashioned."

"I think I'd like to marry you, Johnnie," she said. Again she might have been speaking half to herself. Then at last there was some passion, and it was difficult for him to keep his promise. But at the same time there was the promise of so much more; Aileen definitely had feelings. "When?" she gasped, when at last she got her mouth free.

"Whenever we can. We'll sort something out."

"I'm going to have to tell Mummy and Dad," she said.

"Of course."

"And Lou," she reminded him.

"I hear congratulations are in order," George Brand said. "On two fronts."

"Well . . . I suppose we've had it in mind for a long time, sir." John wished he could make up his mind whether or not the old bugger had been lying when he said he did not know Margo. But then, he also wished he could make up his mind whether or not he was joining this special and apparently secret force simply because he had an idea it might bring him back into contact with her. He was engaged to be married!

"You do understand you'll have to keep it in mind for a while yet, if you're serious," George said. "As a lieutenant in HM forces, marriage is simply not on. One has to be at least a captain."

"We both understand that, sir. It's the commitment, you see."

George nodded. "Oh, quite. Right. Well, as I say, congratulations. Now, you have considered what I said and you have made your decision. This *is* a commitment. Do you understand?"

"Yes, sir."

"Very good." He handed John a piece of paper. "There is the address to which you will report. They are expecting you."

"How long is the training period, sir?"

"That depends upon you. But I wouldn't expect you to be watching much cricket or tennis this summer." He looked out of the window at the steady downpour. "Supposing there's any to watch. You're to report this evening."

"Yes, sir. Ah . . . do I mention your name, sir? I mean, for being there at all?"

"No. You mention nothing at all about this civilian world. You'll answer any questions truthfully, of course. Just do as you are told without question or hesitation. That's a good rule of thumb for surviving in the Army. And in the course of time you'll be giving the orders yourself. That's always something to look forward to."

"Yes, sir. What about gear?"

"Take as much as you think necessary. As I said, you won't be going home for a while."

"Does that mean I'm not going to be in uniform?"

"They'll give you a uniform, I imagine," George said. "More than one. But a lot of the time you'll be wearing mufti. Now, here's a train ticket to where you are going. I'm afraid it's second-class, but that is standard procedure. There is nothing to stop you upgrading it to first and paying the difference yourself. And here," George held out an envelope, "are your travelling expenses. Ten shillings and sixpence."

"To do what with, sir?"

"Anything you like. It's principally intended for food. Of course, it's not going to buy you a bottle of Bollinger . . ."

John grinned. "But I can always upgrade my lunch out of my own pocket. I get the drift. Thank you, sir."

"Thank me when it's all over," George Brand said. "If you're still in the mood."

There was so much to be done, at such short notice; he supposed he was fortunate in that he had tidied up all his affairs before leaving for the Cartwright expedition, and had not had the time to untidy them again, so to speak. But there remained his parents.

"So soon?" Judith Warrey asked, hugging him as he brought his suitcase downstairs. "I thought it was just an idea."

"I suppose you could say George Brand twisted my arm," John explained.

"Are you going into his regiment?" Father asked.

"Ah, no. There are a limit to the number of strings one can pull, I suppose."

"But you're going to an officers' training camp. Which one? Close to home?"

"No, it's some distance away. I'm afraid I can't give you an exact location. The Secrecy Act, you know."

"Anyone would think we were at war already," Mother grumbled. "When do you suppose you'll get your first leave?"

"I didn't ask. I thought it might be rather bad form to ask about leave on the day I'm joining up. I'll let you know."

Then there was Rob, who had chafed a bit when he had announced he was going out into the desert. "Am I glad that you're back in one piece," Rob said. "First trials are on Saturday week. Out of Lymington. And let me tell you, Johnnie my boy, this new boat is an absolute bloody marvel. Cowes isn't going to see us for our wake."

"Sounds tremendous," John said. "But . . . I'm afraid I won't be crewing this summer, Robbie. Something has come up."

"What on earth can keep you from crewing? Your old man okay?"

"Well, of course he is. The fact is, I've joined up."

"Joined up what?"

"The Army," John explained.

There was a moment's silence. Then Rob asked, "Whatever for?"

"I felt I should do my bit."

"But we're not at war, old man."

"Informed opinion seems to think we soon will be."

"For God's sake! What am I going to do for a number one navigator?"

"Look around. Anyone worth a damn will be delighted to hear from you."

"You're the one I want," Robbie said. "Look, can't your call-up or whatever be deferred?"

"I haven't been called up. I have volunteered. Maybe next year."

"Next year," Robbie said disconsolately.

Next morning John was on the train to the village where his training headquarters was apparently established; it was situated in the Midlands. He had no idea what he was going to find, what he was going to. He had indeed supplemented his train ticket to travel first, and he used his meagre travelling allowance to augment his lunch. It was amusing to suppose that Aileen would be doing the same thing. And no doubt feeling the same, that she was being cast adrift on deep waters. But she would have Lou with her, and Lou, being a brigadier's daughter, would know the ropes.

He took a taxi from the station to the house, which was some way out of the village, and set in its own grounds. "You need a pass to get into Blitton Hall, guv," the driver remarked. "Very 'ush-'ush. You got a pass?"

"They're expecting me, I think," John said. "War Office property, is it?"

"You mean you don't know?"

"I'm a visitor," John explained.

There were wrought-iron gates, closed, and a sentry in uniform, armed with a rifle. He inspected the papers George had given John, then telephoned from a box by the gate. After a brief conversation, he returned to the taxi. "You can go in, sir. But not the taxi."

"Just like I said," the driver commented.

"I've a bag in the back," John pointed out. "It's fairly heavy."

"It's not far, sir," the sentry said. "Just up the drive and turn left. You can't miss it."

John paid the taxi driver, who winked as he got the suitcase out of the back. "You're in the Army now, mate."

Chapter Three

The Recruit

The walk to the house was a good deal longer than John had expected and he was out of breath by the time he got there; he had spent most of the previous three months sitting in Margo's truck and was not in the best of condition. It was now quite dark and he was both tired and fed up with the drizzling rain which was penetrating even his mackintosh. He surveyed the brightly lit building with considerable distaste.

A sentry stood at the top of the terraced steps. "Mr Warrey, is it?" he asked, pleasantly enough.

"That's me. Am I allowed to come up?"

"They're expecting you inside, sir."

"Thank you." James lifted his suitcase once again, mounted the steps, pushed upon the door, and found himself in what might have been an hotel lobby, save that there was no soft music, no white-jacketed waiters, and no people. But there was a reception desk, behind which waited a uniformed soldier with a sergeant's stripes on his sleeve.

"Mr Warrey? Colonel Pritchard is waiting to see you, sir. Leave the bag; someone will take it up for you."

"You're not serious?"

The sergeant apparently did not know the meaning of the word sarcasm. "Got something valuable in there, have you, sir? Not to worry; we won't rob you. It's up the stairs and first on the right."

John duly climbed the stairs, turned right along the corridor, knocked on the first door. It was opened by an attractive young woman in uniform, to his pleasant surprise. Not very tall, she wore her dark hair short, had crisp features, and filled her tunic to perfection. Presumably she was one of the new force Aileen and Lou were joining; it was a fascinating thought that one of them, or both, might actually be posted here. But she didn't look either surprised or pleased to see him. "Mr Warrey? Colonel Pritchard is expecting you."

"I'm a little wet," John remarked.

She gave what might have been mistaken for a smile. "I'm sure you'll dry." She gestured at the inner door. John crossed the room, glanced at her, knuckles poised. "Go right in, Mr Warrey."

He opened the door, stepped into a large, warm office. The walls were bare save for a portrait of the King hung behind the desk. The desk itself was the only item of furniture, apart from the three chairs, one behind the desk, the other two, straight-backed, in front of it. There was no carpet on the floor. Standing behind the desk, having just risen, was a rather small, somewhat overweight man, who wore a moustache to go with his thinning dark hair, a sports jacket, an MCC tie, and grey flannel bags. Anything less military could not be imagined. But he had been described as a colonel. John stood to attention.

"Warrey," Colonel Pritchard remarked, and came round the desk to shake hands. "You're a little late."

"I'm afraid the train was delayed, sir."

"Nuisance, what? Sit down." He gestured to one of the chairs before the desk, and John sat. Colonel Pritchard closed the door, then returned behind the desk and sat himself. "Brigadier Brand sent you."

Tell the truth, George Brand had said. "Yes, sir."

"Highly recommended. Experience of North Africa, eh?"

"A little, sir."

Colonel Pritchard ignored the self-deprecation. "Egypt," he said, "controls the Suez Canal, and the Canal is the key to the British Empire. Right?"

"Indeed, sir."

"The last time," Pritchard said, "we had to worry about the eastern side of the Canal. Turks, eh? The Italians were on our side. The next time, we will have to worry about the west. Do you agree?"

"We are not at war with Italy, sir."

"Not yet. But we will be, one of these days. We nearly were, three years ago, remember? And Mussolini and Hitler have this so-called Pact of Steel. If Hitler makes the mistake of attacking Poland or Rumania, we shall fight him. Oh, yes, never fear. Chamberlain has learned his lesson. And if we fight Hitler, we may expect to have to fight Mussolini as well. And when we do that, the Canal is going to be the key to a German-Italian victory, they will suppose. Therefore it is a vital area. Right?"

"With respect, sir, I have never seen the Suez Canal."

"It looks like a poor quality river," Pritchard pointed out. "The only good thing about it is that it's straight. I am not asking you to look at the Canal, Warrey, unless you happen to like brown water. Your business, along with a lot of others, will be to stop the Italians ever looking at it. For this purpose, we need to know how they are thinking, what they are doing, how they are disposing their people in Libya. You are fluent in Italian, are you not?"

"I can make myself understood, sir," John said cautiously.

"Always helps. Now, here is the general set-up. We are creating a force here which will act under cover but which will nonetheless fight the enemy, even before the outbreak of war. However, it is necessary that this force, a very small élite, you might say, is a part of the Army, and therefore subject to army rules, regulations and discipline. Do you agree?"

"Entirely, sir." There was no other answer he could give.

"Quite. Now, to give you the necessary clout, should you ever need it, you will be trained and commissioned as an officer in the Army. You will be Second Lieutenant Warrey, and you will, in the fullness of time, no doubt rise to a higher rank. Right?"

"I hope so, sir."

"Quite. However, while you will receive what one might call normal military training, in addition to your special course, you will be commissioned straight into Military Intelligence. This means that you will never use the clout you may have, except as directed by your superior officer, or in case of the most dire necessity. Right?"

"Name, rank and number, and that sort of thing, sir," John said, as brightly as he could.

"Never," Pritchard said. "If you should fall into enemy hands while wearing mufti and you attempt to give them your name, rank and number, you will immediately be shot. Right?"

John gulped. "I'm sure you're right, sir."

"When I use the term 'dire necessity', that means if the occasion should arise that you need the immediate and total assistance of some of our people, who might otherwise be unwilling to help you or carry out your direction. Right?"

"Yes, sir."

"Good. Now, in addition to your military training, you will receive physical training. You have to be fit. You *are* fit?"

"I think so, sir." John tried to forget the way he had been puffing when he reached the house.

"You will also receive specific training in certain other directions. Cyphers and codes. You know about cyphers and codes?"

"I'm afraid I do not, sir."

"You'll learn. Unarmed combat. You know about unarmed combat?"

"No, sir."

"You'll learn. Politics, and the history of recent politics, certainly in North Africa. You know about North African history?"

"I'm afraid not, sir."

Pritchard studied him for a few seconds, clearly reflecting, why wasn't I told this fellow is as thick as two short planks? "You'll learn," he said. "Reveille is five tomorrow morning. Have you eaten?"

"Not recently, sir."

"You've missed supper, but I imagine something can be rustled up." He pressed the bell on his desk, and the secretary opened the door. "Carson, will you take Warrey downstairs and find him something to eat. And then show him where his bed is. Right?"

"Yes, sir," Carson said, and waited for John to join her.

"The boss appears to be a ball of fire," John remarked, as they went down the stairs.

"He's efficient." She seemed a young woman of very few words.

"Would you put me straight about one or two things?" he asked.

"If I can." She nodded her head to the duty sergeant, led him down a corridor and into a vast pantry. Now he could hear sounds from the back of the building, where the front had been abnormally silent. "Mr Widdicombe," she called, and a large man emerged from a door at the back of the room. "A new guest, Mr Widdicombe. Who is hungry. Can you do something about that?"

"Yes, ma'am. Sandwiches all right, sir? And a glass of milk?"

"Milk?" John asked.

"I'm afraid we're dry," Carson said. "There is a pub in the village for your nights off."

"How often do we get those?"

"Rarely," she said. "Well, Mr Widdicombe will look after the inner man. I'll come back in ten minutes, shall I?"

"I'd prefer it if you stayed."

She looked down her nose at him. "Why?"

"Because of the questions that need answering."

Again she considered him for several seconds, then she sat down. "Well?"

"What do I call you?"

"Miss Carson will do."

"No Christian name?"

51

"Not here."

"Ah. Now tell me, am I your superior, or are you mine?"

"I am yours, at this moment."

"And when I graduate, or whatever?"

"You will be mine. But I wouldn't jump the gun."

"Point taken. Now . . ." he paused as the plate of cold roast beef sandwiches was placed in front of him, together with a very large glass of milk. "Thank you, Mr Widdicombe. The boss gave me the impression I was to get fit, not fat."

"You'll work that off, tomorrow."

He regarded her trimly-belted figure. "Do you participate?"

"I sometimes watch, from the window."

"A spark of humanity at last. How many of us are there?"

"You'll find out."

"Are you always this uncooperative? Even in bed, for instance?"

She leaned forward, her elbows on the table. "The rule here is no prying into backgrounds, foregrounds or present grounds, Mr Warrey. You are here to learn to be of service to your country. Not to have a good time."

"Not even on those rare nights out?"

"Not even then. Eat up. I have work to do."

"At ten o'clock at night?"

"Yes."

John ate, beginning to feel distinctly lonely. On the other hand, as a recently engaged man, he really had no business flirting at all, even with this pretty little thing. He just couldn't get used to the idea that he was a recently engaged man.

His meal finished, Miss Carson led him along various corridors lit by single bulbs. Now there was muted sound and movement all around him, behind the doors to left and right. "Lights out is ten o'clock on weekdays," Carson told him. "But I imagine Room Six will still be awake."

"There were lights on in the front," John argued.

52

"This is the back," she pointed out, and opened a door. There was some startled movement inside. "John Warrey," Carson announced. "They'll introduce themselves."

John caught the door as she was about to close it. "It's dark."

"Are you afraid of the dark?"

"I was thinking of undressing."

"I'm sure you can undress in the dark, Mr Warrey. Good night." The door closed.

"Welcome," said a voice from the darkness.

"Is that what you call it?"

"Oh, don't mind old Knickers-in-a-Twist. She's the only woman in the house so she feels she has to keep a barbed wire fence up front. And down back. Pritchard is a stickler for protocol."

"So no getting too close," Warned another voice. "Peter Jameson."

"John Warrey." John fumbled in the darkness, and found a hand. "Mind if I drop my clothes on the floor?"

"Help yourself. I'm Laurie Clarke."

"How long have you chaps been here?" John asked.

"Arrived yesterday," Jameson said.

To John's astonishment, nearly all the recruits were recent arrivals. HM Government had clearly decided to launch an early drive for above-average intelligence young men, too much above average to be considered as cannon fodder. Not that they were given that impression at reveille next morning. Being mid-summer it was already light, but again it was raining and altogether bleak. Yet the entire establishment of twelve recruits, plus two drill sergeants, were turned out for a long run, then an hour's square bashing. John guessed that most of his fellows had, like himself, at least a school cadet corps, if not a territorial background, and none of them found it very difficult, but it was certainly exhausting.

He kept looking up at the front of the building to see if Carson was watching, but if she was, it was from behind drawn curtains. What fascinated him about her, apart from the fact that he had got quite worked up over Aileen and been rewarded with nothing save a commitment? He wondered if it was because of the possibility that Margo had been trained at an establishment like this? But there was no evidence that any women had ever been included in the training schedule, and he didn't want to ask.

Drill over, they spent another hour in the very well-equipped gymnasium, doing everything from push-ups and pull-ups to punching bags. Then they showered and breakfasted, and got to work. This covered a great deal of ground, from map reading to cyphers, from political lectures to language classes to unarmed combat and being taught the use of firearms. Here again the territorial training of most of the class stood them in good stead. The lecturers came in all shapes and sizes, but they knew their stuff, and John found that he was enjoying the work. It was certainly better than sitting behind a desk in Dad's office, and if, as the summer wore on, he occasionally watched the clouds scudding across the sky and thought of Rob and the others creaming up and down the Solent, he had a sense of purpose he had never known before taking off with Margo into the desert.

Even if some of his lessons were hard to fathom; for at least one hour in every day he was taught to use, understand, strip and reassemble . . . a typewriter. Was it possible he was undergoing all of this training merely to become a male secretary? But as with everything else, it was in his nature to involve himself utterly in whatever he was required to do. However inane.

His companions were similarly dedicated. There were one or two who really let their hair down on Saturday nights in the pub, but they rapidly disappeared. "One thing you must understand," Colonel Pritchard told them. "Only the very best will do for this establishment. Those of you who graduate will be the very best."

And with almost every day they became more aware of that,

as they reached a level of fitness none of them had known before, combined with a level of skill and knowledge none of them had attained either. Miss Carson faded into the background, sometimes present with clipboard and pencil, more often invisible, but equally no doubt with clipboard and pencil. John reckoned he was lucky in that both Jameson and Clarke seemed as dedicated as himself, refrained from getting drunk in the pub, and swotted as hard as he did. Yet it was an extremely odd life. All the trainees were in their middle or late twenties, used to total personal freedom, to whatever sexual mores turned them on in their private lives, and to a reasonably sedentary mode of existence, public or private. John rapidly realised that he, with his Saharan adventure behind him, probably knew more about what it was all about than the rest put together.

Yet they were all being treated as sixteen-year-old schoolboys, their lives, private and public, totally controlled and regimented, even down to their sleep and the food they were given to eat. "Well, they say you can't give orders unless you can take them," Jameson remarked over breakfast.

"They'd never get away with this with enlisted men," Clarke grumbled. "Or even ordinary officers. They'd have a mutiny. Do you realise that we have been here five weeks, and not a spot of leave or a skirt in sight?"

"You wouldn't class Carson as a skirt?" John asked.

"Carson," Jameson sighed. "I dream every night of being shipwrecked on a desert island with Carson."

"She'd say no," John pointed out.

"She wouldn't be able to," Jameson riposted with a grin. "Not if there was just her and me."

"You reckon you could take her? She's trained to the tits."

Jameson continued to grin. "It sure would be fun trying."

Heady stuff. John preferred to dream of Margo. But Carson was closer to hand.

*   *   *

55

"This is Brigadier George Brand," Colonel Pritchard announced. John, standing to attention with his nine companions in the gymnasium was totally surprised. The old bugger! With him there was a uniformed sergeant, a very large man with a severe expression. Carson stood behind him, as always coldly remote, looking at the assembled men but not actually appearing to see them. "Brigadier Brand is in overall command of this operation," Pritchard went on. "He is here to assess your progress. Brigadier."

"I shall see you separately," George Brand said. He had given not the slightest indication that he had ever met John, much less was a friend of the family. "We'll commence with you, Mr Price."

"The rest of you will leave the room," Pritchard commanded. They filed out.

"This is it," Jameson said. "Have you ever considered what happens if we flunk?"

"They send us off with a flea in our ear," Clarke said.

"I don't think they can do that," Jameson argued. "We know too much."

"We haven't been given a scrap of information that could be of the least use to anyone," Clarke said.

"But we know how intelligence officers are trained," Jameson insisted. "That's a lot of knowledge. What do you think, Johnnie?"

"It's a problem," John agreed.

"So all the failures are taken outside and shot, is that it?" Clarke scoffed.

"More likely put into some line regiment doing garrison duty in the Seychelles," Jameson said. "Ooops."

Carson had appeared in the doorway. "Mr Lambert," she said. She was breathing heavily. Lambert hastily got to his feet, looked at the others almost apologetically, and followed her into the other room.

"What happened to Price?" Jameson said.

"As I said, he's probably been taken out and shot," Clarke said. Jameson stared at him with his mouth open.

"Of course he wasn't going to be sent back in here," John said, trying to defuse the incipient panic. "He'd be able to tell us what to expect." Yet the tension was growing. Jameson had put the cat amongst the pigeons. Just what *would* happen to anyone who was rejected at this late stage? Suddenly fear of failure had overtaken ambition to succeed.

John was the sixth man to be called; this was three hours after Price. Jameson had already disappeared, and Clarke was decidedly agitated. So were the other three remaining recruits. Carson waited for him in the doorway. He grinned at her as he passed her, but her face remained stony.

"John Warrey, Brigadier," Pritchard said as John stood to attention before the desk, which was the dais at the far end of the room. To John's consternation, the drill sergeant was now wearing a dressing gown; his uniform – and his underwear! – was neatly folded on one of the benches.

George was studying the file in front of him. "Useful background," he remarked. At last he looked up, but still with no sign of having ever met John before. "According to your file, Mr Warrey, the Italian Army may have saved your life, and those of your companions."

"Yes, sir," John said.

"Have you, therefore, any feelings towards the Italian Army?"

"As you say, sir, they saved my life."

"But if there were to be a war between Great Britain and Italy, would you be prepared to take Italian lives or perhaps cause Italian lives to be lost?"

"In defence of my country, yes, sir."

"And in defence of your country's interests, perhaps overseas?"

"I think so, sir."

"I'm afraid your commitment would have to be more than that, Warrey."

"Yes, sir. I would do it, sir."

"Good. Life becomes much easier when one has a total

57

commitment. Now then, it says here that you are now fluent in Italian, that you are completely *au fait* with the political situation in the Middle East, and that you have been taught survival drill in the desert. Tell me about Egypt. What are we doing there?"

John took a deep breath. "We are in Egypt, sir, because of debts incurred by the Egyptian Government in the middle of the last century. When these debts became acute, the then King of Egypt put up his shares in the Suez Canal for sale. The then British Prime Minister, Disraeli, bought a controlling interest in the shares. That involved political and military involvement to safeguard Britain's investment. When the Khedive again ran into debt, Britain took over Egypt's finances, not without some opposition from both France and Egyptian nationalist elements. When the Great War began, the Khedive revealed an inclination to support Germany. Britain thus took over the entire country and ran it as a colony. After the War there was again considerable nationalist opposition. In 1936 a treaty was signed between Britain and Egypt, restoring Egyptian independence, but giving Britain rights to garrison the Canal area and maintain troops in Egypt for twenty years."

"Very good. The attitude of the people?"

"I understand, sir, that on the whole they hate us, but bow to our superior power."

"In a nutshell. What, in your estimation, should be our attitude should there be a European war?"

"I assume that we would secure the country, as we did in the Great War, in order to safeguard our use of the Canal, sir."

"Absolutely. Now tell me about Libya?"

"Conquered from the Turks by the Italians in 1912, sir, as part of the Italian drive for an African Empire. There was considerable opposition from the indigenous Arab population, the Senussi, but this was officially ended about ten years ago."

"Officially," George agreed. "As you found out. Very good.

58

You understand that you will be stationed in Cairo, as a sales executive in an import-export company dealing in typewriters?"

"Yes, sir."

"Good. But you will also make journeys into Libya, as salesman for the group you will officially represent. Your principal duty will be to make contact with various residents of Tripoli and Tobruk and Bardia, who are opposed to the rule of Mussolini, and are therefore inclined to be sympathetic to our democratic ideas. You will at all times proceed with great caution as regards these people. You will also, obviously, keep your eyes and your ears open for any snippets of knowledge as regards Italian troop dispositions. You may also be required to make contact with certain of the Senussi leaders, who remain opposed to Mussolini. Would this bother you?"

John thought of poor Graham Poultrie lying dead in the sand. "I shall not let it bother me, sir."

"You do understand that when you are required to venture into Italian controlled territory, you will be embarking upon a mission that could well be dangerous. If you are arrested and charged with spying, in peacetime, you may well have to expect a form of show trial followed by expulsion. This would be humiliating, and annoying for us, as it would mean we would be unable to employ you again in your chosen field."

"Yes, sir," John agreed, wondering if the old git had forgotten that he had not chosen this field; it had been chosen for him.

"However, should you be arrested and charged with spying *after* any outbreak of hostilities involving Great Britain and Italy, while there would probably again be a show trial, the outcome would be a death sentence. Do you understand this?"

"Obviously I must endeavour not to be found out, sir."

"Obviously," George said drily. "There is, however, an even more unpleasant possibility, but one that needs to be taken into consideration. If you were to be arrested, either before or after an outbreak of hostilities, you would certainly be interrogated. This can be a most unpleasant business."

"Surely they couldn't knock me about, sir, if they intended to put me on trial?"

"Depends on what you mean by 'knock you about'. I'm afraid that in this twentieth century man has greatly refined the art of inflicting pain while leaving no visible marks. I assume you have no experience of this?"

"I'm afraid not, sir."

"Well, it is necessary for you to be acquainted with it. It has been found that a man is more likely to be able to withstand torture if he knows what is going to happen to him, and perhaps has prepared himself to withstand it. Would you agree with that theory?"

"I don't know, sir. It sounds fairly logical."

"Very good. Now, there are certain tests I must inflict upon you. The first is your proficiency with weapons. Strip."

"Sir?" John could not stop himself glancing at Carson, who was, as always, stony-faced. But from time to time, as she had called them in, she had been breathing quite heavily.

"Undress, Mr Warrey," George said. "It says here that you are a proficient marksman. But that, I assume, is when lying or standing comfortably on the range, with nothing to distract you from the target. Sadly, if you ever have to use your weapon in self-defence, circumstances may be a little more trying than that, and certainly there will be distractions. I am assuming you have never killed a man?"

"I don't know, sir. I have certainly fired at one."

"Of course, the Senussi in Cyrenaica. But we still need to be sure. Undress. Believe me, Miss Carson won't mind." But her cheeks were pink as John removed his clothing until he was down to shorts and singlet. "Everything," George said.

Slowly John laid his last remaining garments on top of the others, cursing himself for his inescapable reaction to the presence of the woman.

"Very good," George said. "Now, behind you on the table is

an automatic pistol. When I give the command, I wish you to turn, pick up the pistol and shoot at the target which will appear on the far wall. I wish you to kill the enemy agent, who otherwise will kill you. Use as many shots as you will, but you will of course be graded on the first bullet, which must at least immobilise your opponent." He held up his finger. "I will tell you when to turn, Mr Warrey. But do please hit the right person, or you could well be hanged for murder."

Carson left the dais, came down the two steps, and moved past John. Whatever was her role in this? He began taking deep breaths. "Now!" George snapped.

John swung round. The table was about four feet behind him, and he concentrated first on that, reaching it in a single stride, picking up the gun, looking up as the butt nestled into his hand, and gazed at Carson, standing between him and the far wall, at a distance of about twelve feet.

She was wearing what looked like a crash helmet with a heavy visor but still John gasped in horror, even as four images were flashed up on the screen. The first was a woman pushing a baby, in the very centre. To her right was a man staring at him with his hands on his hips. To her left was a pretty girl, laughing. And to her right was a man, facing him, with a gun in his hand. John took them all in in a second, but his attention was still caught by Carson, staring at him, lips slightly parted. Talk about dangerous situations! But he had to concentrate. He swung the gun to point over her left shoulder, and squeezed the trigger, and again, and again. The three bullets all entered the chest or abdomen of the man with the gun.

The room was silent for a moment, save for the echo of the shots, the somewhat acrid smell. "Sergeant?" George invited.

The sergeant went forward. "Good shooting, sir," he said. "First bullet, right chest. It wouldn't have killed, but it would have affected the gun arm. Second bullet straight through the heart. Third bullet, in the abdomen. That would have killed, eventually, but the man would already have been dead."

"Oh, very good, Mr Warrey," George said.

John was staring at Carson, who at last moved, coming forward to take the pistol from his hand. Had she really stood there before six naked men, each with a pistol in his hand, knowing that the slightest distraction could mean that she was hit? Her face remained expressionless as she took the gun from his lifeless fingers, but she did mutter, "Well done, Mr Warrey. The best so far." John almost resisted the slight pull, to maintain contact. But then she was away.

"If it is any consolation to you, Mr Warrey," George said, "Miss Carson is wearing very effective body armour beneath her tunic. Had you miscalculated, or perhaps lost your head, she would have received a severe bruise, but she would not have been killed. Even, indeed, had you hit her in the head. But of course you have been trained always to shoot at the body, not the head, which can so easily be missed."

"That does relieve me, sir," John said, and wondered what his parents, who played bridge with George and Juliet Brand every week, would say if they knew what he really did for a living.

"Now we need to see how good you are with your hands," George said.

The sergeant had gone further up the room, and now waited in an open space in the centre. He took off his dressing gown to reveal that he too was naked, then turned away from John and faced the wall of targets. "What I want you to do, Mr Warrey," George said, "is approach Sergeant Bullock, without him hearing you if possible, and kill him. You won't actually kill him, of course, but you must display to us that you could do so. One would hope that if the actual circumstances arise, you might have such a thing as a knife or a cosh which would make life much simpler. Too simple for our purposes. Because there is always the chance that you might not have a weapon."

"Will my victim always be naked, sir?" John could not resist the question.

"Hopefully not. But we are again concerned with the business of distraction. Now . . ." he touched his lips with his forefinger, then held the finger up.

John found himself glancing at Carson. He simply could not get her out of his mind, standing there waiting for him to shoot at her. At least all the distractions had ended his arousal. But now he had to wrestle with a naked man.

George lowered his finger. John took a deep breath, then moved forward on the balls of his feet, muscles tensed and hands held flat, as he had been taught. It was a choice of what to do. Lock his arm round the sergeant's throat and throttle him? Bullock was a bigger man than himself, and probably stronger as well. Alternatively try to land a chopping blow on his shoulder that would temporarily immobilise him and *then* go for his throat? He was now three feet behind the sergeant, who had still given no sign that he was about to be attacked. But as John raised his hand, having opted for the chop, Bullock turned with amazing speed for so big a man. John had the impression that he had run into a moving mountain. All the breath left his body as a fist slammed into his stomach, all the senses were knocked from his mind as he was head butted. His legs gave way and he slumped against Bullock's body.

He felt the sergeant holding him under the armpits, pushing him away, felt rather than actually saw a huge fist hurtling at his face, and slumped again, this time deliberately, while he tried to get both his brain and his breathing under control. The fist passed over his head, but he wasn't sure that he was ahead, as the muscular body again thumped into him, this time knocking him from his feet. As he hit the floor he wondered if Bullock was also under instructions not actually to kill?

The sergeant was coming down on him, and desperately he rolled to his right. He only got to his side, however, before Bullock was half across him, one hand reaching for his neck, the

63

other finding his genitals and starting to squeeze. John gasped in agony, struck behind him with an elbow, and was at least rewarded with a grunt. The grip on his testicles relaxed and he swung backwards again, this time using the full extent of his arm, outflung, and with hand held rigid. His hand slammed into Bullock's neck, and the sergeant hit the floor without a sound. John scrambled to his feet, body wracked with pain, but still serviceable, and Bullock's hands closed on his ankle. He stamped down, and the sergeant let go, and leapt to his feet, clearly dazed, but still a killing machine. John jumped back, trying to get some balance and regain some strength, and George called, "Stop!"

Both men allowed their hands to fall to their sides, and faced each other, gasping for breath. Then Bullock held out his hand. "You're no pushover, sir."

"Thank you, sergeant."

"It was your breathing told me you were that close, sir. You need to control the breathing."

"I'll try to remember that, sergeant."

George came down from the dais to peer at him. "Are you all right?"

"I think so, sir."

"Most chaps just fold up when Bullock gets at them. Tell me, that karate chop, or whatever; was that deliberate or an accident?"

"The blow was deliberate, sir. I suspect I was fortunate in that I caught the sergeant off balance."

"Exactly so. Nonetheless, well done. Now, let us interrogate you."

"If you will sit down, sir," Sergeant Bullock invited. "On this form." Again John could not stop himself glancing at Carson as he obeyed; her face was as impassive as ever, but her breathing had quickened slightly, as she came forward to stand in front of him. "Arms over the back, sir," Bullock invited. Or was it a command?

64

John draped his arms over the back of the form and had his wrists seized and handcuffed, the handcuff itself being linked to a steel rod that ran underneath the bench. Before he could adjust to that, his ankles were also secured, by Carson, one to each upright of the bench.

Never had he felt so exposed, in every possible way. At least Carson had withdrawn. He gazed at George, who was smiling at him. "We cannot, of course, replicate the exact circumstances in which you could find yourself," George explained. "The beatings you will already have had, the verbal abuse, plus of course the humiliation of being placed in your present situation. We believe that you are man enough to withstand any treatment like that. However, there remains the pain threshhold. Sergeant."

"You'll excuse me, sir." Bullock had come round in front, and now for the first time John saw the box on the table, placed there by George. Now he saw, too, the two wires, each ending in an alligator clip, that led away from the box. Immediately he knew what was about to happen to him. He had to force himself to remain still, not to look at the woman, or indeed any of their faces, as one of the clips was attached to his penis. Carson had moved behind him, and now she seized his jaws to force his mouth open. Instantly Bullock had attached the second clip to his tongue. It tasted foul and he realised this was not the first tongue it had been attached to that day. It was also extremely painful, but that was nothing to the pain he suffered a moment later, which began between his legs and raced up his body. He made a choking sound and the pain died, to return a moment later, somewhat more severely.

John's body arched away from the bench as his entire brain filled with unacceptable agony. His fingers bunched into fists that threatened to drive his nails into his flesh. Then the pain was gone again and he subsided, gasped for breath, aware that his head was against Carson's blouse as she removed the electrode fom his mouth. Bullock was doing the same with the other clip. He gasped and panted, and his mouth flooded with saliva. George Brand stood in front of him. "Can you speak?"

John swallowed and got his shaking limbs under control. Bullock was releasing his ankles and Carson his wrists. His arms seemed to come round in front of himself as if of their own volition and he grasped himself. "Yes, sir," he muttered.

"Good lad. They can't do anything worse to you than that. Just remember that."

"What do you reckon?" Clarke asked, when they were at last alone together. It had not been possible to discuss their respective ordeals, or bruises, during lunch, at which the senior staff were present or during the various classes afterwards. But now they were dressing for dinner.

"I damn near hit her," Jameson said. "And do you know, she never batted an eyelid."

"Because she was wearing body armour," John suggested.

"My bullet went by her ear."

"Doesn't sound so good for you, old man," Clarke said. "But do you think that girl has blood in her veins? Or iced water?"

The gong went and they assembled in the dining hall to discover there were only nine of them now. "Whatever happened to Lambert?" Clarke whispered.

George Brand was still with them and took his seat at the head of the table, with Pritchard to one side and Carson to the other; Sergeant Bullock sat beside Carson. To their astonishment, Carson was wearing a dress. And the wine was chateau bottled claret.

"Gentlemen," George said, when they had eaten, "I give you a toast. The King, God bless him."

They drank. "I am informed that none of you smoke," George went on. "That is very sensible. Well, gentlemen, you have completed your course, and those of you who have survived," he looked from face to face to let them know that the two missing men had failed, "are now members of His Majesty's Armed Forces.

You will receive your orders tomorrow. But for tonight, why, you may relax and enjoy yourself. The pub is on limits."

"Hoorah!" Clarke shouted.

"Will you come with us, sir?" John asked.

"Do you know, Warrey, I think I will. And you, Sergeant Bullock."

"And Miss Carson, sir?" Clarke asked.

"Oh, why not. You'll want to keep an eye on your charges, eh, Captain?"

John managed to sit next to her in one of the three command cars as they drove into the village; Jameson secured the other side. "Did the old boy say 'captain'?" John asked.

"I've just been promoted."

"You promised me that when I graduated I'd be your superior officer."

"It'll come," she assured him. "What will you do then?"

"Well . . . what do I call you for the time being?"

"Oh, ma'am will do."

"I didn't know they had ranks like captain in the ATS?" He could not help but wonder if Aileen and Lou would turn out like this.

"They don't," she said. "I'm not in the ATS. I'm in Military Intelligence. And so are you now, Mr Warrey. The rank, as I am sure Colonel Pritchard explained to you, is merely to give us clout if we need it." She actually smiled. "I need it to cope with each batch of recruits."

"You mean you have to do this all over again, with some more poor saps?"

"Starting next week," she said.

"What I don't understand," Jameson said, "is how I passed. I mean, I damn near hit you. Ma'am."

"I know," Carson said. "Your shooting isn't too good. But you scored well on other subjects. He's the only man to put Sergeant Bullock down," she told John.

"And you never told us, you son-of-a-gun," John said admiringly. Jameson winked.

It was a Saturday night and the pub was crowded. The officers made space for themselves at the bar, however, round George, Pritchard and Carson. "You did damned well, Johnnie," George said, when they found themselves together, beers in hand.

"Thank you, sir. Am I now allowed to know you?"

"That was necessary. Couldn't show any favouritism, you know. And if you hadn't come up to scratch, I'd have flunked you out."

"I understand that, sir. And if I had flunked out, like those others . . ."

George grinned. "A line battalion." But John had an idea he wasn't quite telling the truth. "Anyway, it's over," George said. "And my best congratulations. This time next month you'll be in Cairo. Now I think you are due some reward."

"Me, sir?"

"Oh, all of you deserve it. But then . . . there's only one reward to go round, wouldn't you say? There's a dance in the town tonight. It's a ticket affair, and black tie, but you're suitably dressed. I give you permission to take one of the cars."

"To go to a dance, sir?"

"To take Sam Carson to a dance, Johnnie. She deserves a little reward as well."

Chapter Four

The Sphinx

"Is your name really Sam?" John asked, as they drove out of the village.

"Samantha."

"Pretty name, Samantha. So do I call you Sam, or ma'am, tonight?"

"I think you may call me Sam. For tonight."

The country road unfolded in front of the headlights. "I'd like you to know," John said, "that I didn't request this posting. It was all the Brigadier's idea."

"Well, he's a friend of the family, isn't he?"

"You mean you knew that?"

"Of course." Her tone indicated that she knew everything worth knowing about him, or indeed any of the recruits.

"But I would have requested it," John said. "If I had supposed there was the slightest chance of your agreeing."

"I am obeying orders," Samantha said.

"Oh, quite. You wouldn't like to tell me just what those orders were? What I mean is, I really have no desire to go to this dance or whatever. I'm still fairly bruised from my encounter with Sergeant Bullock, I'm fairly exhilarated from having passed, I'm fairly excited at the prospect of going out to Egypt, and . . . well . . ."

"You're still turned on by having me see you in the nude."

"You know how to put things in a nutshell," John agreed.

"Do you reckon you can function?"

69

"I reckon I have never been more ready to function in my life. I'm super-charged with electricity, remember."

"And you don't have a girl waiting for you at home, to go back to and fold in your arms and tell her how successful you've been."

My God, he thought: Aileen! But with every day of his training the image of Aileen had become more nebulous. He was engaged to her because it had always been supposed that he would become engaged to her. They would no doubt get married some time in the not too distant future, have kids, play bridge, go for walks, play tennis and listen to the wireless . . . yet there had been no passion. He had wanted passion, but she had been afraid of it.

"What's her name?" Samantha asked.

John gave a start. "I may never see you again," he said.

"Almost certainly you will not."

"And I think you are the most attractive woman I have ever met." Now was not the time for qualifications.

"How nice of you to say that. So tell me, what would you like to do, if we do not go to the dance?"

For reply he turned down a side lane, very dark between the hedgerows. He drove for perhaps a hundred yards, then found what he was looking for, a gap in the hedge, which allowed access to a field. There was a gate, so he stopped the car, got out, and opened it. There was just room for the car to fit through. Once inside he turned to his left, to seek the shelter of the hedge, then returned and closed the gate. In the distance a cow mooed; now that his eyes were growing accustomed to the darkness, he could make out several of the animals. But they were a good way off and showed no signs of approaching.

While he had been carrying out his various tasks, Samantha had remained in the car, not speaking. But as he closed the gate she got out with a rustle of silk. "You don't suppose there could be a bull amongst those?" she asked.

"Not a chance."

"Good." She stood beside the car, waiting for him to come

70

back to her. "You do realise that it is a most serious offence to rape a superior officer?"

He moved against her, took her in his arms, kissed her mouth, and was surprised by the vehemence of her response. Her tongue scoured his, her nails scraped up and down the back of his dinner jacket so frantically he thought she might tear the material.

"And we thought you were made of stone."

"All those men," she said, fumbling at his belt, while he raised her dress to her waist and slid down her knickers. "Wait," she said. "I want to be naked."

His pants had settled around his ankles. He took them off, watched her lift her dress over her head, fluff out her hair. Then her petticoat joined her knickers on the grass, she stepped out of her shoes, and he could take her in his arms again, feel her against him while they kissed again, and he slid down her body to suck at nipple and groin. For so long he had waited for this. So very long. With a woman he was never going to see again. But wasn't that the best? Certainly the most sensible.

He lifted her into the car, stretched her on the back seat, lay between her legs. "Oh, Johnnie," she muttered. "I always wanted it to be you, this time. I really did."

John was climaxing as she spoke and the words did not at that moment have any meaning. It was only when he was spent, but still lying on her, while her nails scoured his naked back, that he realised what she had just said. He pushed himself up, sat at the far end of the seat, her feet resting on his lap. "How many groups have you had?" he asked.

"You're the third." The feet were withdrawn as she sat up in turn, clearing hair from her face and neck.

"And every time . . ."

"I get my pick. I told you, all those men." She blew him a kiss. "As you said, we are never going to see each other again."

He got out of the car, dressed himself. After a few seconds,

71

she followed. "You're not going to be school-boyish about this, are you, Johnnie?"

"I have an ambition," he said.

She pulled on her knickers. "Tell me."

"That one day I may meet a single woman who is exactly what she seems."

"Tricky."

"More than you know. But . . ." he was going to be school-boyish, after all. Because he was an innocent in this world where the only rule was to be false. "Suppose the opportunity arose, would you like to see me again?"

She settled her dress. "I very much doubt that would be a good idea."

"Because once you've had one, you've had them all."

"Now you are being positively childish. I was thinking of our jobs. We simply cannot afford to become emotionally involved, Johnnie. I may have to sign an order virtually condemning you to death, one day. Or even vice versa; I don't intend to spend all of my life at the training camp. I want a field assignment. So let's just have this one night to remember."

He held her hand. "But supposing things were different, or became different . . ."

She reached up to kiss him. "Then of course I would like to see you again, Johnnie. Again and again and again."

Obviously she was lying. He really was a child in a man's world. Or was it a woman's?

"John Warrey?" The man was very much a colonial expat, from his white fedora through his white duck suit and his striped tie to his brown and white shoes. He even carried a little cane. But amazingly, he did not look the least out of place on the Alexandria dockside, even surrounded by tarbooshes and haiks and yashmaks and dark skins and, in a lot of cases, bare brown feet. He was clearly lord of all he surveyed.

And now he was not alone, John thought, as he left the gangway and went towards him, because he was wearing, on orders, almost identical clothes.

"Charles Skipton." They shook hands. "Had a good voyage?" Skipton signalled an Egyptian porter to bring John's luggage; customs and immigration had been cleared on board ship, which now lay alongside the Sea Passengers Terminal in the centre of the vast inner harbour.

"Splendid," John said, wondering just what position this man held as regarded himself. But he had been told to wait, not lead.

"First time in Alexandria?"

"Ah, no. I was here a few months ago."

"Of course. You were the johnnie who was with that Cartwright female when she was attacked by the Senussi. Right?"

"Right," John said.

Skipton showed him to a tourer, fortunately with the roof up; it was just after noon and the sun was very hot. The porter placed the bags in the back and received a tip with a bow and a smirk. "Some show. You must tell me about it. I'm afraid we've a fairly long drive ahead of us."

"Oh. Aren't we spending any time here? I'd love to have a look around." He gestured at the harbour. "History, eh? Aboukir and all that."

"You can't kick a stone in this damned country without unearthing history," Skipton said, starting his engine. "I thought you'd been here before."

"Very briefly. I didn't have a chance to look around."

"Well, you'll be back, when you've some time off. Not that there's anything to see in Abu Qir Bay now; you have to use your imagination if you want to discover old one-eyed Nelson walking the quarterdeck while the cannon bellowed and the French blew up."

He drove across various railway crossings, through a succession of narrow streets leading away from the dock area and then turned right over a canal, blowing his horn repeatedly at the small boys who ran to and fro in front of the car, the camels which, even when being led, wandered along the middle of the road, and the women who smiled and waved at them. "Not my favourite city, I'm afraid."

"But Cairo is."

Skipton snorted. "I'd rather be in Stockton-on-Tees, old man." He was still concentrating on the road, but a few minutes later the houses started to dwindle and in front of them was a familiar road, with the railway line and then the desert on their left and the sea on their right, and the sun in front of them, just beginning its descent. "Thank God for that."

"Forgive my asking," John said, "but aren't we going the wrong way?"

"What makes you say that?"

"Simply that we are driving west, towards Libya. I thought Cairo was south of Alexandria."

"It is, old man. This way we get a better road. The turn-off is at El Damanhur." He glanced at John. "You do know why you're here?"

"Ah . . . to sell typewriters."

"Exactly. And you need to be an expert. You *are* an expert?"

"Are you?"

Skipton gave another snort, and watched the road. This was necessary, for although they were now clear of the city there was still a great deal of traffic, mainly camels and donkeys, but many bicycles, and even several cars, which raced to and fro at great speed. "The wogs don't understand about cars," Skipton said. "They reckon there are only two speeds, full and stop. You going to buy a car?"

"Not on my salary."

"There's no problem with credit, and anyway, sell enough typewriters and there'll be bonuses. Think of it, old man, you have the whole of North Africa in front of you, waiting to buy our typewriters."

"Even the Senussi?"

Skipton grinned. "Even the Senussi have to modernise some time."

"Is there anything I should be saying to you?" John asked.

"Or anything you should be saying to me?"

"Not a thing, old man. We leave the formal introduction to the company to the old man. Just keep your mind on typewriters."

Once they turned off there was, as Skipton had promised, a long, straight and fairly good road leading for a hundred miles to the south-east. Here there was much less traffic, and the main difficulty was keeping awake; the passengers had been served a very good buffet lunch, complete with champagne, while waiting for customs and immigration clearance. John hoped Skipton was more used to the heat than he was. But the railway line had also turned off and ran parallel to the road, and although it was clearly a subsidiary line, the odd train rumbled by, packed with shouting people, jerking him back to wakefulness. Meanwhile the sun settled steadily into the western sky, but it had not yet disappeared, and the early evening was bright, when Skipton said, "Now there is history."

John sat up to look at the three pyramids, some distance off as yet, but still clearly visible. "Memphis," Skipton explained, "used to be the capital of Egypt. Oh, we're talking about several hundred years ago."

"Do I get a closer look at them?" John asked.

"Of course, old man. They are virtually on your doorstep. I'll take you myself. But we can have a quick look now."

The road he took actually swung very close to the pyramids, when John was surprised to see there were a good many more than three, although the first three were the biggest and the others were further off. "The next three are the Sbu Sir, and that one right off in the distance is the Saqqarah step pyramid. And of course the big lump on the riverbank is the Sphinx." John was lost in wonder.

Skipton swung back to cross a canal. Now they were surrounded

75

by houses and people and inevitably, camels, donkeys, bicycles and car horns. "Cairo," Skipton announced. "Al-Qahirah in Arabic. That means 'victorious'. Actually, this is al-Jizah, it's a suburb. The city is across the river."

Which now came into sight, crossed by a broad bridge. "This is ar-Rawdah Street," Skipton explained, "because we are about to cross ar-Rawdah Island."

John was looking at the smooth-flowing brown water. "How wide is it?"

"That depends on the time of year. Right now, about four hundred yards. The Mother of Waters, eh?" Now they were again on dry land, but a few minutes later they were crossing more water, "The ar-Rawdah Rivulet," Skipton said, before he turned left onto another good road, running beside the water. "This is Maspero Street, and it goes the whole length of the city. Over your shoulder there is the Old City, the Misr ad-Qadimah."

They drove past some very modern-looking hospitals, around which were far more modest and, John thought, suitable dwellings. But of course, the British had been here now, whether wanted or not, for sixty years, and they did have a tendency to make themselves comfortable.

Now the river was opening on their left, much wider than before, but a little further on there were more bridges, and . . .

"Is that another island?" John asked.

"That, my boy, is az-Zamalik. The name may not mean anything to you, but it is the home of the Gezira Sporting Club, where only the élite are permitted. We'll get you in. And here," he swung off the road into a driveway, "is Shepheard's Hotel."

It was every bit as grand as John had expected it to be. The only pity was that he was seeing it in the company of Skipton and not Margo. "You mean this is where I am staying?"

"Only for a day or two, while we sort out your digs. It's bloody expensive."

"But the firm is paying, I hope?"

"Only for a day or two," Skipton repeated, and began spluttering in Arabic as the car was surrounded by eager porters.

"Do you speak the lingo?"

"I'm afraid not."

"Bloody difficult language. And you know, they can all speak English, but they won't let on till they have to. Well, old boy, I'm sure you'll spend a comfortable night. I'll call for you tomorrow morning about eight, and take you along to the office. It's not far, on Ramses Street. Close to the railway station, what? The boss'll see you then." He did some more Arabic speaking. "Tootle-oo." He got back into his car and drove off. Not exactly the warmest of welcomes, John thought.

But the welcome inside the hotel was certainly warm enough. Reception clerks bowed obsequiously as they checked his name and passport, bell hops and lift boys scurried, and he found himself in a room, high in the building to be sure, but with its own bathroom and a magnificent view over the river and the island. He was high enough up even to make out the tops of the pyramids, seen through what appeared a forest of mosques and minarets.

"You like?" asked the boy who had brought in his luggage.

"Oh, very much. What time is dinner?"

"Dinner is served from eight, effendi. But before then, there is the cocktail bar."

"Sounds great." John tipped him, and was left alone. He had a cold shower, desperately needed, and dressed for dinner; he had no doubt that in a place like this black tie was de rigueur. And wondered about the whole thing. He was realising that his life, which had been very much his own up to the beginning of this year, had since then been entirely taken over. From the moment, indeed, he had carelessly volunteered to be Margo Cartwright's navigator. Now he seemed to be on a roller-coaster, commanded by someone else, without a clue where he was going to wind up.

He had fallen in love, he knew that now, with a woman who was not at all what she seemed, but had nonetheless taken control of his life and left him trailing in her wake. He was engaged to be married to a girl who, while he had known her all his life, he really didn't know at all, and had no idea when he was going to see again.

Having become engaged, he had already cheated on her with a woman who was utterly false, at least in her personal relationships, no matter how brilliant she might be at training agents, or even being one herself. He had become a trained spy, equipped both physically and mentally, it was supposed and he desperately hoped, to kill if need be. And to suffer untold pain without surrendering.

And here he was, in one of the world's greatest and most famous hotels, dressing for dinner, without a clue as to why he was really here, save that it was not to sell typewriters, except as a cover. Tomorrow he saw the 'boss'. He wondered who this character was?

He rode down in the lift, found his way to the cocktail bar easily enough. Soft lights, soft music and a multi-coloured array of bottles behind the huge bar. It was also fairly full of people. "What will it be, sir?" asked the white-jacketed Egyptian barman.

"Something exotic," John said. That would fit his surroundings. And his mood.

"How about a cocktail, sir? I have one made with arrack. Very good. Very strong."

"Ideal," John said, and inhaled a familiar perfume.

"Well, hello," Margo said.

She was absolutely stunning in a powder-blue evening gown, low cut to reveal a great amount of faintly freckled flesh; her auburn hair was loose and framing her face to soften the slightly gaunt cheekbones. John hastily stood up and nearly fell over. "I had no idea you were in Cairo. Although one always hopes for a miracle."

"Make that two," she told the barman. "I like to be where I am most wanted."

"Which as far as I am concerned is right here. Dinner? We did have an arrangement."

"I know. But I have a date tonight." She half turned her head, and he saw a table of five people on the far side of the room, three men and two women. And one of the men, at least, was watching Margo quite carefully.

"Are they us, or them?" John asked. "Or shouldn't I have said that?"

"I have no idea what you are talking about," she said. "How long are you going to be in Cairo?"

He studied her. He had only his own instincts to tell him that it was she had recommended him to MI6. But then, he had only Umberto's logical but by no means factual reasoning to consider her a spy. Yet he was here, and she was here . . . but it had to be played her way. "I shall be here for the foreseeable future," he said. "I've got myself a job."

"In Cairo?" Either her surprise was genuine or she was a consummate actress.

He grinned. "Why not? The brief glimpse you allowed me of Egypt convinced me that it was a nice place."

"You have got to be joking."

"Then why are you back? Or have you been here all the time?"

She sipped her cocktail and gave a little shudder. "I'm back. It seems my last photographs were such a success they want me to do another collection. The Nile. All four thousand miles of it, right back to its source. Pity you have a job, you could have come along."

"I shouldn't think you'd need a navigator for going up the Nile. What you do need is a pilot."

"I have one," she said. "I leave next Thursday."

"Well, then . . . tomorrow?"

"That would be very nice. I'll meet you here at seven."

"You mean you're not staying here?"

"Of course." She smiled. "But it is such a big hotel, one really needs a rendezvous."

"John Warrey." The middle-aged man with the trim figure and the pencil moustache held out his hand. "Sandy Carmichael. Good to have you here."

"Thank you, sir." John shook hands and was gestured to a chair in the office, airy because of the revolving ceiling fan which assisted what little air came in the open windows.

Carmichael closed the office door, shutting out the several women typists, half of whom were Egyptian, the various male clerks, all of whom were Egyptian, and the three English seniors, amongst them Skipton, who had just brought him from the hotel to the office. "I'm not going to waste time with preliminaries," Carmichael said. "You're here, and you know why you're here. I'm afraid that things are moving rather more quickly than we expected." He seated himself behind his desk. "Smoke?"

"No, thank you."

"Sensible." Carmichael took a cigarette himself from the silver-plated box on the table, flicked a silver-plated lighter. "Let's hope you can keep it up. You've heard about the Nazi-Soviet agreement?"

"It came through on the ship. No details though."

"The Nazis and the Soviets have signed a non-aggression pact. Thus it would appear that Hitler has secured himself from Soviet interference in whatever he plans to do next. Very pragmatic. I mean to say, the Nazis and the Communists hate each other. One can't trust the buggers an inch. The Soviets were negotiating with us for a restraining alliance *against* Hitler, would you believe it? Still, there it is. Hitler wouldn't have done such an abrupt volte-face if he wasn't looking for action. As he has involved the Soviets, that action will be against Poland. Well, we have known for some time that was where he was heading, which is why old umbrella-man gave them a guarantee.

"I won't discuss the rights or wrongs of that with you, Warrey. We aren't allowed to hold opinions in this job, merely do our duty. The point is, we could be within a week or two of war. If it doesn't happen within a week or two, it probably won't until next year, because of the weather in Europe from October onwards. But we must assume the worst."

"I see, sir. And the Italians will come in on the German side?"

"They are contracted to do so, certainly. Whether they will or not is what we are trying to find out. I'm informed that you know Libya."

"I don't actually, sir. I've driven through Cyrenaica, that's all."

"Hm. Well, anyway, I want you to go to Tobruk, leaving today."

"Today, sir?"

"I'm afraid so. This afternoon. We have an agent in Tobruk, for our typewriters. You'll take a sample of new ones. I'll give you a covering letter to Roberto Quesmi. He manages the local retailer. You may trust him absolutely."

John's mind was still whirring. This afternoon! Of all the damned bad luck. But then . . .

"Do you know a woman named Margo Cartwright, sir?" he asked.

"Margo Cartwright? I've heard of her. A Rosita Forbes type."

"In a manner of speaking, sir. Did you know she's here in Cairo?"

"No reason why I should. Why? Is it important?"

"I am supposed to take her out to dinner tonight."

"I see. I'm afraid you will have to put duty before pleasure in this job, Warrey."

"It's not that, sir." Which wasn't altogether true. "I was with Miss Cartwright back in March when we were attacked by Senussi and rescued by the Italians."

"By Jove, so you were." As if he hadn't known that all the time.

"And, well, we, or at least I, got rather pally with the Italian CO, and he told me they suspect Miss Cartwright of being a British spy."

"Good lord, whatever will they think of next?"

"I would like to know where I stand, sir. I was given this job, and the day I arrive here who should I bump into but Margo Cartwright. That's too much of a coincidence. I think I am entitled to know if she is one of us."

"One of us. What a dramatic phrase. I'm afraid I can't tell you that, Warrey. Simply because I don't know. MI6 is inclined to work on the principal that its left hand should never know what its right hand is doing. Certainly when it concerns junior operatives like ourselves. Miss Cartwright may very well be a British agent, but it would be best for all if you didn't ask any questions about her."

"Did you say, junior operatives, sir?"

"I'm afraid so, Warrey. We are an information gathering office. Whatever information we gather is sent off to London. What they do with it, or if they do anything with it, we are never told. I know this probably doesn't add up to whatever romantic ideas they may have planted in your mind at training school, but there it is. Information, that is what we're after. Roberto may have information to give you, or he may be able to put you in contact with people who do have something of value. In either event, gather what you can, sell a few typewriters, and then return here. You will of course carry whatever you are told in your head. Nothing must be written down. Now, Skipton has some digs for you. He's waiting to take you along there now. I suggest you transfer your gear from the hotel to the digs, and be prepared to leave."

"Yes, sir. May I ask a question, sir?"

"You may. But understand that I am not obliged to answer it."

"Is Skipton *au fait* with what I am doing here?"

Carmichael frowned. "He didn't say anything to that effect, did he?"

"No, sir. He didn't say anything about anything. Except the Pyramids."

"Which is as it should be. The one rule I make is that my people do not discuss their job under any circumstances. That goes for you, too, Warrey. Anything else?"

"Just one thing, sir. Why me? I am just out of training school, and here I am, in Cairo, and not just in Cairo, but setting off on a mission."

"I do wish you would abandon these dramatic ideas, Warrey," Carmichael said. "You are going to Tobruk to sell typewriters. That is hardly a mission."

"I would still like to know the reason for my being pitchforked into this situation, sir. What *about* Skipton, and the others out there?"

"They have their duties."

"But visiting Cyrenaica is not one of them."

"No. You are a replacement for our Libyan salesman, Warrey. I agree, you are being hurried a little, but as I have explained, events are moving somewhat quicker than we had anticipated."

"And the man I am replacing, sir?"

Carmichael's eyes were hooded. "He met with an accident. Now you really need to get on. Good luck."

"Best we could do at short notice," Skipton explained, showing John into the fairly large bedroom of the house situated just off Clot Bey Street. "I'm afraid you have to share the bathroom. But just down there are the Azbakiyah Gardens. Very pleasant."

"I'm sure it'll do very well," John agreed.

He wasn't that sure of his landlady, a remarkably young and doe-eyed Egyptian lady, who affected Western dress, worn rather short, and heavily mascaraed eyes, to go with long, thick, black hair. He was going to share a bathroom with this exotic creature?

"Her name is Arsinoe," Skipton explained, "and it is her husband who actually owns the house. His name is Mustafa."

"Does she speak English?"

"Doesn't everyone?" Arsinoe asked, her voice as liquid as her eyes.

"There you have it," Skipton said.

"You no 'ave luggage?" Arsinoe inquired.

"Yes. At the hotel. I'll just fetch it. Would you mind, old man?" Skipton turned right onto Al-Bustan Street to gain the river front and Shepheard's. "Play your cards right," he remarked, "and you won't lack for company."

"What about the husband?" John inquired.

"He's a Suez pilot. Spends a lot of time away from home."

"And if he finds out I am shagging his wife?"

Skipton grinned. "That wouldn't be too good. Egyptians are more inclined to a knife in the dark than a co-respondent's suit in court."

"I'll keep that in mind."

"She serves meals as well," Skipton said.

John found it intensely difficult to be sitting beside a comrade-in-arms and yet be unable to discuss the facts of life with him. They had telephoned from the office, and his suitcases were waiting for him in the concierge's office. "I need to leave a note," John explained.

Skipton raised his eyebrows. "Something important?"

"I'm cancelling a dinner engagement."

"You're a quick worker. Arsinoe may have a job to keep up. I'm afraid I will have to read it."

"Are you my minder?" John inquired, aggressively.

"You're a new boy," Skipton pointed out. "New boys tend to be indiscreet."

John snorted, pulled the pad of hotel paper towards him,

Arsinoe sighed heavily. "My 'usband comes 'ome in a couple of days."

84

"You must be happy about that."

"But then 'e goes again, a couple of days later."

"How sad."

"I am a lonely woman," she explained. "Most of the time."

"I can see that. Why do you not have children?"

"My 'usband . . ." she shrugged.

"Don't tell me he doesn't, ah . . ." he realised he was getting into deep water.

"Oh, 'e does. Like a . . . what you say . . . Macdonald, eh?"

"You mean, Old Macdonald? Good lord. You mean you know that song?"

"Doesn't everyone?" It seemed her favourite expression. "But 'e 'as no, what you call it?"

"I have a train to catch," John explained, finishing his stew.

"You 'ave not 'ad coffee." She got up, went to the stove, hips moving provocatively beneath her short skirt; she wore no stockings, and had very good legs, as she was undoubtedly aware.

How am I going to get out of this? John wondered. It was not a problem in the short term, but in the long . . . on the other hand, he couldn't really afford to offend his landlady, and having to stand Margo up after having waited so long and now come so close . . . "Coffee would be very nice."

She did various things at the stove – the procedure was as complicated as if she were brewing alcohol – and then came back to stand beside his chair. " 'Ow long you stay 'ere?" she asked.

"A long time, I should think."

Her hip brushed his shoulder, and he inhaled her scent. "This is good," she said. "We get to know each other. When my 'usband is not 'ere, eh?"

"I think that would be a very good idea."

She returned to the stove, poured two small cups of coffee, placed one in front of him and sat down in the chair beside his.

"No milk or sugar?" he asked.

"Why you wish these things?"

"Just a thought." He sipped, and nearly choked, not merely from the heat.

"You no like the coffee?" Arsinoe frowned at him.

"It's . . ." John got his breath back. "It's very nice."

"It stimulates, eh? It . . ." Arsinoe placed her left hand in the elbow joint of her right, and brought her right arm up with a sudden movement. "You know this?"

"Ah, yes."

She looked down at his pants. "But not for you?" She sounded more curious than concerned.

"I have a train to catch," he explained, again.

The afternoon was intensely hot, but there might be any one of several reasons for that, apart from the actual temperature. As promised, an Egyptian clerk from the company was waiting for him with a travelling case presumably filled with typewriters. It was certainly heavy. This was placed on board the train by a porter, who was tipped by the clerk. "Good fortune, Mr Warrey," the clerk said, and saluted.

John had a reserved first-class seat, and sank into it with a sigh of relief. Once the train began moving, the breeze coming in the window did something to dry his perspiration, and an hour after leaving Cairo they reached Alexandria, following which, and a lengthy stop, they joined the seaside track and he could look out at the Mediterranean. By then he had already nodded off more than once; it had been an exhausting couple of days, and not merely physically. He felt he needed to think, quite seriously, about a whole lot of things. But for the time being it was necessary to concentrate on the job; time enough to think when he was on his way home again.

From Alexandria the railway followed the coast road he already knew, but at Mersa Matruh, where he and Margo and Safyun had arrived following the road from Siwa, the line turned away from the coast and crossed the desert. This was interesting, not because the desert was interesting – John felt that he had seen enough desert to last him a lifetime – but because it was an interesting logistical exercise.

"First time in Egypt?" asked the man sitting opposite. He had been there since Alexandria, occasionally appearing to nod off himself, but more often studying John.

"No," John said shortly.

"Name's Portman."

"Warrey."

"Travelling, are you?"

"Typewriters."

"Quaint. Do you sell a lot to the natives?"

"What are you in?" John asked.

"Women's corsets."

"I imagine you do a roaring trade in those." Portman gave a snort, and considered the situation. But before he could think of another topic they were at the border, at a place apparently called Salum Sidi Omar, and were once again in sight of the sea.

Here, as John had been warned, it was necessary to disembark but there were ample porters, one of whom took his travelling bags through Italian Customs and Immigration without the slightest check, and out onto a dusty street.

"Signor Warrey?" The man wore European clothes and a topee, but had a dark complexion. "I am Grimaldi," he explained. "I am Signor Quesmi's chauffeur. The car is here."

The car turned out to be a somewhat old Mercedes. "How far to Tobruk?" John asked.

Grimaldi grinned. "Sixty miles. We will be there tonight."

"I never doubted it for a moment," John said, and looked around for Portman; as he had been rather rude to the fellow on the train he presumed he could offer him a lift. But Portman had disappeared.

Once again they drove away from the sea, and across empty desert. "You know the desert?" Grimaldi asked.

"A little," John said.

"Out there is a very big desert," Grimaldo said. "The Sand Sea. Very bad."

"And then?" John decided to be ignorant.

"After a long way, Tibesti. Mountains and lakes. But bad people. Tuaregs, eh?"

"Don't you have some bad people in Libya? Senussi?"

"Ah, they were bad once. Not now."

"Is that a fact."

"Tobruk," Grimaldi said, with some pride. Now John could see the sea again, and the town and the harbour. It looked quite attractive, the buildings an odd mixture of the Arab and the European. "You know this place?" Grimaldi asked.

"No."

"Ah, you know, it is one of the oldest settlements in Africa. The Greeks had a colony here. They called it Antipyrgos. Then the Romans kept it as a fortress, to guard the frontier of Cyrenaica."

"It's a long way from the frontier," John suggested.

"But it has the only natural harbour on this entire coast, until Alexandria," Grimaldi explained. "Very important."

"I can see that," John said, as they drove close to the waterfront and he could see the ships loading and unloading. He was fairly sure what was being unloaded was military supplies, but presumably Carmichael knew that. Now they were in the town itself. He knew the Italians had first occupied it in 1911, only twenty-eight years before, but they had certainly given it an Italian flavour, and on the whole the people looked happy enough. But there were far more soldiers to be seen on the street than there had been in Cairo. "Is it still guarding the frontier?" he asked. He had no means of knowing whether Grimaldi was also on the books of British Intelligence.

"Of course. But Il Duce, he likes lots of soldiers. He says, every Italian should be a soldier."

"You are not a soldier."

"I have served," Grimaldi said, and John decided to drop the conversation.

"Here is your hotel." Grimaldi pulled into the forecourt, and porters hurried forward.

"And Signor Quesmi?" It was now quite dark.

"He expects you at the office tomorrow morning. I will pick you up at nine."

John nodded and had his bags taken inside. *Déjà vu,* he thought. Only this wasn't Shepheard's, and there was no Margo to be bumped into in the bar. But it was comfortable, the staff were friendly, and his recently acquired knowledge of Italian made it easy for him. He showered and had a drink in the bar, avoiding the attempts of various people to engage him in conversation, had a light dinner, and went to bed. The heat was still intense, and with his windows open he was assailed by all the sounds of the town, principally barking dogs.

But he eventually went off, and slept heavily, only awaking when the waiter wheeled in the breakfast he had ordered. The man was looking extremely agitated. "The news," he said. "You have heard the news, signor?"

"I'm afraid not. Something happened?"

"Some thing," the waiter said, rolling his eyes. "The Germans have invaded Poland, signor."

PART TWO

Practising

'But war's a game, which, were their subjects wise,
Kings would not play at.'

William Cowper

Chapter Five

Soroya

With a great effort John refrained from leaping out of bed. "Can
that be true?" he asked.

"Oh, yes, signor," the waiter said. "It is on the wireless."

"But . . . what is the reason for the attack?"

The waiter shrugged. "It is the Poles. They are terrible people.
The wireless says they attacked the German frontier guards."

If you believe that, you'll believe anything, John thought, and
realised that was the exact truth; people like this waiter would
believe anything he was told.

"It will soon be done, the wireless says," the waiter confided.
"Poland will be conquered in a week. That is what it says."

"Was there news of Britain and France?"

"They have protested, signor." The waiter grinned. "They are
always protesting, eh? But what can they do? They cannot help
the Poles. They cannot fight Hitler, eh?"

John did not feel in the least like breakfast, but made himself
eat something, then showered and dressed. His instincts were to
get back to Cairo as quickly as he could, but that simply wasn't
on; more than ever he needed to find out what the Italian attitude
was. At the same time, to stay here in Tobruk, surrounded by
Italians . . .

He went downstairs into the lobby, bought himself a newspaper,
sat down to read it. It was exactly as the waiter had said. Polish
border guards had attacked a German radio station. An act
of criminal madness, the newspaper said. Certainly an act of
madness, John thought. Something must have provoked them.

93

"Ahem," Grimaldi said. John stood up. "Roberto is waiting for you," Grimaldi continued. "Where are the typewriters?"

"My God, I forgot all about them. They're in my room."

"We must have the typewriters," Grimaldi explained. "You have come to Tobruk to show Roberto the newest machines, eh? We must have them."

John fetched the typewriters, sat beside Grimaldi as they drove through the town. "You've heard the news?" he asked. "Do you have any idea what will happen?"

Grimaldi shrugged. "It will be as with Czechoslovakia. There will be much talk and at the end of it, Poland will be part of Germany."

"Just like that," John suggested.

"It is the way of the world, signor."

Roberto Quesmi was a short, fat man with a bald head, who perspired constantly. Or perhaps, John thought, he was perspiring more than usual this morning. But he appeared as reassuring as everyone else. "This was bound to happen, once the Nazi-Soviet pact was signed," he explained, having shaken hands and gestured John to a chair in front of his desk. "I would imagine Poland is to be once again partitioned, as it was between Prussia, Austria and Russia a hundred and fifty years ago. This is bad for the Poles, but . . ." he shrugged.

"Do you believe they actually attacked Germany?" John asked.

"No, no. That is – how do you say? – a put up job, in my estimation. The Poles are a foolish people, but they are not that foolish."

"And how does the situation affect us?"

"Hopefully, not at all."

"Great Britain has given a guarantee to Poland that if she is invaded we will fight on her side."

"Well, you know, that is not very practical, as Britain and Poland are at opposite ends of Europe. I do not think that

94

guarantee means a great deal. Oh, your people will huff and puff, and there may even be a vote of censure, but with his parliamentary majority Chamberlain will survive that easily enough. Now, you have the typewriters? I have fixed up some appointments for you. People who wish to buy typewriters, eh? The codeword is the letter Z, eh? It sticks. Here are the addresses."

John took the typewritten list, glanced over his shoulder. They were out of earshot of the various members of Roberto's staff. "You know all of these people. You know who are our agents and who are not. Why do you not just collect the information yourself and forward it to Cairo?"

"It is very simple, Signor Warrey. I am an Italian citizen. Perhaps I do not agree with everything Signor Mussolini does, but if I am required to do so, I will stand on the street and wave my tricolour and scream my approval as loud as the next man. That way I get to see my grandchildren, eh? You come here with typewriters to sell. I am happy to be of service. I know of people who would like to buy typewriters. I ask them, why you wish to buy English typewriters instead of Olivetti, eh? And if they say they prefer English goods, I suggest they may wish to speak with you further."

"And when they are arrested, and repeat that conversation?"

Roberto grinned. "I do not speak in front of witnesses, signor. It is their word against mine. And in Tobruk, my word is a good word."

"I see. But suppose I am arrested, and give the authorities your name?"

"You would do this?" Roberto looked genuinely shocked.

"I might be tortured," John pointed out. "And unable to resist the pain."

"Then again it would be your word against mine. But, as I am the agent for your typewriters here in Tobruk, would it not be obvious for you to name me as your agent for other things as well? I do not think anyone would believe you."

"Probably not," John said, beginning to feel somewhat nettled.

"But supposing, just supposing, things escalated and Great Britain honoured her guarantee to Poland and declared war on Germany, and thus Italy came in on the German side, as I believe she is obliged to do by the terms of your Axis treaty, and the British Army came storming into Tobruk, which side would you declare for then? Or is that a rhetorical question?"

Roberto continued to smile. "Oh, indeed, Giovanni. This a rhetorical question." He raised his hands and ticked off the fingers. "You say, supposing Great Britain went to war on behalf of Poland? That is hardly practical. You say, supposing Italy then went to war on the German side? That is hardly necessary. And then you say, supposing the British Army comes storming into Tobruk? My dear Giovanni, that is hardly possible. There are two hundred thousand Italian troops in Libya. Are there not perhaps thirty thousand British troops in Egypt? I do not think that would be a contest the British would risk."

"Absolutely," John agreed. "One last question: whose side are you on, really?"

"I do not wish to see war between Italy and Great Britain. I do not, in my heart, support Il Duce in his plans for a vast Italian Empire. Let us first of all sort out the social and economic problems of Italy, eh? Despite what your imperialists say, I think you will find that your British Empire has, on the whole, been a drain on your resources, not a source of profit. I exclude the very few men who have made fortunes out of places like India or South Africa. Italy can do without such drains on our resources. Therefore it follows that the more Great Britain knows about our strength and intentions, the less likely it is that our people will go to war. Do you follow me?"

"Not entirely," John said. "But I suppose I will have to wear it. So, if anything goes wrong with my mission, or any future mission, I cannot expect any help from you."

"My dear fellow, I will utterly disown you. But so will Sandy in Cairo. Did he not explain this to you?"

* * *

"Very neat," said Signor Cartagani. "I especially like the siting of the capital locks. This is new, is it not?"

He ran his hands over the typewriter.

"Designed for greater speed," John explained, watching the somewhat pudgy fingers moving over the left side of the querty keyboard.

"I can see that," Cartagani agreed. "Maria, come and try this machine." His secretary, an extremely buxom Italian young woman, sat at the desk, smiled at John, and began typing at great speed, her somewhat tight shirt front almost wobbling in time to her fingers. "I enjoy watching Maria work," Cartagani explained.

"Absolutely," John agreed, as the deft little finger depressed the Z without apparent discomfort.

"What do you think?" Cartagani asked.

"It is very nice, signor," Maria said. "But . . . it is not so good as my Olivetti."

"An excellent machine," said Signor Armanto. "Indeed. A work of art." As the morning had worn on, John had lost his enthusiasm through heat and disappointment; Armanto was his fifth customer, and he had sold but one machine, but no one had remarked on the Z. "May I try it?" Armanto asked.

Armanto did not rise to such adornments as buxom, white-shirted secretaries. His store was on the street, although it stretched back a good way; it was heavily scented with herbs and vegetables. His staff were local Arabs, selling, in addition to food, leatherware and cottons to passers-by. The rear of the shop was protected from the glare and was somewhat gloomy. Armanto had placed the typewriter in the centre of his large, scarred desk, clearing a sheaf of papers to do so, and now he inserted a sheet and banged a few keys. "Very good," he said. "But . . . the Z sticks."

John, looking around at the large and varied stock in the emporium, turned back very sharply. "Yes," he said. "It does."

"Ah," Armanto said. "This news from Europe, Signor Warrey, will Britain go to war?"

"I have an idea she may well do so," John said. "If only as a token gesture. She has pledged her word, and that is important. What will Italy do?"

"Italy will stay out of the war," Armanto said. "Certainly in its early stages."

"How do you know this?"

Armanto smiled. "I have a close friend, who also sleeps with one of General Graziani's aides. She tells me these things. Italy is quite unprepared for war. She has no oil, not sufficient bullets, and economically the country is in a state of catastrophe. She cannot fight a war without massive German aid, and for the moment the Germans require all their resources for themselves. Besides, they do not need Italian help to beat Poland. Do you know that the Italians, even Mussolini, I understand, did not know of this German coup until it had happened? They reckon that absolves them from all obligations under the Axis treaty. Not that they wish to let Germany down. They will never repudiate her actions. But the Italian scenario is that Germany should conquer Poland, and as you say, the British, and perhaps the French, will fire a few token shots and then realise that they are faced with a *fait accompli*, and the war will be over. Oh, it will certainly spring up again in a few years time, when Italy will be ready."

"You can guarantee this?"

"As near as it is possible to guarantee anything. I can tell you for certain that Graziani has no orders to move troops towards the Egyptian frontier."

"That could be because no war has as yet been declared."

Armanto grinned. "You are too much of a gentleman, Giovanni. In this modern world, the tendency is to move troops to the frontier first, and declare war second."

"But there are sufficient Italian troops in Libya to fight a war, are there not? I have heard the figure of two hundred thousand mentioned."

"That is true. But this figure is well-known. And they are here because the Italians fear the British, after that Abyssinian business, rather than the other way about." He tapped his nose. "That is the official line."

"Got it. But . . . no war."

"No war, Giovanni. Unless the situation changes dramatically."

"I hope you have had a successful day," Roberto remarked, when John returned to the office that evening.

"Exhausting, but I think, successful. Is it possible to return to Egypt tomorrow?"

"It is possible, certainly. But why do you wish to do this?"

"I think it is necessary."

Roberto tapped his desk with his pen. "I have an appointment for you, tomorrow."

John frowned. "With whom?"

"A man named Ali Selim bin Fuad. He is a Senussi sheikh."

John's frown deepened. "A Senussi wishes to speak with me?"

"Yes." Roberto grinned. "He wishes to buy a typewriter. An English typewriter. This could be a lucrative outlet for you. For us, eh?"

Grimaldi picked John up at dawn. John hoped Roberto knew what he was doing, as they drove out of town and followed a track leading south-west, absolutely straight into the distance, although the surface was sufficiently uneven to prevent them going too fast. Behind them a column of dust rose into the air. "This is Marmara," Grimaldi explained. "It is a big, sandy plain, eh? But you see, there is more stone than sand. It is good for – how do you say? – playing at soldiers?"

"Manoeuvres," John suggested.

"That is it. Manoeuvres." He braked without warning, and John saw several more columns of dust rising into the air perhaps three miles away, and heading north. "A squadron of tanks."

"Where are they going?"

"Home to base. They have been out on these manoeuvres, eh?"

"How far south would they have been?"

"Not far. Only fifty miles away is the great sand sea. That is not good, even for tanks." They drove for another hour, then Grimaldi turned off onto a side track, even more bumpy and not so straight. Suddenly there were people. John remembered the scenario well, the line of armed horsemen on a low ridge to their right. And this time he was totally unarmed, as was Grimaldi. But this time he was a friend. So it seemed.

The car bounced round another corner and the end of the hillock, and they saw palm trees. "It is a small oasis," Grimaldi explained. "But it suffices for Ali Selim bin Fuad."

Dogs barked, goats bleated. Children of both sexes swarmed out of the brightly painted – in pastel shades of blue and yellow and white – little houses that clustered round the water. Behind them rose the tower of the minaret. A whole civilisation, John thought, only a few miles from that of the Italians, but a million years away in culture and belief.

The car stopped, and was surrounded by the children and dogs. But these scattered as the men came forward. Grimaldi spoke to them in Arabic and they grinned and inspected John as he got out himself. "The sheikh awaits you," Grimaldi said. "Don't forget the typewriters."

John followed Grimaldi through the crowd, carrying his suit-case, sniffed at by the dogs, stared at by the women, whose eyes were the only parts of their bodies visible behind their haiks and yashmaks. Arab women always made him uneasy. They walked up a narrow, dusty and dung-littered street, and came to a house only slightly larger than the others in the village. There was a bead curtain and several more men, who conversed with Grimaldi and then parted the beads to allow John into the house. It was so dark after the glare outside that he had to stand quite still for several seconds to accustom his eyes to the gloom.

"Signor Warrey," said a quiet voice, to his utter surprise speaking perfect English. "Come and sit down."

The sheikh sat on a pile of carpets on the far side of the room. He was dark-skinned, wore the conventional jibbah and burnous and sandals, and was alone save for a cat, which sat on his lap to be stroked, and purred gently. It did not appear alarmed at the sight of a stranger, not even when John sat down as invited. Grimaldi had remained in the doorway, but now he was waved away, escorted by the guards. "Don't tell me," John said. "You were educated at Oxford."

Ali Selim bin Fuad's teeth gleamed through his beard as he smiled. "Sadly, I have never been to England. I was educated in Cairo. Tell me, do you trust that man? The Italian?"

"Thus far," John replied.

"Well said. Nowadays, it is difficult to know who to trust. But I am told I can trust you, Mr Warrey."

"Who told you that?"

"Roberto Quesmi."

"Who employs Grimaldi."

The two men gazed at each other for several seconds, then Ali gave a short bark of laughter. "As you say. Show me your typewriter." John unpacked his case, laid the instrument before Ali, who inserted a sheet of paper and tried a few keys. "The Z sticks. Am I right?"

"You are, Sheikh Ali."

"Will Great Britain fight against the Nazis?"

"I believe she will."

"And against the Italians?"

"Great Britain will not declare war on Italy, if that is what you mean. She would have to be provoked. I am told there will be peace. Because the Italians wish it so."

Ali struck a few more keys. "If there were to be a rising of the Senussi against the Italians, would the British help?"

"No." Ali's head came up, his brows drawing together over the huge beak of a nose. "Great Britain will not interfere in the internal affairs of another country," John said.

"Not even if it would be in her interests to do so?"

"Not even then," John said. "If we were at war with Italy, now, that would be different."

"Your people play a waiting game," Ali grumbled. "You would forfeit the friendship, and therefore the help, of my people."

"I would beg you to do nothing rash. We must wait upon events."

Ali gazed at him for several seconds. Then he clapped his hands. "Food!" he shouted. "Food and drink for our guest."

They ate with their fingers, in the company of most of the village, it seemed to John, then everyone was waved away again out of earshot as Ali and John drank thick black coffee.

"I will tell my people what you say," Ali said. "I will beg them to be patient. This will be difficult, but I can do it. But they will need – how can I put it? – encouragement. Were there to be a war between Great Britain and Italy, in which we would take part, we would be outnumbered. Not so much in men, but in arms, and the quality of the arms. It would encourage my people greatly were they able to procure modern weapons." He gazed at John over the rim of his cup.

"How would we get these arms to you?" John asked.

"Across the desert. My people know ways that are not known to the Italians."

"I can promise nothing," John said. "But I will tell my superiors what you have said. Supposing they were interested, how may I contact you? Through Roberto?"

"No," Ali said, very definitely. "When do you return to Cairo?"

"Tomorrow."

"And you are living there? You have a house?"

"I have an address."

"Write it down for me and I will make contact with you. How long will you need to procure these guns?"

"I have said, I can promise nothing," John reminded him. "I must put the project before my superiors. And they must put it before *their* superiors. This will take time."

"How long?" Ali asked again.

"Contact me in one month."

"One month." Ali did not look very pleased.

"It would, however," John said, "both please my masters and convince them of your determination were you to help them in any way possible."

"How can I help them, when I am not allowed to start a war against the Italians?"

"You can give them information," John said. "I am sure there will be a war, eventually. The Italians believe this too. Thus they are preparing for it. In the desert, a modern army needs fuel and bullets and shells as much as water. The Italians are preparing stocks of these at certain places in the desert. We call them dumps. My superiors would be very grateful, and the more inclined to help you, if you were able to give us the situation of these dumps. Or some of them, at any rate."

Ali stroked his beard. "In the desert, how can one say something is there? There are no streets, eh?"

"Send someone to me, one month from today," John said, "and I will give your messenger a map, with grids and co-ordinates. Then you can mark the position of the dumps, and return the map to me."

"You realise that if I am caught doing this I will be hanged?"

"When we go to war, a great many people will die," John pointed out.

Ali considered him for several seconds, then he grinned. "Very good, one month. Now, you have a servant?"

"Ah . . . no."

"Every man must have a servant. I give you one." Ali clapped

103

his hands, said something in Arabic to the man who bowed before him. "You may take your pick," Ali said.

John blinked at the six young women who presented themselves before him. Each was totally enclosed beneath haik and yashmak, but they were at least slender of thigh and shoulder.

"You mean you wish me to take one of these?"

"That is what I mean, yes."

"As my servant?"

Ali shrugged. "As your servant, certainly. But you may use her for whatever purpose you wish."

Imagination boggled. Even more at what Carmichael might say. "I really couldn't do that," he protested.

"You refuse my gift?" Ali's brows drew together. Then he gave a shout of laughter. "Ah. I understand. You would prefer a boy. Then it shall be a boy."

"And will he also expect to be used for whatever purpose I wish?"

"But of course. He will be your slave."

"Ah. Then . . . I think I would prefer a girl." He had no wish to offend the sheikh, and besides, having a female servant might keep Arsinoe at bay. "But suppose the girl I choose does not wish to be my . . . servant?"

"These girls are my slaves," Ali said. "They will do whatever I tell them to do, now and for the rest of their lives. They will protect you, and care for you . . . and serve you in any way possible."

"As long as I serve you?" John suggested.

Ali's teeth gleamed. "Is that not a fair arrangement?"

"You mean she will not actually belong to me."

"In effect, yes. She will be a loan. A permanent loan, perhaps."

"But her ultimate loyalty will always be to you. Therefore my ultimate loyalty will have to be to you, as well."

"In matters that concern us both, Giovanni, great matters, we must always be loyal to each other. Does that not please you?"

"I'm sure. There's just one problem: I do not speak Arabic."

"My girls speak Italian," Ali said. "Uncover yourselves," he said, in that language. Each girl in turn reached up and released her yashmak, allowing it to fall beside her cheek. They were certainly pretty enough, although their smiles had a coquettish quality John did not appreciate. "You wish to see more?" Ali inquired.

"Ah . . . no. Not at the moment."

"Then choose."

John surveyed the women. They all seemed eager enough, and he presumed they knew for what purpose they had been lined up. "That one," he said. She had the most serious face.

"Soroya. Yes, that is a good choice. She can cook, too."

Soroya smiled at him and he felt more uneasy yet. She was the tallest of the girls and perhaps the eldest, although he did not suppose she was a day over twenty. Her face was strongly handsome, her eyes dark pools. He estimated she had a full figure. Ali was watching him with interest. "She will also be able to assure you that any messenger who may come to your Cairo house is from me," Ali pointed out.

"Excellent," John agreed.

Ali clapped his hands and the girls scurried off, including Soroya. "She is fetching her things," Ali said. "Now, my friend John, you will treat her well, eh? When you beat her, do not break the skin."

"You think I should beat her?"

"Well, of course," Ali said. "How else may a man please a woman?"

John scratched his head as he wondered how Aileen, or Margo, or most of all, Samantha Carson, would react to that philosophy.

"He gave you this woman, just like that?" Grimaldi asked, as they drove back to Tobruk.

"Actually, she's a loan. The sheikh felt I needed a servant,"

John explained, and looked over his shoulder at Soroya, seated in the back, yashmak and haik fluttering in the breeze, her somewhat small bundle of personal belongings clutched to her side. He saw the face mask inflate as she smiled at him. He really had no idea what the rest of her looked like, but he was an optimist. Of course, any idea of 'using' her as Ali had suggested was out of the question, he told himself. But it was a heady feeling. He had never actually owned a woman before.

"We all need servants," Grimaldi grumbled as they rumbled into the town.

He pulled into the hotel forecourt, and porters hurried forward. Grimaldi came inside with them, and they presented themselves at reception. "This young lady intends to spend the night here," John explained to the clerk. "I wish a room for her."

The clerk scratched his ear while he looked Soroya up and down. "Bedouin?" he asked.

"Senussi, you droppings from a goat's arse," Soroya informed him.

"Oh, shit," John commented, anticipating a punch-up.

But the clerk remained extremely relaxed. "If I thought you knew how to use a bed I'd give you one."

"Listen," Grimaldi said. "Just do it."

"Who is to pay?" the clerk demanded.

"She goes on my bill," John said.

The clerk snorted and handed over a key. "I will wish you a good night," Grimaldi said, and rolled his eyes.

But it was not to begin yet. As John escorted Soroya towards the stairs leading up, Roberto emerged from the lounge. "Where have you been? I have been waiting all afternoon for you." He looked at Soroya, eyebrows arched.

"Please don't say anything," John begged. "I don't think she's in a good mood."

"She's from Ali?"

"Yes. A sort of go-between he thought I should have."

"Go between what, eh? Or who?" Roberto gave a brief shout

of laughter, which ended as Soroya turned her gaze on him. "Listen, while you have been enjoying yourself, there have been developments. The British, that man with the umbrella, has issued an ultimatum. To Germany. Would you believe it?"

"I said it was probable. What has he demanded?"

"That they withdraw all troops from Poland, and renounce hostilities, by eleven o'clock tommorow morning. Can you believe it?"

"What has been the German response?"

"There has been no response. Nor will there be. Hitler must be sick with laughing."

"Yes. Well, in all the circumstances, I think I need to be out of Libya before eleven o'clock tomorrow morning. Can you arrange it?"

"Grimaldi will pick you up at seven. You are taking this woman to Egypt with you? Does she have a passport?"

"Yes, I have a passport, jackass," Soroya said, speaking Italian.

"I wish you joy of her," Roberto said, and held out his hand. "We will meet again."

"I am sure of it. And many thanks for your help."

"One does what one can," Roberto said, looking Soroya up and down again, and hurried off.

"I do not trust him," Soroya remarked.

"I suspect the feeling is mutual. I'm starving. How about you?"

"Food will be good," she said, and waited. He realised that however vigorous her response to masculine insults, he was supposed to mount the stairs first. There was a lot about this young woman that was going to take getting used to.

"It never occurred to me that you would need a passport," he said over his shoulder. "Or that you would have one."

"I belong to Ali," she said. "Therefore I have a passport." John couldn't quite make the connection at that moment.

"What I do not understand," Soroya said, "is why I am to sleep in a separate room. Do you not like me?"

"I like you very much," John assured her, not wishing to be compared to the droppings of a camel or whatever. "But it is correct, you see. As we are not married."

"I am your concubine."

"Ah . . . no. You are my servant. There is a difference."

They had reached the first floor, and he led her along the corridor. "You do not like me," she said again, and he checked and turned at the change in her tone, and saw to her utter consternation that there were tears in her eyes. She had rather lovely eyes.

"I do, I do," he promised her. "I like you very much. We are going to be great friends. Who knows, we may even become concubines. I mean, you may become my concubine. In the course of time. When we get to know each other better. Right now, there is a lot going on and I have a lot on my mind. This is your room." He opened the door. "I suggest you have a shower, change your clothes and join me in the bar downstairs in half an hour. Okay?"

"Bar?" she asked.

"The place where one meets to have a cocktail before dinner. Ah! You're a Muslim."

"I am a believer."

"Quite. Well, you don't have to drink alcohol. You can have orange juice."

"I can have ass's milk."

"Why not? If it's available. See you in half an hour."

She stepped into the room, then turned. "What is this, shower?"

"There is a room through there, in which you will see a nozzle in the ceiling. Turn on the tap, and water will come out."

"It is to drink?"

"No, I wouldn't recommend that. It is to stand beneath and get clean. And cool."

"My clothes will get wet."

"You take off your clothes first," he explained.

She frowned at him. "You will come for this?"

"No. I'll be showering in my room. But I'll be thinking of you."

He didn't think there would be any doubt about that.

Then why not go the whole hog and take the girl? It was a great temptation, the more so after his second recent frustration with Margo. How he cursed his inhibitions. But there was more to it than that. There was the memory that the woman he had sought so desperately, with the image of Margo in his mind, had turned out to be as deceitful as any woman could be. There was also the consideration that Soroya, however much she might claim to belong to him, actually belonged to Ali. Whatever she did would be because Ali had told her to do it. That included sleeping with the Englishman, and making him desire her more and more. There was heady thought, but a treacherous one. He had no idea how many men she might have slept with because Ali had told her to. Or how often she might have slept with Ali himself.

The shower felt so very good after the long day in the desert. And truth to tell, he was very pleased with himself. He felt he had accomplished a great deal in his two days. He would have accomplished even more but for Hitler jumping the gun and Chamberlain responding so vigorously. He was not responsible for that. But Carmichael could not help but acknowledge that he had covered a lot of ground. And Ali could prove a great asset . . .

A hand reached past him and switched off the water. "You will drown, or catch cold," Soroya said, severely.

John's initial response had been to react violently to the intruder, and before he could stop himself he had begun a blow to her midriff which, only half-checked, had her gasping and bending double. Now to his consternation he discovered not only who it was, but that she was naked, as she had removed her clothes before stepping into the shower stall behind him.

Any fears as to what might lie beneath the haik were immediately dissipated; Soroya was a very well endowed young woman, in every direction, from flowing black hair past heavy breasts to strong thighs and long legs, all a delicious golden brown, to another mass of black hair. She was also apparently in pain, which figured, as she half turned away from him and sank to her knees. He knelt beside her, water dripping onto her back, and held her shoulders. "I'm sorry. I didn't mean to hurt you. But you shouldn't creep up behind a man like that."

For response she crawled away from him, reached the bed and draped her torso across it, leaving her buttocks exposed. "No, no," he said. "Get up." He didn't really want her to, but it simply wasn't on.

"I have offended you," she said, her voice issuing from the sheet into which her face was pressed. "You must beat me."

He gazed at the rounded flesh. There was so much he would like to do with that. But for God's sake, he reminded himself he was an officer and a gentleman, on a mission. "I do not wish to beat you. Get up."

She looked over her shoulder. "You are not angry with me?"

"No, no, not in the least. Or I won't be when you stop soaking my sheets."

"Then you must want to fuck me. I can see that you do."

"Oh, for God's sake." He hastily turned away from her, towelled himself.

"You hate me," she said.

He kept his back to her. "Listen, I do not hate you."

"But you will not fuck me."

"No, I will not. Not right now, anyway. You must understand." He pulled on a pair of underpants and felt safer. "We are working together, you and I. We are working for Ali. And right now, we must concentrate on that work."

She stood up. "We work better if we fuck," she suggested.

"When we get back to Egypt," he said.

"You swear this?"

"No, I do not swear this. But that's the soonest it's going to happen. Now get dressed." He peered at the discarded clothes, which consisted of a short underskirt, and a longer sort of shift; there was also the haik. Hardly cocktail wear. "Have you nothing else?"

"Why I should have something else? I have my yashmak."

"Then they will have to do. Would you mind getting dressed?"

She did some more pouting and sighing, but put on her clothes and wrapped herself in the haik. "There will be no need for the yashmak," he said.

"You wish strange men to look on my face?" she asked, in tones as injured as Aileen might have used had he suggested she walk down the street with her breasts bared.

"You have a beautiful face," he said. "Why should not men look at it? It is the rest of you that matters, and that belongs to me, does it not?"

Almost he thought she was going to scratch her head. But she liked what he had said. "You think I am beautiful?"

"Indeed I do."

"But you will not fuck me." She shook her head sadly, and waited for him to finish dressing.

Actually, he felt a considerable sense of pride as they descended the stairs together. She *was* a beautiful woman, far more so, classically, than any of the other three who had played so important parts in his recent life, and she moved beautifully too, her carriage upright, her face severe, her chin tilting up from time to time. He reckoned she was highly nervous, as this was the first time she had ever appeared in public with her face exposed. "All these men," she muttered as they entered the bar. "Staring at me."

"They are all admiring you," he told her. And then checked, still hanging on to her arm, as one of the Italian officers forming a group at the bar detached himself and came towards them. Umberto!

111

Chapter Six

War

"John Warrey!" Umberto seemed genuinely pleased to see him. "I had not expected to see you in Tobruk. Or anywhere in Libya, after your experiences."

"Ah . . ." John was desperately trying to think; he was no believer in coincidences. And Umberto had been promoted over the summer; he was now wearing a colonel's insignia. "I hadn't expected to see you either."

"But this is my – how do you say? – patch? Tobruk is my headquarters. You did not know this?"

"Nobody told me," John said, and wondered why they hadn't.

"But it is not your patch, eh?" Umberto asked.

"Well, old man, actually it is. I'm a salesman for a firm in Cairo. Selling typewriters."

Umberto gazed at him for several seconds. "Cairo," he said. "But you were not working for this firm when we met in the desert."

"No, no, I was navigating Miss Cartwright, remember? But I liked Cairo, Egypt, so much, I applied for a job there, and got it."

"Who is this arsehole?" Soroya inquired. Umberto raised his eyebrows.

"I do beg your pardon," John said. "Her Italian is limited mainly to expletives. This gentleman is a friend of mine," he told Soroya. "He saved my life." Soroya's gaze became more benign.

112

"And the lady?" Umberto asked.

"A friend."

"Who is staying in this hotel with you?"

"Is there a law against that? We have separate bedrooms."

"She is a Senussi," Umberto pointed out.

"Is she really? I had no idea. How can you tell?"

"I would not have thought you would ever wish to get close to any Senussi again after your experience," Umberto said. "As for a Senussi woman . . . they are fiends in human form."

John gave Soroya an anxious glance, afraid that another explosion might be on the way. But she seemed pleased with the description. "Oh, well, they're not all bad," he remarked.

"May I ask where you obtained her?"

"My dear fellow, she's the daughter of a friend. I am taking her to Cairo to complete her education."

Umberto considered this, while John mentally cursed his luck at the so inopportune meeting. "You have a friend who is a Senussi?" Umberto asked.

"Chap I met in Cairo. Like I said, they're not all bad."

"And when are you returning to Egypt?" the Italian asked.

"Crack of dawn tomorrow morning."

"That is probably wise. You are selling typewriters, you say. May I look at these typewriters?" He grinned. "I may wish to buy one myself."

"Certainly." John escorted Soroya to a table and sat her down, ordered her an orange juice; there was, apparently, no ass's milk available. "Now," he said. "You sit here and sip that and don't speak to anybody unless you can think of something nice to say. I'll be back in a few minutes."

"You prefer him to me?" The question was disparaging.

"By no means. We have business together."

He led Umberto upstairs, opened the suitcase and displayed one of the two remaining typewriters.

"Very good," Umberto said, and ran his fingers over the keys.

Now, John wondered, what do I do if he says the Z sticks? But he didn't.

"Very good," Umberto said again. "Giovanni, I am sorry I felt it necessary to check. I do not like this Senussi business. What is she really to you?"

"Well . . ." John tried to look embarrassed and did not find it the least difficult. "Actually, I bought her."

"Explain?"

"I went to a party last night, and these girls were for sale, and I was feeling randy, and before I knew it, bingo. I suppose I was drunk."

"Slavery is forbidden in Libya," Umberto said severely. And then shrugged. "But it goes on. And the girl looks contented enough. I have no intention of stopping you taking her out of the country. But how will you get her into Egypt?"

"Believe it or not, she has a passport."

Once again Umberto considered for some seconds before speaking. Then he said, "I wish you joy of her. May I ask you another question?" He had suddenly switched to Italian.

"Certainly."

"I did not know you were fluent in our language. You did not speak it when last we met."

"Well, you were speaking English. As a matter of fact, I only had a few words then. But I learned it during the summer. It was necessary, you see, in order to obtain this job. Selling typewriters."

"Ah," Umberto said.

Obviously he knew he had been told a great many lies, John reflected. And once again felt regret that it had to be so; he thought that Umberto was a man he could genuinely like. But tomorrow the whole world was going to explode, and he had no idea what would happen after that.

"I do not think he likes me," Soroya remarked as they had dinner. "All those other men liked me. But not that one."

"He has a suspicious nature," John told her. He could believe it about the other men, who had stared at Soroya; those of them dining were still doing so, while the waiters were in a state of some agitation. No doubt they were unused to having an Arab woman dining in their restaurant, but there were other reasons.

"What is this thing?" Soroya asked, daintily conveying a piece of meat to her mouth between finger and thumb.

"It's called a fork, and it is for lifting the food to your mouth, instead of your fingers."

She made a few not very successful attempts, then uttered a noise like a low-flying aircraft. "I prefer my fingers."

"Now," she announced after dinner. "I dance for you."

"That really isn't necessary."

"It will make you hard with wanting me."

"I'm sure it will. But I do not want to be hard with wanting you tonight. I have said, when we get to Cairo . . ."

"Cairo," she sighed. She was easily distracted. "I will like Cairo."

"And Cairo will like you," he said. Hopefully. "Now," he patted her bottom. "Off to bed. We leave at dawn."

"I do not understand you," she remarked.

"You will, in the course of time."

He wondered if he should lock her in, but she seemed prepared to obey him in all things, at least for the time being, and he was both desperately tired and desperately anxious to get out of Tobruk. He could not doubt that Umberto was attempting to find out just where he had picked up his Senussi woman. If he somehow managed to trace her back to Sheikh Ali . . . What had he been doing in the hotel anyway? Someone must have tipped him off that his old friend John Warrey was in residence.

He slept heavily and awoke to find Soroya standing beside his bed. The sight of her nearly gave him a heart attack, for she was naked and carried a straight razor in her hand. Senussi women! He sat up and she placed a hand on his chest and pushed him flat again, and then straddled him. "I am to shave you," she ssaid. "Sheikh Ali told me that you would wish to be shaved, every day, first thing in the morning."

"And he was quite right. But I have always shaved myself. And you need water and soap, not just a knife. So if you don't mind . . ."

She wriggled her bottom to get herself into the position she required. "Now," she said, "you fuck me."

John reflected that it would be risking a great deal to reject a Senussi woman sitting astride his thighs with a naked razor in her hand.

"What is that?" Soroya inquired, as Grimaldi stopped the car outside the railway station.

"That is a train," John explained.

"I have heard of this," she said.

"But you've never seen one?"

"There is a train in Benghazi," she said. "I have been told this. But I have never been to Benghazi," she added darkly.

He reckoned she had the mind of a twelve-year-old girl. But as she had the body of a twenty-year-old woman, and in certain directions the knowledge of a fifty-year-old, that did not make her any the less dangerous, or attractive . . . or sensual. My God, he thought, only two hours ago I was being raped by this magnificent creature – to all intents and purposes. And not once, throughout her surges, had she let go of the razor. He suspected his hair might be turning white.

He wondered if Grimaldi guessed that he had had her. But no doubt Grimaldi accepted that he would have jumped into bed with Soroya the moment he had got her upstairs in the hotel. This morning the Italian was pensive. "Will we meet again, signor?" he asked, as he carried John's bags onto the platform. Soroya was left to bring her own bundle.

"I would say that is entirely in the lap of the gods," John said, shaking hands. "You and Roberto have been a great help to me. I appreciate it, and so will my employers."

"We must hope for the best," Grimaldi said, enigmatically.

The Egyptian customs officer peered at Soroya, who was sitting absolutely motionless, petrified with a mixture of fear and delight as the train moved the few hundred yards to the border. "She is with you, effendi?" he asked.

"She is the daughter of an old friend and is going to visit her aunt in Cairo," John explained. "I am her chaperon."

The official raised his eyes to heaven, but he stamped the two passports; John could not be sure whether he merely envied the white man who had so easily picked up the girl of the month or whether he disliked being treated like an idiot. John also wondered if he was aware the world was about to collapse into war?

"I do not feel well," Soroya announced, as the train rumbled east.

"It is the motion," John told her. "Take deep breaths."

At least it kept her out of mischief, allowed him to study her without an immediate and embarrassing response. What was he going to do with her? Because having tasted, as it were, possession, he did not think she was going to give it up, however she might be temporarily sated. But then, having tasted what she had to offer, he didn't think he was going to give it away, either. What price Margo now? Or Aileen? Or Samantha Carson? History.

It was several hours to Alexandria. He bought them a picnic lunch in Alamein, which she seemed able to stomach, as the train was stopped to allow her, and all the Muslim passengers, to perform their midday prayers. But she also seemed to have got slightly more used to the motion. "Perhaps I will like this," she remarked. "We always travel, so?"

"Just as far as Cairo."

They reached Alexandria in the middle of the afternoon and there were the newsboys hawking their papers up and down the platform. "What is this war?" Soroya inquired.

"I reckon you might consider it man's natural state," John suggested, and wondered if she wouldn't be right?

Cairo was in a state of vast agitation. Perhaps Alexandria was by now also, but it was five in the afternoon and the news had had time to sink in. Again newspaper headlines were being flashed, people were gathering in little groups to discuss the news, soldiers were hurrying to and fro looking terribly important, but as they couldn't possibly have received any meaningful orders yet John reckoned they were really looking for the nearest bar. A taxi took them to Arsinoe's house, where the door, to his enormous relief, was opened by a large Egyptian man. "You must be Mustafa," John said. "I'm John Warrey. I'm your tenant."

Mustafa looked him up and down suspiciously.

"Mr Warrey!" Arsinoe hurried through from the back, wiping her hands on her apron, dark eyes sparkling. She checked at the sight of Soroya, dark eyes losing some of their lustre. "What is this?"

"My servant," John explained.

Mustafa stepped aside to let them into the house. "How you have a servant?" Arsinoe demanded. "Where is she to go?"

"I go with him, arsehole," Soroya said, her voice somewhat disembodied beneath the yashmak.

"What she say?" Arsinoe enquired, uncertain whether or not to take deep offence.

"Don't you speak Italian?" John asked with some relief. "She said, hello, how are you, so pleased to meet you."

"Ha! And where she is to sleep? You have only one bedroom. And only one bed," she added for good measure.

"We'll make her own arrangements," John assured her.

"You turn my house into a brothel!" Arsinoe declared.

"Your house is only fit for camel shit," Soroya informed her, apparently understanding something of what was being said.

John turned to the master. Hopefully. "Do you have any objection to my servant living with me?"

Mustafa no doubt knew enough about his wife, and his wife's habits when he was not around, to feel very comfortable at having another woman – and what a woman – about the place. "I have none, effendi."

"Ha!" Arsinoe repeated.

"Well, then," John said. "We'll just move in."

"I do not think she likes me," Soroya remarked, when the door had closed on them.

John felt he had to report right away. He did not suppose it would do a lot of good to request Soroya not to become engaged in a fist fight before he returned; he put his faith in Mustafa. "Just be a good girl," he begged. "And tonight I'll let you dance for me."

That seemed to please her and he hurried along to the office, where the lights were burning as the dusk closed in. "Warrey! Thank God you're back," Carmichael said. "You've heard the news?"

John nodded. "My information is that Italy will not be involved."

"That ties in with our other reports. Have you anything else? Sit down, man, sit down."

John sat before the desk and outlined his conversation with Sheikh Ali. Carmichael stroked his chin. "You were sent to him by Quesmi?"

"My information is that the sheikh asked for the meeting."

"Hm. Do you trust him?"

"In so far as he wishes to do business with us, and believes we wish to do business with him, yes. Attitudes can change."

"Quite. Well, we must see what he comes up with regarding Italian fuel dumps. That was a clever move on your part. But you will be careful. You have no means of knowing if his messenger is genuine."

"Er, I do, as a matter of fact."

Carmichael raised his eyebrows.

"Sheikh Ali gave me a servant, partly, I think, because he

119

wished to impress me with the command he has over his people, and partly so that any messenger purporting to come from him could be identified."

"Hm." Carmichael looked embarrassed. "You need to be careful of these young Arab lads, Warrey. But I expect you know that."

"I will be careful, sir. May I ask about the possibility of supplying weapons to the Senussi?"

"Tricky business, that. I shall forward your report to London, of course. We'll have to see what they say. You understand that it would be in our interest not to offend Mussolini until we have sorted Hitler out."

"I understand that, sir."

"So, as I say, we'll have to wait and see. Of course, were the Italians to go to war now, then we would give the Senussi all the help we can. But you've done well, Warrey. Very well. Now, for the time being, while we wait to see which way the Italians go, you will carry out your normal work here in the office. Did you actually sell any typewriters?"

"I sold two, sir."

"Oh, well done! Well, fill out the invoices and what have you and present them to the chief clerk. We must keep up appearances, eh? Now, my wife and I are having a small supper party tomorrow night. We'd be delighted if you would come along."

While the lights might be going out in Europe, they continued to burn very brightly in Egypt, certainly once it was realised that Italy was *not* going to enter the war. Indeed, as Poland was rapidly overrun by the Germans from the west and the Russians from the east, repeating the historical partition of a century and a half earlier, the whole world seemed to have settled into a kind of equilibrium, two armed camps eyeing each other with mutual suspicion, but each afraid to make the first aggressive move. At home of course things were still being taken very seriously. John received regular letters from both his mother and Aileen, depicting blackouts and rationing, false alarms and various items of domestic news. Aileen, it seemed, had settled in very well as a soldier, and was having the time of her hitherto uneventful life.

It all seemed a million light years away from the round of cocktail parties, and, as Christmas approached, dances and garden parties that filled the Cairo evenings. These were what he wrote about in reply. There was nothing else he could, or dared, tell them. The small British army in Egypt, while quietly strengthening their frontier posts, were anxious to let sleeping dogs lie; they were well aware they were outnumbered by more than six to one by the Italian forces in Cyrenaica, much less in all Libya, and equally, that the Egyptians themselves had no desire to be involved in a shooting war, even if not all of them hated the British to the extent of their king, who secretly sent Hitler a message wishing him an early victory.

Domestically, somewhat to his initial concern, Soroya and Arsinoe appeared to become friends very rapidly; he surmised that both women were basically lonely and had hitherto had only sex to consider as an outlet. Now perhaps they still did, with each other; they were able to converse in Arabic, although Soroya set to work to learn English as rapidly as possible. As she did most of her learning from Arsinoe's somewhat limited vocabulary she was actually merely extending her already extensive knowledge of swearwords. John was very content with the arrangement. Soroya remained an eager bedfellow to him when he was there, and in that respect he had to consider himself the most fortunate man alive. Her presence certainly eliminated the lingering, unhappy, memories of both Margo Cartwright and Samantha Carson. But she was also there to work, and within a month an Arab duly presented himself at the door of Arsinoe's house.

"What is this?" the landlady demanded. "All these desert Arabs . . ."

"He's a friend of Soroya's," John pointed out, and summoned her to interpret.

The Arab had brought the map, which he showed John in the

privacy of his bedroom while Soroya leaned over them both to tell John what he was saying. And he had pinpointed three other fuel dumps, close to the Egyptian border. "This is very good," John said. "Tell Sheikh Ali I am pleased."

Soroya interpreted, and the man spluttered in reply. "He says, the sheikh wishes to know about the delivery of guns," Soroya said.

"Ah. Yes. Well, we haven't heard anything from London yet," John explained. "I did tell the sheikh that it might take a few months to get a response. But there will be one, to be sure."

"Sheikh Ali will not be pleased," Soroya pointed out.

"He must be patient."

Soroya blew through her teeth to indicate that her master was not a patient man.

Christmas came and went and John heard nothing further from the English side. Life was very pleasant, with Soroya forming a delightful bridge between himself and Arsinoe, almost literally, and even, possibly, in Mustafa's direction – John was glad for all the help he could get when it came to coping with the women. He was pleased to discover that Skipton's suggestion that he would find credit easy was exactly right; he bought himself a second-hand car in which he took a delighted Soroya for drives in the evenings, around Cairo and across the river to look at the Pyramids. She was not impressed. "That stone would build a lot of houses," she remarked.

Presumably Skipton, and thus Carmichael, by now knew of his domestic arrangements, but they pursued their policy of non-interference in other people's affairs. Easter also came and went, and the Germans invaded Norway, which attracted an immediate Allied response. It seemed definite that the phoney war was over, and having received two more requests from Ali, John felt obliged to bring up the matter again with Carmichael. "London aren't keen, as I indicated," Carmichael said.

"The sheikh delivered his half of the goods, sir," John pointed out.

"Well, we don't know that, do we?" Carmichael asked. "I mean, we have no proof that those marked dumps are genuine. I think we need to find out. You say the sheikh's messengers come to you across the desert. Then they can take you back across the desert. Right?"

"Me?"

"You are our contact, Johnnie."

"Right. Well, I can have a go. It may take a week or two to arrange; the sheikh is getting a little impatient."

"He can't blame us for wishing to check out his information. Arrange it."

John told Soroya, who did another of her whistles. "This is a bad business," she said.

But when next the messenger arrived from the sheikh, which was at the beginning of May, she told him they were going to pay Ali a visit. He gargled a bit, but Soroya seemed pleased. "We go now," she said.

"Now?"

"Tomorrow morning."

"Ah," he said.

There was a dance at Shepheard's that night.

It often amused John to consider the possible reactions of his fellows Brits were he to turn up at one of their functions with Soroya in tow; it did not bear consideration. He had actually taken her shopping and bought her some western clothes, which she enjoyed wearing, if in the oddest fashion; if she was pleased with the dresses and fascinated by the brassieres, she hated the knickers and would never wear them. But she was even more fascinated by the wristwatch he bought her; it had to be waterproof as she never took it off, even in the bath. "She is a strange creature," Arsinoe commented. "But very loveable."

Which confirmed his suspicions as to what went on when he was out and why Arsinoe had gone off the boil – at least as regards him. But the same thoughts had clearly been roaming Soroya's brain. "You go out," she said, sprawled across the bed while he coped with his black tie. "I never go out. You do not take me out. You do not like me, arsehole."

"I adore you," he insisted. "But you would be bored by this function. All very old people."

She rolled on her back and kicked her feet in the air. As usual she was wearing her brassiere and her watch but nothing else. "Tomorrow," she said. "You and me . . . and the desert."

He wondered if that was a threat, or a promise?

There was the usual throng at Shepheard's, although oddly, it was raining outside. This did happen from time to time in Cairo and was treated as a joke by everyone. "Johnnie!" announced Miranda Carmichael, the boss's wife. "There is someone you must meet. An old friend of yours."

John felt as if he had swallowed a lead weight, because there could be no doubt who she meant. "Johnnie," murmured Margo, and presented her cheek for a kiss. "I have heard so much about you."

"In which direction?"

"How you have a live-in lady. An Arab, no less."

Now, how did she know that? he wondered. "Ah, well . . . it's a long story."

"Which I wish you to tell me. But first . . ." she introduced him to some of her friends, none of whom registered in the least.

But there was an orchestra, and a dance floor, and he managed to get her on it. "How did your trip go?"

"Boring." She smiled at him. "Because you weren't along."

"You say the sweetest things. So, what now? Back to England?"

"I think I may hang about Cairo for awhile. I'm told there are things to see."

"I would have supposed you have seen everything there is to see in Cairo."

"I meant out there," she waved her hand in the general direction of the desert.

"Ah. Yes." He cursed the fact that having had to make Soroya happy before coming out tonight, he was feeling not the slightest bit randy. But he simply had to find out just where Margo stood – and things might develop. "Do you remember a certain agreement we had?"

She nestled against him as the orchestra seeped into Artie Shaw. "I do indeed."

"Well, we're both under Shepheard's roof. And the way things are, and have been, it might be a long time before we are both here again."

"Absolutely. All right. I think you've waited long enough. But we can't just depart now. People would talk." She looked at her gold watch. "Half-past nine. Give it another hour. Circulate. Leave at half-past ten. Only, when you leave the ballroom, instead of going out into the street, go upstairs. My room is number forty-seven."

"Will the door be open, or do I wait in the corridor?"

"You're sounding suspicious again. The door will be open. If I am not there, just make yourself at home."

He wondered that he was not as turned on as he should be. Had Soroya really exorcised Margo's charms? Or had he managed to become more interested in his job than in the woman? He passed the time easily enough, chatting with acquaintances, dancing with Miranda Carmichael, staying sober with difficulty. From time to time he tried to catch Margo's eye, but she studiously avoided his. "What an exciting woman, don't you think?" Miranda asked. "When I think of you and her, alone in the desert with the Senussi . . ."

"And half the Italian Army, to be sure," John pointed out.

She giggled girlishly.

Slowly the hands of his watch crept round, until ten-thirty finally arrived. Then he said goodnight to the Carmichaels, receiving a knowing nod of the head from Sandy, and emerged from the heat and noise of the ballroom into the comparative quiet of the lobby. There were two staff members present, but neither made a move to stop him as, instead of heading for the exit, he went to the lifts. A few minutes later he was at the door of number forty-seven, in an empty corridor. As far as he had been able to make out, Margo had still been on the dance floor. But he had also to assume she had made whatever arrangements were necessary. He hesitated for a few seconds, then turned the handle and stepped into darkness. Gently he closed the door behind himself, while registering that it was extremely unusual to leave an hotel door unlocked in Cairo, even in Shepheard's Hotel. As he did so he inhaled a most definitely masculine scent. He turned back to the door, and the light came on. "Not leaving already?" the man asked.

John mentally cursed the way he had again been taken in and suddenly realised that he was definitely coming to dislike the Famous Cartwright. He turned again, gazed at the man seated in an armchair on the far side of the bed. He wore a dinner jacket, had smoothly brushed black hair and looked entirely at ease. Thus he must appear the same. "Do I have the wrong room?" he asked.

"You have the right room. Sit down." He spoke with a reassuringly Welsh accent. John hesitated and realised that there was another man in the room, standing behind him. This man also wore a dinner jacket but he did not look as if it was his usual evening wear; he reminded John of Sergeant Bullock. "My bodyguard," the man in the chair said pleasantly. "He even has a gun, which he will show you, if you wish."

John sat down on the straight chair by the window. "Are you Margo's boss? Or do you work for her?"

The man smiled. "I am her boss, Mr Warrey."

126

"And are we in the same business?" John asked.

"Only in the slightest manner of speaking. If I may give you an analogy, when a German bomber, or a squadron of them, appears over England, they are, hopefully, spotted by various observers, who may or may not have radar. This information is then relayed to the nearest squadron of fighters, who take off and do the business. Well, in our peculiar profession, you, working for Sandy Carmichael, can be compared to an observer on the ground. Your business is to collect information and pass it to the necessary channel. How that information is collated and then used is no concern of yours. Are you with me?"

"Yes," John said. "And you are the fighter squadron, is that it?"

"Perfectly put, old man."

"And Margo?"

"Oh, she is one of us."

"And she, and you, are finding me something of a nuisance."

"By no means, my dear fellow. We think you are very good at your job. After all, it was we put you up for it. I did, as a matter of fact. But on Margo's recommendation."

"How do I know any of this is the truth?"

"George Brand recruited you, didn't he?" John gulped. "Dear old George. I'm happy to say they've taken him out of cloak and dagger mothballs and given him a command. He's in Norway. That's by the by. You're off into the desert tomorrow, right?"

"How the hell did you know that? Carmichael?"

The man shook his head. "Sandy keeps his nose to the grindstone, does his job and asks nothing more. But we keep tabs on him. As we keep tabs on everything. What were you going to tell the Senussi sheikh?"

"Same as I've been telling him for the last nine months, that the arms he wants cannot be supplied at this time."

"There are six cases of rifles and ammunition and one of dismantled machine-guns waiting at an address where you can pick them up tomorrow morning," the man said. John's jaw dropped. "Which is why you are here tonight," the man pointed out. "Ah, here is Margo."

Knuckles had brushed across the door and a moment later it opened. Margo looked slightly breathless and somewhat relieved, John thought, to see him sitting there, still in one piece. "No trouble?"

"Good lord, no. Mr Warrey has been the ultimate in understanding. But of course he needs to understand a little more."

Margo sat on the bed, stared at John. "I am sorry to have had to trick you."

"It isn't the first time," he reminded her.

"It is a tricky business," she said, and smiled.

"Greetings over," said the man.

"Not quite," John said. "I don't even know your name."

The man smiled. "You may call me Jones. Because I am Welsh. I am sure you have gathered that." He leaned forward. "It is fairly well understood, in military intelligence, that some time in the next month or so Hitler will invade France. His probable route will be the same one the Germans took the last time, through Belgium, to turn the Maginot Line. This time he may well take in Holland as well. As I say, this is fairly well known, and from a number of sources. There was the German officer who was forced to crash land in Belgium with a full set of invasion plans in his pockets, and who failed to burn them in time. There was the information given by the German ambassador to Italy to the queen of that country, who happens to be the King of Belgium's sister. There are the German troops movements towards the Belgian frontier."

"But what about Norway?" John asked.

"A diversion. Necessary for Germany, to be sure; they couldn't let us take over the country and be in a position to interfere with their shipments of iron ore from Sweden. But it is not supposed this will delay their plans to any great extent.

"Now, for various reasons, the allied high commands are refusing to accept the evidence of their own eyes. The Dutch and the Belgians are simply terrified to believe it, feeling as

128

they do that any move towards mobilisation on their parts might actually encourage Hitler to invade. The French prefer to think it is all an elaborate hoax on Hitler's part; they are indulging in wishful thinking because they know their much vaunted most powerful army in Europe is actually so riddled with Communist sedition it couldn't even take on Belgium. And of course the British military high command has placed itself, or been placed, under the French. However, the facts are there. The Phoney War is about to end. Our business is to anticipate and evaluate that situation. And our evaluation is that at an appropriate moment Italy will enter the war on the side of Germany. Information from Italy is that Mussolini has overcome his various shortfalls in men and materiel, and that Germany is now prepared to supply him with what he needs in the way of fuel. This being so, we must anticipate an attack upon Egypt and the Canal some time this summer.

"Now, sadly, our superiors still refuse to become involved in the business of pre-emptive strikes. But they are at least prepared to ripost with as much vigour as we can manage."

"The Senussi," John muttered.

"Exactly. Most of them continue to hate the Italians. We shall arm them, and we shall have them attack the Italians the very moment the Italians go to war on us. Our information is that this Sheikh Ali whatever, with whom you have made so valuable a contact, is the man to lead this attack. If he is happy with this idea, you may tell him that there will be more arms to follow this shipment. Understood?"

"Yes," John said. "But there is one problem. How do we keep Sheikh Ali from attacking the Italians until after we are at war?"

Jones smiled at Margo. "Leave that with Miss Cartwright. She is going with you, as our official representative."

Chapter Seven

The Guns

John stared at Jones for a moment and wished he hadn't had that last glass of champagne. "With respect, sir," he said, "you cannot be serious?"

"I am always serious, Mr Warrey."

"But. . . it simply will not work. Margo, the Senussi, remember? We fought against them last year."

"*You* fought against them, Johnnie," she reminded him. "I was simply an onlooker."

"If they'd come down . . ."

"I would have survived, I'm sure."

"Miss Cartwright met some Senussi chieftains on her last Saharan expedition," Jones explained. "One of these was Sheikh Ali. Who happens to be the nearest sheikh of consequence to Egypt, and also happens to be the man with whom you have struck up that very useful acquaintance."

"And those people who attacked us?"

"We will never know, will we? You never let them get close enough."

John turned back to Margo. "Did Sufyan and Graham know this?"

"Of course not."

"But they had been with you on the previous expedition. When you met up with the Senussi?"

"So we had a meeting. They do not know what I talked about with the sheikhs."

What a swirl of confusion surrounded him. He supposed he

should be grateful that he had at last been included in a part of it. But a very lowly part, till now; Jones was operating on a totally different level to Carmichael, and poor Carmichael knew nothing of it – or of the fact that he had a Secret Service mole in his establishment! And now he had just been told he was to play his part in starting a war! Supposing he could believe a word of it. He also needed to remember that Margo, pursuing her own plans, had been responsible for the death of Graham Poultrie – and if she had appeared to be genuinely sorry about that, it had not deflected her from her purpose.

"Well," Jones said, "now that you are *au fait* with the situation, as it were, I think we should all have an early night. I understand you have a guide to the desert track leading to where Sheikh Ali can be found?"

"Yes," John said, and reflected that he had a secret of his own. He wondered how Margo was going to cope with that.

"Very good. You will rendezvous with Miss Cartwright, and the guns, at the Wadi el Farigh at dawn tomorrow morning."

"And transport?"

"Miss Cartwright will provide her own. Oh, by the way, the password is 'duce'."

John prodded Soroya. "Wake up."

"Eh? Eh?" She blinked. "It is not time."

"Yes, it is time. We are leaving early."

She pushed black hair from her face, got him into focus. "This is a trick."

"No trick, my dearest girl. But the situation has changed." He got up, went to the bathroom.

She joined him. "What has happened?"

"Nothing, yet. But London has decided to go along with your master's wish for guns."

She looked back into the bedroom, as if expecting to see it full of stacked rifles. "You have these guns?"

"We are going to pick them up. Now, no noise. We must leave without Arsinoe knowing."

She pouted. "She will be angry."

"Don't tell me you are afraid of Arsinoe?"

"She can be very hard when she is angry."

"And I bet you love every minute of it. Hurry."

She got dressed, needless to say wearing her brassiere, although she was exchanging her city clothes for desert wear; she also retained her watch. John buckled on a service revolver, hung his binoculars round his neck; he felt vaguely ridiculous, but it was necessary to anticipate some kind of trouble. Then they crept out of the house and into the cool pre-dawn of a Cairo morning. Around them the city was just beginning to stir. John drove the car round the corner and across the ar-Rawdah Bridge on to the road leading west. This soon enough disintegrated into a rough track, as he knew it would, but as it grew light the track was easy enough to follow.

Behind them the sun rose as they approached the village. Here their arrival in a motor car aroused the usual great amount of interest, surrounding them with children of all ages, dogs, chickens and goats. "Effendi, you are early," the camel herder complained.

"It's such a nice day," John explained. "Now, will my car be safe here? I may be gone a few days."

"I look after it my very own self," Hamdi promised.

"See that you do, arsehole," Soroya told him.

He waggled his eyebrows and looked at John for help. "She doesn't like early rising," John explained, and they mounted up.

For all his now several months of practice he still felt extremely uneasy on the back of a camel, and it took him some time, to the amusement of the populace, to get the beast under control. "Hit him," Soroya recommended. "That is all they understand. Hit him."

John determined to rely on patience, just in case the beast took offence at being hit and at last they moved out of the village and along the track leading to the desert. This was still the stony desert and the going was comparatively easy. But they had only been travelling for an hour when Soroya reined in. "People," she said.

"Where?" He could see nothing save the undulating, brown, arid country.

"There," she pointed. John levelled his binoculars and saw a man on a camel, perhaps half a mile away, watching them. "They will rape me," Soroya remarked.

He couldn't tell whether she was apprehensive or anticipatory. "I doubt it," he said. "He is using binoculars too. Let's go."

"You wish to speak with this man?"

"I'm partial to conversation."

They cantered their camels towards him, while he remained motionless, watching them. He was armed with a rifle, but this he left lying across his knees. John, however, loosened his revolver in his holster, just in case he was making a mistake in his assumption. "Good morning," he called as he approached. "Duce."

The man gazed at him for several seconds, then turned his camel and rode over the brow of the hill. "What is that you said?" Soroya asked.

"I really have no idea. Shall we follow?"

"This is not good," she muttered, but she followed him up the rise, to pause in consternation at the sight in the valley beyond – a caravan of some fifty camels, each heavily laden, with a dozen drivers – and Margo, looking every inch the sheikh's girlfriend in a topee, white silk shirt, and jodhpurs. She was presently dismounted, and walking up and down, cutting at her boots with a riding crop.

"You're late," she commented as John and Soroya rode into the midst of the caravan.

"So are all the best people."

"Where is your guide?"

"This young lady. Please be careful what you say," he advised. "Her English is not good, but convincing."

"Just what is she to you?"

"She is my servant."

"I am his woman, arsehole," Soroya stated.

"As we're late, we'd better move out," John suggested, endeavouring to pre-empt open warfare.

"Is this the woman you have been keeping in Cairo?" Margo inquired. "You bastard! While you were making up to me?" Obviously, while she had been prepared to accept the idea that he had accumulated a female servant, she hadn't expected her to be quite so good-looking.

"You have fucked this woman?" Soroya inquired, her voice dangerously low.

"No, I haven't,"

"That is good. If you had, I would cut out her eyes and stuff them up her arse."

"Are you going to let her speak to me like that?" Margo demanded.

"Actually, she was speaking to me. If you must know, she was a loan to me from your friend Sheikh Ali."

Margo gave up, mounted her camel and they rode off.

"The way lies across the Great Sand Sea," Soroya said. "You understand this?"

"I had a notion it was going to be difficult."

"Does *she* know this?" Soroya chuckled, a sinister sound. "Maybe she will drown."

"I know about the Great Sand Sea," Margo said that night when they camped. "We were trying to avoid it when last we were out here, if you remember." Her tone remained cold. "But first there is a small sand sea, which they call the Qattara Depression. I hope your ladyfriend knows the way."

"I'm sure she does. Margo, she was literally foisted on me by Sheikh Ali. Well, he insisted I have someone, and he offered me

a choice between a boy and a girl. I took the girl. Would you
have preferred me to choose the boy?" She snorted. "And, well
. . . my lodgings aren't very spacious, so we have to share a good
deal . . ."

"Including the bed, no doubt."

"As a matter of fact, yes," he said, beginning to get nettled.
"Where do you get the right to criticise my private life? You
and I have never got together, no matter how much I may have
wanted to."

"I am your superior officer," she said, more coldly than ever.

"And you never sleep with the help. That's a very good rule.
But who the help sleeps with is their business, right?"

Next day she was very stiff, the more so as she was well aware
that John and Soroya had shared the same blanket. It had been
a very cold night but the day rapidly grew very warm, much
warmer than before, and they had not gone far when the track
disappeared, and before them was nothing but sand, undulating
in windswept dunes. Even the camels found the going difficult,
while the humans poured sweat. The sand wisped into the air,
settled on their clothes, their faces and hands, and then got
inside their clothes. There was no great temptation to speak,
because then the sand got into their mouths, and Margo kept
them rationed to a few mouthfuls of water every other hour.
There was absolutely no temptation to get too close to each
other, even on Soroya's part.

They wrapped their scarves round the heads, over their noses
and mouths, and plodded onwards. John and Margo at least had
sand goggles, but the Arabs did not seem to mind, even Soroya,
whose eyes had faded into little slits. "How many days to cross
this?" John asked, when they stopped for lunch.

"It is one hundred and fifty miles to the end of the Depression,"
Soroya said. "That is maybe a fortnight. Then we will be south of
Siwa. Then we must cross the Great Sand Sea to find the track
leading up to Sheikh Ali's village."

"And that is?"

"Another fortnight, maybe."

"Did you hear that?" John asked Margo.

"Yes," she said grimly.

John realised that crossing the desert by truck had been sheer luxury compared with crossing the desert on a camel. He soon got used to both the animal and its movements, but it remained intensely uncomfortable and he was sure he was losing all the skin off his buttocks. But as neither woman complained, he had to grin and bear it. Soroya was right in her estimation of time and a fortnight later they emerged from the Qattara Depression onto reasonably solid ground. "Where is Siwa Oasis?" John asked, standing with his hands on his hips and gazing around at the empty desert.

"Over there," Soroya pointed. "You wish to go there? They have baths, eh?"

"We do not go near Siwa," Margo snapped.

"Isn't there an oasis nearer here?" John asked. "I would give a lot for a bath."

"No oasis," Soroya said.

"And now we tackle the Great Sand Sea," he said sadly.

"But you wish bath? I give you bath."

Even Margo turned her head in interest.

"There." Soroya pointed at a wadi some hundred yards away, and led them over. She stood on the edge of the dry water course and pointed again. "You see those?" John took off his goggles to peer at the cluster of tiny pink and white flowers peeping through the stones. "In the desert, the water is often only a few feet beneath the surface," Soroya explained. "But you must know where to look. In the sand sea, you cannot see. But in the stony desert, where there are flowers, there will be water."

"Under there?" John asked incredulously

"Oh, yes. It is there. Maybe several feet. But it is there." She spoke in Arabic to the drivers, who grinned and climbed down into the wadi to dig with their spades. John joined them, careless of the sweat pouring out of his hair and soaking his shirt. If there was water . . .

They dug for perhaps an hour, and then suddenly he realised clear brown liquid was seeping about his boots. "Holy hallelujah," he said. "You were right."

"I am always right," Soroya said. They dug some more and soon had a pool several feet across and several inches deep. "Now you bathe," Soroya suggested.

"Well . . ." he looked at Margo. "Ladies first."

"In front of these natives?"

"You are ashamed of your body?" Soroya enquired, and removed her haik to throw it on the ground. Then she removed her brassiere as well – her ultimate act of disrobing – and stepped into the water, kneeling to scoop it over herself. The watching Arabs applauded. "It is cool," Soroya said.

Margo gazed at John for several seconds, then began removing her clothes. The Arabs applauded some more as she joined Soroya in the pool. Soroya splashed water over her and Margo responded with a giggle. They made a fascinating sight, voluptuous brown skin against slender white, tossing black hair and red, glowing sexuality and scattering water. John looked at the Arabs, who gave shouts of appreciation and joined the women. For a moment he feared he was about to witness a gang rape, but they had only enjoyment in mind. So he joined them.

He supposed it was the weirdest orgy in which he had ever participated, because although there was a good deal of touching and pulling and squeezing, it was all in the purest fun. They stamped and rolled about, while the water grew as filthy as themselves, and then dissipated into mud. Then they collapsed on the dry sand. "We must not lie here," Soroya said, putting on her brassiere. "It will not be good."

"Why does she wear that thing?" Margo asked.

"She likes it," John explained.

"And I presume you gave it to her?"

137

"Of course. Don't you think it might be an idea for us all to be friends?"

She allowed her gaze to drift slowly up and down his body. "Yes," she said. "It might be an idea."

"But not till we get back to Shepheard's?"

"Who knows?" she asked enigmatically, and ran her hand up the smooth flesh of Soroya's arm. "Who knows."

"I think she is growing to like me," Soroya said.

Within twenty-four hours the delights of the bathing party had dwindled into distant memory as they entered the Great Sand Sea. Here the going was even harder than in the Qattara Depression, for the sand felt softer and the Sea itself covered a much greater distance. Day passed interminable day, with the sun seeming to hover directly overhead, burning them even through their cloaks and burnous. They prayed for darkness, but with the temperature dropping to close to zero they would awake shivering, and pray for a sight of the sun all over again.

They had replenished their waterskins at Soroya's waterhole, the Arabs digging again to restore the upwards seepage, but even so it was necessary to ration themselves. "I hope your friend knows where we are going," Margo grumbled.

"At least there is no wind," Soroya said, watching the wisps of cloud in the sky somewhat anxiously.

The wind came two days later. They actually felt its effects before it got to them, when John found himself brushing wisps of drifting sand from his face. Then he felt the breeze on his shirt. It was a hot breeze, but was nonetheless refreshing. "Quick," Soroya commanded. "We make camp."

No one argued, not even Margo, who had apparently endured a sandstorm on one of her earlier forays into the desert. The camels were hobbled in a circle, their loads taken down and stacked beneath tarpaulins, which were then stretched out and pegged down to make a shelter, sloping towards the breeze. Which by dusk was blowing a full gale.

The noise was tremendous, the roaring of the wind being accompanied by the hissing of the sand, which piled up against the improvised half tent and soon found its way inside. The eleven humans huddled together behind the makeshift shelter, each confined entirely to his or her own thoughts. "How long does this last?" John bellowed into Soroya's ear.

"Not long," she shouted back. "Maybe until tomorrow."

It lasted longer than that, for by John's watch it was about nine in the morning before the wind dropped. For some fifteen hours they had had nothing to eat and only a few sips of lukewarm tea from their thermoses to drink. Now they had to dig themselves out, for the sand was mounded against the lean-to in a fresh dune. But they were alive and so were the camels. The Arabs reloaded the guns. "What a way to live," John commented.

"What a way to die," Margo riposted, her face lost beneath the coating of sand. "Do I look anything like you?"

"Far worse," he assured her.

Now they were heading north-west. John had no idea whether or not Soroya had been following any landmarks through the desert, but if she had, they had to have been obliterated by the storm. Yet she never hesitated for a moment, led them steadily, crouched on her camel, her haik gathered about her, never once appearing to look even to left or right. "Is she that purposeful in bed?" Margo asked.

"Yes, she is. Are you still meaning to find out for yourself?"

She smiled. "I believe in experiencing everything at least once. Oh, you're on the list, Johnnie."

He had a feeling they were all close to total hysteria. But after another fortnight, Soroya reined in her camel and pointed. "My people," she said.

*   *   *

139

There were three horsemen on the next rise and as usual, they did not approach, but waited for the caravan to come to them. Soroya however had taken off her scarf and was waving it in the air long before they were close enough to speak. Then she shouted at them in Arabic, of which John could understand only the words, Sheikh Ali.

The men inspected the caravan, gazed at Margo and grinned at John. He understood that they remembered him from his last visit to their village; he certainly could not remember them. Having listened to them, Soroya became very excited. "There is a great battle in France," she said. "The Germans have invaded and there is much fighting."

"Who is winning?" John asked.

"They do not know, but they think it is the Germans."

"That's not possible," Margo objected. "The Germans can't get past the Maginot Line."

"Sheikh Ali will know more," John assured her. "At least the Italians don't seem to have joined in as yet."

Ali's men had apparently been sent to look for them, because it took them another three days to emerge from the Great Sand Sea. Then they crossed the track over which the Italian soldiers had escorted John and Margo the previous year. By now Margo had her map out. "That dump is marked, here," she said. "I wish to have a look at it."

Soroya explained what was required to their escort, who looked sceptical. "It is very dangerous to approach the dump," she explained.

"But that is what we are here for," Margo told her.

Another chat with their escort, who seemed to be of the opinion that they were there simply to deliver the guns. But at last one of them agreed to take them to within sight of the dump. The caravan was to continue to Ali's village. "You'd better stay with it," John suggested to Soroya.

"I am your servant," she said. "Where you go, I go."

He found that remarkably reassuring.

*   *   *

140

The four of them walked their camels back along the track for some distance before the Arab led them away into some low hills. "Down there," he said.

They lay on their bellies while both Margo and John used their binoculars. This was a different angle to that from which they had first seen the dump, the Arab having wisely led them to where they were backed by the sun, and therefore there would be no reflection from their glasses. Now they realised that the dump, or fort, was far larger than they had supposed; they had seen a gate leading between two hillocks; now they were behind the hillocks and looked at a considerable military establishment. "Do any of your people ever get inside places like that?" Margo asked.

Soroya translated. The Arab grinned and replied. "He says if they did, they didn't come back out again," Soroya said.

"That is a big dump," Margo said. "Fuel storage tanks, what could be a magazine, and all only maybe seventy miles from Siwa."

"You'd think they would have something closer," John suggested.

"They do." She prodded the map, where there was another mark, situated very close to the border. "We need to have a look at that."

"Let's get these guns to Sheikh Ali first," John suggested.

They reached the encampment the next day and were greeted with much firing of old matchlock rifles and clashing of swords and spears. Everyone was in a high state of excitement. "You have heard the news?" Ali asked, embracing both John and Margo.

"We have heard nothing save that the War has started in earnest, in France," Margo said.

"In France, pouf! That is all finished."

"Say again?"

"France has surrendered. It belongs to Germany. And Italy."

"But what about the British?" John asked.

"The British have fled. They got into their boats and hurried back across the water. Hitler is master of Europe."

141

"Shit," John muttered.

"Did you say that France belongs both to Germany *and* Italy?" Margo asked, concentrating on essentials.

"That is so." Ali was watching the boxes of rifles and ammunition being unloaded. "By Allah, but there is a sight. We fight now, eh?"

"Let me get this straight," Margo said. "Italy is in the war?"

"Oh, yes. A week ago. They invaded France."

"Are they at war with England?"

"I believe so." He signalled his men to open one of the crates. The lid was lifted off and the first rifle was taken out. Even heavily coated with grease it was still covered in sand. Ali gave orders to his men to start the clean-up. "Now," he said, "we will eat, and you will tell me what orders you have brought me. When will the British attack the Italians?"

"I'm afraid I have no idea," Margo said. "We have been on the road for six weeks. When we left Cairo the only fighting was in Norway."

"Ah," Ali said, disappointed.

"And what I would like even more than food is a bath."

"Of course. And you, Giovanni, eh?"

"Indeed. But we'll share."

"Bugger off," Margo told him. "That was a one-off."

He shared with Soroya instead. She was on a high, being reunited with her friends and relations. "That woman does not like you," she remarked.

"I have a feeling you're right," John agreed sadly.

"But you like her, eh? Why?"

"It's a long story."

"You should not like other women," she pointed out, "when you have me. It is not right. And it is difficult."

He wasn't sure whether she was considering the number of women whose eyes she would have to pluck out and stuff up their backsides. But in any event, he had more serious matters to consider. Matters he had hoped to discuss with Margo in the privacy of their shared bath. If Italy was at war with Britain, then he and Margo were enemy aliens and worse; neither was wearing uniform. It also meant that Ali was close to being in open rebellion against the ruling power, at least here in Cyrenaica.

Every instinct was to get the hell out of there as rapidly as possible and regain the comparative safety of Cairo. But his sense of responsibility told him that would indeed be a dereliction of duty. It would take him not less than a month to get back to Egypt, even supposing they would be able to travel faster in a smaller party and without having to lug the guns. In that month, anything could happen, judging by the amount that happened during the past six weeks when they had been incommunicado. He could arrive in Cairo to find it occupied by the Italians!

There was also the matter of the dumps. They had been sent to ascertain that the information given them by Ali was correct. Ascertaining that was surely more important than ever, now. There was also Ali himself, just itching to start shooting Italians, who had now been presented with the wherewithal to do just that, at least in the short term. Obviously, if the Italians were about to begin a push into Egypt, his job, and that of Margo, was to stay with the Senussi and direct them to the best possible use as regards sabotage and sneak attacks.

All with a firing squad at the end of it.

Margo had apparently been brooding on the same lines. Having had her bath she appeared as *soignée*, sweet-smelling and sophisticated as if they had just left Shepheard's, wearing clean shirt and jodhpurs, wet hair lying damply on her shoulders, teeth cleaned and even lipstick. John had shaved, or rather, had been shaved by Soroya, who enjoyed handling a razor. Ali was still in a state of high excitement, as were his people, who continued to fire guns into the air and generally make conversation difficult. "The attack," he said. "Tell us where to attack? Where are the British?"

"Oh, they will be attacking, certainly," Margo agreed, avoiding John's disparaging gaze. "Our job must be to strike at the Italians' line of communications."

"Ah, yes," Ali said. "I have read of these lines of communication."

"I beg your pardon," John protested, realising that Margo saw herself as a latter-day Lawrence of Arabia. El Margo of Libya! "There are no trains to blow up here; there is only the coast road."

"That can be blown up, too," Margo argued.

"What with?"

She considered this point; they had brought the Senussi rifles and ammunition, and some machine-guns. But no high explosive. "Well, then?" she demanded. "What do you think we should do?"

"Exactly what we were sent to do. Pinpoint the Italian ammunition dumps, and get back to Cairo."

"And these people?"

"Us," Ali shouted. "We are at war!" He brandished his rifle.

"I would suggest that you sit tight, recruit as many people as you can, train your men and await orders from Cairo."

"Sit tight?" Ali bellowed. "Do nothing?"

"It is vital," John said, "that you time your attack upon the Italian lines of communication with the British advance from Egypt. There is absolutely no sense in your advancing towards Tobruk, and perhaps cutting the road, even if you had the means to do so effectively. The Italians would wipe you out and they would repair the road within hours. If you were to wait until the British attack and *then* cut the road . . . we would of course provide you with explosives," he added winningly.

Ali stroked his beard. "You would give us dynamite?"

"Of course. If you will agree to use it as directed from Cairo."

Ali stroked his beard some more, and looked at Margo.

"I think what Lieutenant Warrey has to say makes a lot of sense," she said.

"I will speak with my people," Ali conceded.

John retired early, but not early enough. He hadn't yet closed his eyes – Soroya not being as exhausted as he was – when his tent flap opened. Soroya made a noise like a hissing snake and moved forward, knife in hand; John just had the time to catch her by the hair to save the life of the intruder.

Margo switched on her flashlight and shone it over the naked woman, the knife held in front of her, and the equally naked man beyond, kneeling on the blankets. "How disgusting," she commented.

"You come for some, arsehole?" Soroya inquired. "I cut your tits off."

Margo retreated to the flap again. "Can't you control her?"

"That depends what you *have* come for."

"I have come, as your commanding officer, to discuss the situation with you."

"No sex?" Soroya inquired.

Margo gave her a scathing look. "We are not all as animal as yourself."

Soroya snorted.

"Relax," John said. "This really is business."

"And what I have to say is confidential," Margo added.

"Would you take a walk, Soroya?" John requested. "And please, no listening."

Soroya glared at him. "You touch this woman . . ."

"I know. But I think you're both on the same side there."

Soroya picked up one of the blankets, wrapped herself in it as if it were a sarong and went to the door. Margo obligingly jumped aside to let her through. "I come back, in fifteen minutes," Soroya announced, tapping her watch.

"Does she know how to read that thing?" Margo asked.

"It's her current god," John said. "Come and sit beside me."

145

"I will," Margo said, "if you keep yourself covered up, and keep your hands to yourself."

"Absolutely. What's on your mind?"

She knelt beside him and began to whisper. "These people, do you really suppose they are going to take your advice?"

"I hope they do, for their sakes."

"We need them. One of us has to stay here and make sure they do nothing except on orders from Cairo."

"That being me, right?"

"Well . . . you could hardly expect me to stay. Women don't really count for much with these people. They'll never take orders from me."

"And you think they'll take orders from me?"

"They're already doing so. And besides, you appear to be almost one of them. This is your big chance, Johnnie. I'll get on back to Cairo and put them in the picture. And then when we attack . . ."

"That being? At odds of six to one?"

"Well, obviously, there'll have to be reinforcements from England—"

"What reinforcements? If Ali is right, our troops were virtually wiped out in France."

"Then we, everyone, including Ali, will have to be patient, that's all. No one ever expected this war to be over in a few days, or even weeks."

"And supposing the Italians invade Egypt?"

"I would say that is highly unlikely."

"Even at odds of six to one?"

"Listen, just stay here and keep these people quiet until we can get back to you. Radio. We'll send you a radio set."

"Across the desert, after you have gone back across the desert . . . Margo, we're talking about Christmas. This happens to be June."

"Patience," she repeated. "Now I'll leave you to your little friend. Stay whole."

She got up, moved to the doorway and was checked by a

huge noise, a combination of grinding engines, spitting guns and shrieking people.

"You forgot," John said, reaching for his pants and his revolver at the same time. "The Italians know where we are."

Chapter Eight

The Crime

Margo ran for the door, colliding with Soroya who, blanket discarded, was coming in just as quickly. The two women fell with mutual grunts, then Margo was out and into the darkness. As she took her torch with her, inside the tent was utterly dark. "Italians!" Soroya gasped unnecessarily.

"Put something on," John told her, and went outside, revolver in hand. Here he could see a little more clearly. All around him was pandemonium, as Arab women ran to and fro, followed by their children, dogs barked, goats bleated, men fired rifles into the air, some shouted orders, which were entirely ignored – while from the north there came a constant ripple of light, and more than that. Instinctively he dropped to his hands and knees as something thudded into the ground beside him. He rolled over to gain the shelter of the tent and was joined by Soroya. "Ali," he said. "We must find Ali. And then Margo."

Soroya snorted, but she began making her way into the village, wriggling on her stomach. Here several of the houses were on fire, while from others there came the crackle of rifles as the Senussi returned fire. The street was already littered with dead bodies, amongst which dogs ran and snarled; several of them had also been hit, and whined piteously. Soroya crawled through the debris to reach Ali's house. "Who is in there?" she called.

For reply there was a mini-fusillade of shots. John fell to his face and pulled her down with him. "It is I, Soroya," Soroya called. "With Mr Warrey."

The shooting stopped, close at hand; the Italians were still blazing away, but they did not appear actually to be advancing. John and Soroya crawled into the house past a huddle of terrified women and children and reached Ali, who had several men with him, peering out of the narrow windows. "How can this be?" Ali demanded.

"Seems the Italians knew where to find you," John suggested.

"But I have not warred upon them."

"They know you mean to, I would say."

"I have been betrayed," Ali shouted. "Betrayed!" he screamed. "When I get hold of the motherfucker who has done this, I will cut his prick into strips and feed them to the dogs! Who is that?"

"Soroya."

"Soroya! It is she who has betrayed us. Seize her! I will cut—"

"Simmer down," John advised. "Soroya didn't betray you. This was done, and this attack planned, long ago. Don't you think the Italians have long known you are hostile? They have just been waiting for an excuse."

Ali considered this, while one of his men peered out of the window. "The firing has stopped. They have gone away."

"I wouldn't count on it," John said. "They just wanted to pin you down and wait for daybreak. They don't want any more casualties than they can avoid."

"Bah," Ali said. "At daybreak, we will see them and shoot them down like dogs."

"If my guess is right, at daybreak they will send in aircraft."

"We cannot shoot aircraft down with rifles," someone said.

"What are we to do?" Ali asked.

"Withdraw into the desert," said someone else.

"That is what they want you to do," John told them. "You cannot travel more than a few miles before daybreak. Then their airplanes will find you easily, and on the open desert you will be helpless."

"You are telling me that we cannot go, but also we cannot stay?" Ali demanded.

John sighed. "I think you must surrender."

"Me? Surrender? I have never surrendered. Besides, if I surrender, they will shoot me."

"I don't think they will," John said. "After all, they attacked you. You have attacked nobody. You have attempted to defend yourselves, but now you understand that is impossible, you must surrender."

Ali considered. "They will lock us up."

"Only for a little while. Until the British take Tobruk. Then you will be freed to fight again."

"And these weapons? They will wish to know where we got them."

"Tell them," John said. "There is no need to tell them you asked for the guns. Just say that they were delivered by Miss Cartwright and myself to encourage you to attack the Italians. But that you refused to do so. It could work out quite well for you."

Ali pulled his beard. "And you? And Miss Cartright? They will certainly shoot *you*."

"We will leave now under cover of the darkness, make off into the desert and return to Egypt."

"And will the Italian planes not find you in the desert?"

"No, because they will not look for us. Tell the soldiers that we left several days ago."

"All this telling of lies," Ali grumbled. "I do not like it."

"Let us hurry," Soroya recommended.

"You stay here," Ali told her.

Soroya grasped John's arm tightly. "I need her," John said.

"For your bed? Now is not the time to think of bed."

"I need her," John said again, "firstly to guide us back across the desert, and secondly so that I can send you a message when necessary."

They found Margo sheltering in another of the houses, rounded up six camels, three of which they loaded with food and water. The Italians were now definitely waiting for dawn, and only the occasional shot winged out of the darkness. "Now remember," John told Ali, "at first light send out a man with a white flag and surrender."

"Surrender," Ali muttered. "I do not like this surrender."

"You'll stay alive until we come back to you." He mounted, and he and Margo followed Soroya south into the darkness.

"This has been a disaster," Margo remarked.

"Absolutely. But not one of our making. Our employers just did not realise that Hitler would make a decisive move so quickly and so effectively. Or that we would be thrown out of France so easily. Mussolini's coming in was dependent upon those events."

"We have still quite failed in what we were sent to do," she pointed out morosely. "All we have accomplished is to deliver five hundred good rifles into the hands of the Italians."

"So we lost this one," John said. "It's the last battle that matters."

She relapsed into silence. Even Soroya did not seem to have anything to say as they walked their camels to the south. By dawn they were back in the sand sea, plodding in single file, Soroya leading the pack camels. Now she looked over her shoulder and pointed. John drew rein to look back, and saw the aircraft, hardly bigger than birds at that distance, wheeling over Ali's village. And now too they could see columns of smoke rising into the still air. "Shit!" he said. "Why hasn't he surrendered?"

"Because they wouldn't let him," Margo said. "It will serve as an example to keep the Senussi in order."

John looked at Soroya, who was staring at the smoke. Under that smoke were her people. The fold of her burnous was across the lower half of her face, but her eyes burned. God help any stray Italian we come across, he thought. "Let's move," he said. "We can do nothing to help them now."

By eleven o'clock they had covered about twenty miles and could no longer see either the planes or the smoke. It was now very hot, so they halted for a rest and a meal, intending to resume their journey in the middle of the afternoon when the sun would be declining. It was while they were eating, mainly dates, that they saw the plane, high, obviously searching. For them! "We have to get out of here." Margo scrambled to her feet.

"To go where?" John asked.

"There is nowhere to go," Soroya said. "Sit down, arsehole, and keep still, and maybe they will not see us."

Margo sat down again, sulkily. But the plane was coming closer. It flew overhead at a height of about a thousand feet, John estimated, and continued on its way. "Missed us," Margo said. "Talk about luck."

"We haven't any," John said, for the plane was turning back. Now it came lower, until it was only a few hundred feet above the desert.

"Wrap yourselves up," Soroya commanded. "They may think we are out of the desert."

They obeyed her but the plane dropped lower yet. "It can't land on this soft sand, surely," Margo muttered.

"They'll think of something," John said.

A moment later there was a burst of machine-gun fire. Margo and Soroya threw themselves flat on the sand. John also lay down but as he did so he noted that the shots had all ploughed into the sand some distance behind them. Of course, the Italian gunner might just be a bad shot . . . He watched the plane circle. Now it was lower yet, barely a hundred feet off the ground. "Let us shoot him," Soroya decided.

"I don't think that would be a good idea," John said. "Not unless we were certain to hit him."

He stared up at the plane and the man leaning out, waving his gloved hand and then pointing. "He's telling us to return," Margo said. "Shit!"

Another burst of fire, this time ploughing into the sand in front of them. The camels became restless. Once again the pilot pointed to the north. "I think we have to go along with him," John decided.

"We'll be arrested," Margo pointed out. "We'll be shot."

"Doesn't it look as if we're going to be shot here?"

He stood up and waved his arms. The plane waggled its wings. "He cannot stay for long," Soroya said. "He must go for fuel, yes?"

"I think he's thought of that," John said. "Come on, make a move."

They remounted and began to head back along their tracks to the north. "We go slow, eh?" Soroya said. "Then when it is dark, we can go back again."

"I wouldn't count on it," John said.

"Why you in so much a hurry to surrender?" she demanded.

"I'm in a hurry to stay alive."

"They shoot you anyway, arsehole."

"She has a point," Margo said. "What's our defence?"

"If Ali has indeed been wiped out, we can juggle with the truth. We were sent to make contact with him. When we left Cairo, Italy and Britain were at peace. The moment we learned war had started, we turned back."

"Do you think that's going to work?"

"We'd better hope it does."

He kept remembering how charming Umberto had always been.

As he had anticipated, their guard plane was replaced by another after an hour. And then another, two hours later. It was still broad daylight when they left the sand sea for the stony desert, where an Italian armoured car waited for them. "Up, up," said the sergeant in command, waving his rifle at them. "Dismount."

They raised their arms above their heads as they slid from their saddles and landed on the sand. Now they were covered not only by the plane overhead, but also by three soldiers with rifles, who left the armoured car to advance on them. The sergeant led the way. He peered at them, then pulled open John's burnous to uncover the revolver holster. He unfastened the flap, took out the

153

revolver, handed it to one of his aides. "Kneel," he commanded. "Hands on the head."

John obeyed, and the sergeant moved on to Margo. Her revolver he also plucked from the holster, handing it to one of his people, then running his hands over the front of Margo's shirt. "Bastard," Margo said.

He grinned. "Kneel. Hands on head."

She hesitated, then obeyed. "You don't think they mean to shoot us out of hand?" she asked in English.

The sergeant placed his boot on her back and pushed, and she fell forward with a faint shriek. "No talking," the sergeant said. "Kneel. Hands on head." Margo did her best to brush the sand from her hands and face before obeying.

The sergeant had reached Soroya and pulled open her cloak as well. But Soroya was unarmed. He squeezed her breasts, and she hissed at him. "She is Senussi," said one of his men. "Let us have her."

The sergeant gazed at Soroya, obviously considering having her himself. But he had his mind on his duty. "Kneel," he said.

Soroya knelt, clearly exerting a great effort to keep herself from swearing at them. Then John saw the sergeant walk round behind the Arab woman, revolver in hand. My God, he thought; they *do* mean to execute us out of hand – or at least Soroya. "Wait," he said. The sergeant looked at him. "Colonel Umberto," John said. "We wish to be taken to Colonel Umberto."

"You know Colonel Umberto?"

"Very well." John drew a long breath. "It is he we are on our way to see."

The sergeant frowned. "You are from the camp of Ali."

"No, no," John insisted. "We are on our way to see Colonel Umberto."

The sergeant clearly found this very confusing. But he opted for the simple answer, as John had hoped he would. "Up, up," he commanded.

"They should be searched," suggested one of the soldiers, rolling his eyes.

"That is correct military procedure," said the second.

"They may have concealed weapons," added the third.

"Yes," the sergeant agreed. "You must be searched."

The women were made to bend this way and that as the Italians enjoyed themselves. "What sort of weapon am I supposed to keep up there, arsehole?" Soroya inquired.

For reply, she was struck a blow across the face which had her sprawling on the sand. "You speak when we ask a question," the sergeant advised.

Slowly Soroya climbed back to her feet, body glowing, as she brushed away some of the sand. She was storing up a great deal of hatred, John reckoned.

Their wrists were bound and they were inserted into the armoured car, where space was extremely limited, so that they were crushed together, John in the middle. They then set off back towards the coast, the camels being trailed behind them.

"I have never had an experience like that," Margo said in English. "I can still feel those shitting fingers."

"Pretend it was me," John suggested.

"Do you think we've gained anything?" Margo asked.

"We're still alive," he pointed out.

It took them two hours to regain Ali's village, or what was left of it. It was a trying journey for the two women, as they were also huddled against the Italian soldiers, who could not keep their hands off them, fingering their shoulders and squeezing their thighs, running their hands up and down their arms, fingering the nipples and breasts through the thin material of Margo's blouse and Soroya's haik. The searching had clearly turned them on. One bold fellow even put his hands back between Margo's legs, but now she was protected by her jodhpurs, although her shriek attracted the attention of the sergeant, seated in the front beside the driver. "Do not harm them," he said over his shoulder.

Which was not what the soldiers had in mind.

"Arseholes," Soroya growled. "When I get my hands free . . ."

"Patience," John recommended.

Ali's village was a bombed and burned-out wreck, the minaret collapsed, most of the houses destroyed. It was still littered with dead bodies, dogs and camels as well as humans. "Did they not surrender?" John asked.

"These bastards do not know the meaning of the word," the sergeant said.

"Did they not *attempt* to surrender?" John persisted.

"The only good Senussi is a dead Senussi, eh?"

John pressed his shoulder against Soroya's in an attempt to keep her from exploding. They drove on, and soon afterwards saw smoke billowing upwards in front of them too. "What happened to Tobruk?" John asked.

"The English swine, they bombed it, last night," the sergeant said.

"How terribly uncivilised."

"We are going to bomb Alexandria," the sergeant told him.

"And the best of luck."

They could see the sea, a very busy sea, with far more shipping that the last time John had been here – a good percentage were warships. The coast road was crowded with vehicles travelling both east and west, and men marching, principally east. "Are you invading Egypt?" John asked, as innocently as he could.

"That is not for me to say," the sergeant said.

There were several fires in Tobruk, causing the smoke, but there did not seem all that much damage. Certainly the port was busier than the last time John had seen it. There were quite a few people on the street, and fire engine and ambulance sirens were still wailing. "I tell these people you are English, they string you up by the heels," the sergeant said, chattily.

"Then let's keep it to ourselves," John said, trying to be as insouciant as possible. "Geneva Convention and all that." Of course he knew they were in grave danger, as they were not in uniform; he was pinning his entire faith in the essential Italian sense of fair play.

They drove into a courtyard and were disembarked. Armed sentries stood to attention as they were marched into one of the buildings, along a corridor and up a flight of stairs. "Three prisoners, Colonel," the sergeant said, opening a door.

"The orders were, no—" then Umberto checked, as he came to the door. "My God! Do you have a death wish?"

"I am hoping you will let me explain, Colonel," John said.

"And I am hoping you will be able to do that. Come in. Miss Cartwright? I had hoped not to see you again."

"The feeling is entirely mutual," Margo assured him.

"And the beautiful slave girl," Umberto said with a smile.

"Listen, arsehole," Soroya said. "I have been assaulted. By those men." She pointed with her chin at the sergeant and his soldiers, who had remained in the corridor.

Umberto raised his eyebrows. "Is this true?"

"She was searched, Colonel," the sergeant said. "Military procedure."

Umberto looked at John.

"In England it would be classed as indecent assault."

"Sit down." Umberto waved them to chairs. There were only two chairs. John held Margo's for her, then nodded to Soroya.

"I am a slave girl," Soroya said contemptuously. "I cannot sit before my master."

John sat down and Umberto returned behind his desk. "Were you searched also, Miss Cartwright?"

"I was also indecently assaulted, if that is what you mean," she retorted.

"These are clearly two difficult women," Umberto remarked. "Clearly you do not beat them enough. Mr Warrey, kindly tell your servant that if she is rude to me again I will have her flogged."

"You heard the man," John said. Soroya snorted.

"Now, explain to me what you were doing in Ali's camp?" Umberto said.

"What was happened to Ali?"

"I am the one asking the questions, Mr Warrey. However, as I am sure you know, Sheikh Ali was an enemy of Italy. Having received information that he was planning to lead a revolt, we decided it was necessary to place him under arrest. He resisted this arrest and was shot, together, I am afraid, with several of his supporters."

"Quite a number of whom were women and children." •

"That is unfortunate. But we are at war and we cannot permit any subversive activities. Now I must tell you that we found a considerable amount of modern equipment in Ali's village. I am speaking of rifles and ammunition and machine-guns. These would appear to have arrived yesterday. With you and Miss Cartwright. And your slave woman, of course."

"I have no idea what you are talking about," John said.

"You are saying that it was not you who delivered those rifles? Can you prove this?"

"Can you prove I did? It was careless of you to kill Ali, Colonel. He would have been able to testify one way or the other."

"I will remind you, for the last time, Mr Warrey, that we are now fighting a war. I have not the time to play games. I have sufficient circumstantial evidence to prove that it was you delivered those rifles. I also have the power to force a confession from you, or," he glanced at Margo and then at Soroya, "from either of your charming companions. Or both."

"Do you know, I had supposed you were a gentleman, Umberto," John said. "We all make mistakes, I suppose."

"Those rifles," Umberto said, "were intended to kill Italian soldiers. When one is dealing with spies and assassins, it is difficult to be a gentleman. It is the end result that matters. You say you had nothing to do with that delivery of rifles to Sheikh Ali. Then what were you doing in that village?"

158

"We were visiting Sheikh Ali, certainly. But it had nothing to do with weapons. Miss Cartwright is planning another journey into the Sahara and the Sheikh had promised to help her. You may remember that I visited him last year to begin the negotiations."

"Do you take me for a fool? Do you really suppose that you and Miss Cartwright can traipse about Cyrenaica in time of war?"

"Small correction," John said. "When we left Cairo there was no war. We travelled across the desert and it took us several weeks. We did not learn of the situation until we reached Sheikh Ali's village last night. Having been told by the sheikh that Italy and Great Britain were at war, we decided to leave immediately and return to Egypt. We have no wish to get mixed up in a war. We were returning when we were attacked by your aircraft."

"You crossed the desert to visit Ali? Why did you not come by the coast road?"

"We wished to use the desert. Our expedition was to be into the desert. So, if you would like to let us return the way we came . . ." John said, optimistically.

"You are enemy aliens. You must at the least be interned."

"I am sure there must have been quite a few British people in Italy when your Duce decided to go to war. Have all of them been interned?"

He had made a point. Umberto began flicking the papers on his desk. Then he said, "I believe you are agents for the British Government. I believe that you did deliver those guns to Sheikh Ali, to enable him to launch an insurgency movement against us. But as you say, I have no proof of this. I could have you interrogated by our secret police, but that would be a nasty business. So, I will let you go." He grinned. "For the third time, I think, Mr Warrey. You wish to return the way you came. I give you permission to do that. But let me tell you this: the next time I see any of the three of you, I will have you shot."

*   *   *

159

"Being rescued by Umberto was probably the luckiest thing that ever happened to us," John said, as they were again squeezed into the armoured car.

"We're not back in Egypt yet," Margo said.

"Arseholes," Soroya muttered. "One day I kill them all."

"Sssh," John recommended.

It was dark before they regained Ali's village, now occupied by soldiers, who had done some clearing up. Here waited a string of camels, and some food. The rest of their equipment, including their changes of clothing, had been confiscated. "You are sending us out into the desert without arms?" John asked the sergeant.

He grinned. "Who are you afraid of? If you encounter the Senussi, they are your friends, are they not? And if you encounter the British, well, they are your friends too, eh?" He pointed at the desert. "You go now."

John looked at Soroya. "I can see in the dark," she said.

"Well, then, it's been nice knowing you," John said, and mounted. The women also got up, and the little caravan walked out of the village and down to the sand sea.

"That was a near one," John said.

"It's been too easy," Margo said.

"Don't you trust Umberto?"

"Umberto is one man. He doesn't control the whole Italian scene."

"You're a pessimist," John said.

But he realised what she meant when, after a walk of several hours, they reached the edge of the sand sea and found two more armoured cars parked across the track.

"Shit," John muttered. They had been given no passes, as they had not expected to encounter any more Italians. But these were definitely waiting for them.

"What are we going to do?" Margo asked.

"We certainly can't run for it. Those cars carry machine-guns. We'll have to talk our way through."

They walked the camels forward, trying to ascertain how many men were in front of them; the moonlight made the desert almost as bright as day, but at the same time where there was shadow it was darker than night. "Halt!" commanded a voice. John reined in his camel. "Get down, Signor Warrey. And the women."

So they knew who they were. This had definitely been arranged. John dismounted and walked forward, leading his camel.

"Where are you going?" the man asked, now emerging from the shadow of the first vehicle. He wore the uniform and insignia of a lieutenant, and behind him were six men and a sergeant. The sergeant carried a tommy-gun.

"We are returning to Egypt," John said. "On the express orders of Colonel Umberto."

"We know this," the lieutenant said. "Colonel Umberto is a friend of yours, eh?"

"Yes," John said. "He is a friend of ours."

"And he is a senior officer and must be obeyed," the lieutenant said. "But he said you must not come back, eh?"

"That is correct. We shall not come back."

"I intend to make sure of that," the lieutenant said.

John frowned. "Just what do you mean?"

"Come," the lieutenant said. "Sit with me." He gestured to the camp table which could now be seen beside his car. "And have a cognac. My name is Renaldo, by the way."

"I wish to know your intentions."

"Why, to have a drink with you, while we are amused. And while you, or your women, answer some questions."

John felt his belly fill with lead. "Are the women to have a drink, too?"

"Perhaps later, when they will need it. Before then, I give them to my men. Flog them," he commanded.

"You bastard!" John stepped forward and looked down the barrel of the lieutenant's revolver. Behind him he heard Soroya cursing, and Margo screamed, a sound which was cut off abruptly as someone hit her in the stomach. He turned round, and saw her being stripped of her clothing and stretched on the sand. For the

161

moment Soroya was still dressed and on her feet, but she knew her turn was next. "Colonel Umberto will have your guts for garters," John snarled.

"But Colonel Umberto will never know," the lieutenant said. "Because you are never going to come back, are you, Signor Warrey? Tell me who is your contact man in Tobruk? Is it the man Quesmi? I do not think this. Your meetings with him were too open and above board. It is to do with the typewriters, eh? What about Signor Armanto?"

"I have no idea what you are talking about," John said. "Signor Armanto is a customer of my firm. He bought a typewriter."

The lieutenant grinned. "I do not believe you. But perhaps you are telling the truth. The woman will tell us. Make her squeal," he told his men. Margo was stretched on the sand, on her face, her wrists and ankles held by four of the men, while two more took off their belts and began slashing them across her buttocks. She screamed and writhed, but was helpless. "Tomorrow you will not ride for a while, eh?" the lieutenant asked with a grin.

John had no idea how to cope with the situation. He had been taught to withstand pain himself. No one, not even that old buzzard George Brand, had told him how to withstand pain being inflicted upon others, when the other was a woman he was almost in love with, and who was being utterly humiliated as well as physically destroyed. "She knows nothing," he shouted. "She has never been to Tobruk before."

"She works with you," the lieutenant said. "I do not think she is screaming loud enough," he told his men.

Margo had, in fact, run out of breath, and John was afraid she would choke as she swallowed dust and sand in her efforts to breathe. He saw red and, revolver or no revolver, lashed out at the fellow. The lieutenant went down with a thud and a startled exclamation, and John turned back to go to Margo's assistance.

"Stop there, signor."

He checked at the command, and saw that one of the two men

holding Soroya had drawn his bayonet and was pressing the point into her throat. "You move, she dies," the man said.

John hesitated, totally confounded. To let Margo be so tortured was unthinkable, but to have Soroya's throat cut was equally so. "That's enough." The lieutenant was regaining his feet and rubbing his jaw. "She will tell us nothing. Try the Senussi bitch."

Margo was ignored, lying in the sand, moaning and twisting. This enabled all of the men to deal with Soroya, and they needed all of them, as she fought them with a vicious anger, sending one man reeling back with both hands to his face, where her nails had ripped the flesh open. But there were too many of them, and a few minutes later she was stretched on the sand and the belts were flailing. Soroya uttered not a sound, nor did she move, save to clench her buttocks as tightly as she could. "One day, signor," John said. "One day, I will come back with the British Army, and then you and I will have a reckoning."

"The British Army," the lieutenant sneered. "It is only good for running away, signor. It ran away in France, it is running away in Somaliland as I speak, and soon it will be running away in Egypt, when we are ready to march on Cairo. Maybe you see me there, eh? But then, I will still be in command. Enough."

The men released Soroya. She did not move for several seconds. Then very slowly she pushed herself up to her knees, her dark hair hanging about her face, stiff with sweat. "Now you use her," the lieutenant told his men. "And the other one. They will not resist you now."

John felt he was about to burst with anger. "You have not had your cognac," the lieutenant said, and poured two glasses. "To Il Duce and victory."

John threw glass and liquid on the ground. He could hear Margo groaning and whimpering as she was stretched on her back, allowing the sand to eat into the weals on her back. Three men knelt around her, one holding her arms, one parting her legs while the other knelt between. The other three men were dealing with Soroya. That left the man with the tommy-gun, overseeing

163

the proceedings, and the lieutenant, now refilling John's brandy glass. "You are so hot-headed," the lieutenant said. "And this is good French cognac. Not to be wasted." He pushed the glass across the table. "Again I give you, Il Duce."

There was a shout of pain and one of the soldiers rolled away from Soroya, who had bitten him. With his pants round his ankles he stumbled when he tried to rise and fell down again. Before his two companions could react, Soroya had swung her arms to and fro and knocked them over as well, in the same instant hurling a handful of sand into the face of the sergeant with the tommy-gun. He gasped in turn, hands coming up to his eyes, dropping the gun. Soroya reached it in a single bound of naked litheness, picked it up and was struck by the bullet fired by the lieutenant, who had dropped his own cognac to level his pistol. Soroya made a gurgling sound and fell, but as she did so she squeezed the trigger of the tommy-gun. The hail of bullets struck the sergeant in the chest and he fell backwards in a splatter of blood.

By now John was reacting. The other men were getting up, reaching for their weapons. But the lieutenant was closest and was again levelling his pistol. John reached him in a great leap, kicking him over and then leaping for the tommy-gun that Soroya was still grasping, while slowly being surrounded by a pool of blood. John snatched up the weapon. Firing a tommy-gun had not been included in his training, but he found it a most satisfying experience, as he swung the weapon to and fro, spraying the doomed men as they tried to throw themselves right and left. He fired for only a matter of seconds before the drum ran out of bullets, but then he was able to pick up the lieutenant's revolver and deal with the others.

He swung back to face the lieutenant, saw him running for the nearest armoured car and getting into it. John fired and hit metal, then the car was driving straight at him. He threw himself to one side and the car roared by away into the darkness. Then suddenly it was over and John found himself standing there, empty revolver in his hand, in a night where the only sound was the gasps and sobs of dying men.

And women. He knelt beside Soroya, muttered, "Jesus!" as he looked at her more closely. She had been struck just below the right breast, and there was a mass of shattered bone, while from the amount of blood coming from her mouth a bullet had also pierced the lung. "Did you kill the arseholes?" she whispered.

"Yes. I have just killed seven men. But the one I really wanted got away."

"Then go," Soroya said. "With the woman."

"We cannot go without you."

"Yes you can. Use the sun. But they will have compasses in their cars. Go south until tomorrow morning, then west. They will not find you. Go."

"And leave you here?"

"I am dead," she pointed out.

He laid her on the sand, made sure all the Italians were also dead. I have killed seven men, he thought.

He knelt beside Margo. She was huddled in a tight ball, her face hidden in her arms and her hair. For a moment he thought she might also have stopped a bullet, but when he touched her she stirred. Then she sat up with a scream and tried to roll away from him. He caught her shoulder and brought her back to him. "It's me. John."

"Those men . . ."

"Are all dead. Now we have to get out of here." Their camels, fortunately, had remained standing together, alarmed but not driven off by the shooting; no doubt they were used to gunshots from Ali's village. "I'll just hunt through that armoured car and see what we can find of use. We need bullets, and there'll be food and water as well. I know you're in pain, Margo, but it'll wear off. So if you'd like to get dressed . . ."

Margo was on her hands and knees. Now she slowly

stood up. "You killed all those men? You? Jesus, you're a hero!"

"Not really."

"Nevertheless, I'm going to see you get a medal."

"The medal," John told her, "belongs to someone else."

PART THREE

Winning

'There's nothing worth the wear of winning.'

Hilaire Belloc

Chapter Nine

The Raid

"Warrey!" Sandy Carmichael exclaimed. "We thought you were dead. Sit down, man. Sit down. What happened?"

John sank wearily into the chair before the desk. He had not yet returned to his lodgings, had spent the night at Shepheard's; he felt he needed that much rest and recuperation, and pampering. He needed to regain his equilibrium. If he was ever going to do that. "You name it, Mr Carmichael," he said. "And it happened. All the wrong way."

"Tell me," Carmichael invited. "Good God," he commented when John had finished. "You mean the Cartwright woman is an agent after all? And you brought her out. Well done."

"At a cost of God knows how many lives," John said.

"Well, old man, there is a war on. Pity about Ali; he might have been useful. Pity about the guns, too. And I assume you didn't have the opportunity to obtain any information?"

"I'm afraid nothing more than we already have. That one dump."

"Pity. You know, there's one thing puzzles me. You say you managed to escape from the Italians, and their two armoured cars. I make that eight people. How did you manage that?"

"I shot them, sir. Well, seven of them."

"You did *what?*"

"Well, sir, as you have just reminded me, there *is* a war on. Unfortunately, their commanding officer got away."

"Good God! You shot seven Italian soldiers just like that?"

"I'll admit I was fairly uptight at the time, sir."

"You'll have to have a gong," Carmichael said.

"I think that's already in hand, sir. Miss Cartwright, you know."

"Ah. Oh, quite. Well, I think you need a few days R and R, don't you know? I'll have to report all of this, of course. I'm sure they'll think of some use to put you to. Meanwhile . . ."

"Could you give me an update on the exact situation, sir? I understood that the Italians were invading Egypt."

"Well, it's all a little confused," Carmichael said. "The Italians certainly invaded Egypt, oh, some weeks ago, now. They stormed across the frontier, thousands of them, with tanks and armoured cars and trucks and aircraft and you name it. Well, we simply didn't have the strength to oppose them, so we fell back. They came on as far as Mersah Matruh and we really thought we'd be fighting in the streets of Alexandria. But then they stopped. Called a halt, dug themselves in and they've been there ever since."

"Isn't that odd, sir?"

"Well, I suppose there are several factors involved. One is the supply problem. Every gallon of petrol they burn, every bullet they fire, has to be brought across the Mediterranean, to Benghazi or Tripoli, Bardia or Tobruk, and then driven along the coast road to wherever their front line happens to be. That takes time, and as you may imagine, our navy is sinking everything it sees between Italy and Libya, and at the same time we are bombing their ports as hard as we can too.

"Then there has been a diplomatic problem with the Government of Egypt. Would you believe the beggars in the beginning refused to declare war on Italy? I ask you. And the Italians, of course, claimed that they were fighting us and not the Egyptians. Well, we've got that sorted out at last. Egypt and Italy are now officially at war.

"But the third and most important factor is probably the invasion of Greece. You know the Italians have moved in there?"

"No, sir. I have been quite incommunicado for the past four months."

"Well, they have invaded. I imagine Musso thought it'd be a pushover. But the Greeks are defending themselves damned well. So right now that's the centre of the main Italian war effort. I suppose they feel that once they have taken Greece and the islands they can get at us here from two directions, as it were. But that's none of your concern, Warrey. You've done well, damned well. Is Miss Cartwright still in Cairo?"

"Yes, sir. I think she also means to indulge in some R and R."

"Absolutely. Well, enjoy her, Warrey. I would say you have earned her."

"Sadly, sir," John said, "I don't think that is a practical possibility."

But he had to say goodbye, at the least. Even if he was not sure he ever wanted to see her again, or that she wanted to see him.

It had taken them, without Soroya's leadership, more than four months to cross the desert and reach Siwa, and even then their anabasis had not ended; Siwa had been evacuated in the face of the Italian threat; such Egyptians as remained were not interested in helping two British scarecrows who had looked more like ghosts than human beings, and it was back to the desert, with only their food and water replenished. Three weeks later they had encountered a British patrol just south of the Qattara Depression. In those sixteen weeks they had shared everything, down to the drinking of their own urine to keep alive. He had often wondered why they bothered.

In the beginning, they had been slightly bolstered by the elation of having fought and won, and escaped. But always the death of Soroya and what both she and Margo had suffered, no less than the massacre of Ali's people, had weighted on them as if they were carrying tons of lead. John had felt utterly inadequate, unable to soothe either Margo's body or her spirit, while his own was so crushed. And she . . . he had supposed that perhaps she felt he had valued Soroya more than herself. Well, that would not have been very wide of the mark. Soroya had attacked life with a laugh

171

and a swear word. She had also been his mistress and he had been closer to her than to any woman in his life before. She made both Sam Carson and Margo seem irrelevancies. He was not prepared to think of her in relation to Aileen at that moment.

And she had died for him. It did not matter that he had a suspicion she had been prepared, and preparing, to die from the moment Ali's village had been wiped out. With the village had gone her friends and even perhaps her relations. She must have had some, even if she had never mentioned them. But the actual act of dying had been that he might live. And he was the one to get the medal.

While that bastard of an officer, Renaldo – it was not a name he intended to forget – had survived, no doubt to torture some other woman just as soon as he could get his hands on one! It had been Soroya's memory that had driven them on, over the sand sea, or was it through the sand seas, huddled together when the desert winds had blown and almost buried them, forcing themselves to dig for water, to eat their iron rations alleviated by a few dates, while their bodies had become encrusted with sand.

They had seldom spoken, because there was nothing to speak about. Quite apart from Ali and his people, and then Soroya, they were obsessed by a deadening sense of failure. They had been sent to lead a Senussi revolt against the Italians, and merely caused the deaths of more than a hundred people. They had been sent to pinpoint the whereabouts of the Italian supply dumps, and they had not had the chance to do any of that, save for the one they knew about anyway. And Lieutenant Renaldo had got away!

The only plus, from John's point of view, was that the Italians apparently did not know the identity of the other British agents in Tobruk, and thus, presumably, in the whole of Libya. But Margo did not know their identities either, and thus did not even know the reason behind her torture. And in the tangled and, he felt, internicine, world of British intelligence, he did not feel he could tell her.

He knocked on her door, ignoring the Do Not Disturb sign.

When he got no reply, he returned to his own room and tried the phone. "Miss Cartwright left orders she was not to be disturbed," said the man on the switchboard.

So that was that. He had been given a very ill-fitting uniform by the British soldiers who had rescued him. There was nothing else. He checked out, telling the clerk to send the bill to the typewriter company, and took a taxi to his lodgings.

Arsinoe greeted him with her hands on her hips. "You!" she remarked. "You know it is six months? I do not know why I did not relet the room."

"Because the rent was being paid," he told her.

"Ha!" She walked round him. "You are burned all black."

"To a crisp."

"And where you get those clothes? You a soldier, now?"

"I was rescued from the desert by some soldiers and they lent me these. Believe me, I want to get them off as quickly as possible."

"Ha! I help you." And she began doing so.

"Listen," he said, "I just want to be alone."

"Alone," she commented. "And where is the girl?"

"Soroya is dead."

She stared at him, and to his consternation he watched tears gathering in her huge black eyes. "Dead? How she is dead?"

"An Italian soldier shot her."

"Soroya?" His consternation increased as Arsinoe appeared to be going mad. She seized her kaftan and tore it open, establishing that she wore nothing underneath. She wrenched the garment from her shoulders, flung it to the floor and jumped on it several times. Then she threw herself on the floor and began what might have been a snake dance, while she grasped her hair and seemed to be attempting to tear it out by the roots, meantime wailing and screaming and gnashing her teeth.

"Here, I say," he protested, attempting to grasp her shoulders and being forced to jump away to avoid her sweeping nails.

"You killed my friend," she moaned.

173

"No, no, not at all. I told you. She was killed by an Italian soldier.

Arsinoe stopped her gyrations, and stared at him. "You avenged her?"

"Well, yes, I did, actually."

"How you did this? You cut off his balls?"

"No. I shot him."

"And *then* you cut off his balls."

"Well, no. There wouldn't have been much point. He was dead."

"Dead men still have balls."

"Yes, but they don't know they do, do they? They can't feel anything, so they wouldn't know if they were cut off or not. Oh, for God's sake, what a conversation!"

"You should have cut off his balls," Arsinoe said severely.

"I'll remember that next time," John agreed.

"Now we have sex, eh?"

"Not on your nelly." Hastily he attempted to make amends. "I mean, not right now. I am quite incapable. I am exhausted. I need rest. I am going to bed."

"I come and see to you." He was too exhausted and confused to refuse her, and she duly undressed him and tucked him in, regarding him sadly as she did so. His claim was all too evident. "Ass's milk," she remarked.

"I'm sure you're right," he agreed, nestling into the pillow.

"I bring you ass's milk to drink," she explained. "That puts the lead back in the pencil, eh?"

"Does it?" It actually tasted like nectar.

John awoke to find Mustafa standing by his bed, only then remembered that he was naked.

"You have been sleeping for two days," Mustafa pointed out. "Where is your car?" No doubt he considered it useful collateral.

John sat up. "My God! It's still at Hamdi's village."

"After six months? He will have sell it by now."

"Jesus! I hope not, I must get down there."

"I will see," Mustafa said.

"Ah! Right. You are not still a canal pilot?"

"I am enlisted," Mustafa said. It was difficult to be sure whether he was proud or resentful.

"Well, there is a war on," John agreed. "Enlisted in what?"

"I am in transport corps," Mustafa explained. "I will go see about your car."

"Would you? I would be most awfully grateful."

Mustafa went to the door, and there checked. "My wife say the Arab woman is dead."

"I'm afraid she is," John acknowledged.

"That is a pity. She was a good woman," Mustafa remarked. John wondered just how far Soroya had spread her favours.

"Yes," he agreed. "A very good woman."

"Now my wife is sad," Mustafa said. "You have sex with her?"

John decided his best chance was attack. "You mean you wouldn't object?"

"When she has plenty sex, she is good woman," Mustafa explained. "When she has little sex, she is bad woman. She throw things."

No wonder she and Soroya got on so well, John thought. "I'm afraid I haven't actually, had, well . . . I didn't know if you'd object," he explained.

"I leave tomorrow, for your car," Mustafa said. "You have sex, eh?"

"Well . . . it's a delightful prospect, old fellow, but I really am done up. Not feeling well," he explained as Mustafa was clearly getting hold of the wrong end of the stick.

Now he grinned. "She do you up." Again he turned to the door, then checked again. "Two men downstairs," he said. "Army people. They wish to speak with you."

"Now you tell me, for Jesus' sake." John got out of bed, hunted for his clothes, discovered they had all been removed, presumably by Arsinoe. "Send them up."

"They take you away from here, maybe," Mustafa said.

"That could well be true."

"Then who has sex with my wife? You want her to take someone off the street?"

John had no doubt that she did, when the mood took her. "We'll work something out," he said. "Send those men up."

He managed to find a towel, in which he wrapped himself, sat on the edge of the bed, then stood up again and saluted, because the first of the two men who entered was wearing the crown of a major on his shoulder-straps. "John Warrey?"

"Yes, sir." He wondered if he was under arrest.

"Is that all the clothing you possess?"

John retrieved the towel from round his ankles. "Laundry, sir."

"Well, sit down and try to stay decent." The major waved a hand and his aide, a lieutenant, hastily brought forward the only straight chair in the room. "The name is Blanchard." He peered at John. "Are you all right?"

"Just came in from the desert, sir. Bit of sunburn. Sunstroke too, I would say."

"Have you seen a doctor?"

"Yes, sir. Some days ago. He prescribed rest."

"Yes. Well, you've had that." Blanchard suddenly frowned, and then jerked his head.

The lieutenant moved to the door, quickly and quietly, and wrenched it open. Arsinoe tumbled in and landed on her hands and knees. "Shit!" she commented in English.

"Friend of yours?" Blanchard enquired.

"My landlady," John explained. "Really, Arsinoe," he remonstrated, "listening at keyholes?"

"I have to know when you are here," she explained, getting up and rubbing her arm where it had struck the door jamb. "Now you are here, now you are gone. How am I to know?"

"To know what?" Blachard asked.

"When he is here, stupid."

176

"If she is a friend of yours," Blanchard told John. "tell her that now we are going to leave the door open and that she is to take herself into the furthest place in the house and stay there until we leave. If I see her again or hear her creeping about, I am going to arrest her under the official secrets act and lock her up for the duration."

"You cannot do this," Arsinoe protested. "This is my own house." She looked at John. "He can do this?"

"I think he probably can," John said. "Don't push it too far. Go and keep your husband company."

"My husband has gone out. He has gone to see about your car."

"Ah. That is good of him. Well, go and keep yourself company then." Arsinoe glared at him, then retreated down the stairs.

"You stay on the landing," Blanchard told the lieutenant. Then he turned back to John. "Quite a dish. Do you have her?"

"My God!" John said. "With respect, sir. Does no one in this place think of anything other than sex?"

"With the food the way it is, and the wine the way it is, and the beer served cold, what else is there to do?" Blanchard asked. "Except think about beating the Eyeties, of course. That's why I'm here." He glanced through the open door, but his lieutenant was firmly entrenched at the top of the stairs. "This is confidential. Absolutely top secret. We are about to make our move."

"You mean we're going to attack, sir?" John's heart leapt. "But . . . aren't we outnumbered?"

"That doesn't mean we can't lick the beggars. A lot of his best people have been withdrawn to Greece. We reckon we can drive him out of Egypt, at the least. But we need to play all our trumps at the same time. Penetration, that's the key. You know the desert, right?"

"Ah . . . yes, sir."

"You've crossed into Cyrenaica several times."

"Twice, sir."

177

"Good enough. You found your way in and you found your way out. We propose to send a squadron of tanks across the desert and round the Italian flank. You will guide them. How much do you know about tank warfare?"

"I know nothing about tank warfare, sir. I have never been in a tank."

"Well, you'll pick it up. I will be in command. Now the first thing I want you to understand is that tanks do not operate in soft sand. You have to get us behind the Italian lines without also getting us involved in any sand sea. Can you do that?"

"Yes, sir." It would be covering country he had first experienced with Margo eighteen months before, and which he had come to know very well over the past six months.

"Right. We leave at dawn. Do whatever you have to with that woman, and report to my headquarters outside Memphis at zero five hundred. Understood?"

"Yes, sir. I should point out that the doctor who examined me recommended at least a fortnight's total rest, with as little exposure to the sun as possible."

"Is that so? And how much rest have you had?"

"Well, sir, actual rest, forty-eight hours."

"That will have to do, Lieutenant Warrey. There is a war on. Oh five hundred," Blanchard said again, and stood up. "Don't bother to salute; it is incorrect when you are not wearing a hat. Didn't they teach you that? When I see you again, I wish you to be in uniform." He left the room, tapped his lieutenant on the shoulder and they went down the stairs.

John scratched his head and waited for Arsinoe to appear, which she did in seconds. "They are sending you away."

"I'm afraid they are."

"For how long?"

"I have no idea. I'll be back as soon as I can."

"You bring another woman?" She seemed to assume he was her pimp, backwards.

178

"I very much doubt that, Arsinoe. When I come back it'll be just you and me. Won't you like that?"

"It is just you and me now," she pointed out. "My husband has gone out."

"Yes, but you see, I need as much rest and recuperation as I can get over the next few hours. So . . ."

"I look after you," she said.

It was difficult to be sure whether she considered him a large baby in her care or an exhausted man who needed resuscitation, but with her looking after him all thoughts of another attempt at reaching Margo had to be forgotten – not that he was in the mood, anyway. And he awoke the next morning at four o'clock feeling vastly restored.

"You come back soon," Arsinoe admonished. "And bring woman," she reminded him.

She had even got one of his two uniforms – which he had never worn – out of the wardrobe and pressed it. He wondered how she would get on with Margo?

The squadron consisted of seventeen A9 Cruiser tanks. "To take on the Italian Army?" John asked.

"Too many breakdowns," Blanchard explained. "Sand, you know. It gets everywhere. But we are a raiding party, not the main thrust. That's going to be along the main road, out of Mersah Matruh. Now, show me your plan."

The maps were spread and the tank commanders gathered round. They were all disturbingly young, even to John's eyes, and he was pretty certain not one had fired a shot in anger till now. In that respect he was light years ahead of them, even if he didn't know one end of a tank from the other. "My idea is that we take the road south to Bahariya Oasis." He prodded the map.

"How far is that?" Blanchard enquired.

"A hundred and seventy-odd miles."

"And the surface is good?"

179

John grinned. "Good enough for a tank."

"Right. Eight hours' driving, a couple of hours' break, we'll be there this afternoon. Is there fuel in this oasis?"

"I would say so."

"We'll take our own tankers, of course." He pointed to the waiting bowsers. "But it would be useful to be able to top them up. And after that?"

"We take the track across the stony desert south of the Qattara Depression, to Siwa Oasis. Say another hundred and seventy miles. This isn't such a good surface."

"Hm. Better allow double, I suppose. Right. Two days. And at Siwa?"

"Well, sir, there is a possibility Siwa may be occupied by the Italians. It wasn't the last time I passed through there, several weeks ago, but it had been evacuated by British troops."

"How far from Siwa to the border?"

"Thirty miles, maybe. My suggestion would be that we swing up from Siwa, cross the border and make for Al-Jaghbub. There's a garrison there and a fuel dump not too far away."

"Show me?"

"I can't, exactly. I have only a rough idea where it is. But I think we may be able to persuade someone on the spot to show us."

"Hm. Well, I suppose you people in intelligence know how to do these things. Right. We have three days to hit this place Jabberwock or whatever. The offensive starts on the ninth of December at dawn, and today is the sixth. One day to to Bahariya. Two days to Siwa. Reconnoitre, then enter Siwa and hold. Cross the border at dawn on the ninth and shoot up Jabberwock, then destroy the fuel dump, except for what we need, then make for the coast to disrupt traffic. Understood?"

The commanders saluted and returned to their tanks.

"Just one question, sir," John asked. "Are we supposed to return from this mission?"

"I have no orders about that. My orders are to search and destroy." John gulped, as Blanchard grinned and gave him a beret. "You're in the tank corps now, Warrey. Even if only temporarily."

Travelling by tank, John discovered, was every bit as nauseating as travelling by camel, save that the tanks went considerably faster; on the road they maintained a steady twenty miles an hour when they were free of traffic. But this was not always the case, as apart from the inevitable donkeys and goats and bicycles, the people gathered in groups to gaze at the armoured monsters rumbling to the south. "Don't they know there's a war on?" Blanchard asked.

As the sun came up it was very hot, but at least they were able to ride with their hatches open. Unfortunately, only one man at a time could comfortably stand in the cupola, and this was usually the tank commander. The rest of the four-man crew – or in John's case, five-man – had to exist as best they could inside an armoured coffin. Soon the air was acrid with partly human and partly fuel fumes; John could not even imagine what it must be like in battle, with the hatch closed and presumably human bowels more activated than usual by fear. He supposed he would soon find out.

They stopped every second hour to stretch their legs and perform whatever necessaries were needed. This was an opportunity for a cup of tea, on which the tank crews seemed to thrive; every machine had its primus ready to be thrust into action. While behind them their supply trucks emerged from the dust clouds left by their tracks.

But this was the easy part and although the crews were exhilarated when they arrived in Bahariya Oasis in late afternoon, he hoped they knew the real stuff lay ahead. Blanchard reported by radio to Cairo, then summoned his men. "General O'Connor says, good work. I know they haven't actually done anything yet," he confided to John over their evening meal, "but it helps morale, what? Shoo those people off, Layton," he bawled at the lieutenant who was his assistant.

Sentries were posted to keep the inquisitive Egyptians away

from the tanks, and they slept as best they could before leaving just before dawn.

Now they were in an altogether different situation, crossing the stony desert. This did not mean there was not a great deal of sand about, merely that there wasn't enough of it to make a tank sink; it plumed behind the column in a vast pillar, which presumably could be seen for miles, and certainly from the air. But down here there was no one for miles and no aircraft. The heat grew ever more intense; the outside of the tanks grew too hot to touch, and when they stopped for lunch the crews amused themselves by frying eggs on the decks.

Water was, as always, strictly rationed, each man being allowed a gallon a day to cover everything; shaving very rapidly dwindled to the bottom of the list. "I suppose you've done all this before," Layton remarked to John.

"Several times," John said, with some satisfaction. His business was to protect his already burned and tortured skin from the sun.

Inevitably, the trucks couldn't make it, and by mid-afternoon on the second day two had broken down. "You'll have to repair as best you can and then go back to the oasis," Blanchard told the sergeant in command. "But first, give us every drop of petrol you have, apart from what you need to get home."

"Will they make it?" John asked.

"I've told them to give us twenty-four hours and then radio for assistance," Blanchard said. "They'll be pulled out and by then it'll be too late for the Eyeties to work out just why we are down here, supposing they pick up the signals."

"And do we have enough petrol?"

"We'd better," Blanchard said, supervising the strapping of as many five-gallon jerrycans as possible to the topsides of the tanks.

If we're seen by aircraft and strafed, and a bomb hits this lot, John thought . . .

Layton seemed able to read his thoughts. "Don't worry about

it, old man. With or without the petrol, if we get hit, it's boom and bye-bye. This tin plate won't keep out a bomb."

Cheerful fellow, John thought.

But apart from losing the supply trucks, things were going surprisingly well. They were actually ahead of schedule, according to John's reckoning, when they stopped for the third night. "Twenty miles to Siwa," he told Blanchard.

"And not an Eyetie in sight. If you're right about Siwa, Warrey, there'll be a mention for you. You've done an excellent job of navigating."

"Thank you, sir. There's another hour of daylight. We could move on it now."

"No chance. What we need to remember is, once we get to Siwa, if there are Eyeties about, the whole world will know what's happening down here. We'll stick to the game plan, eh?"

"Yes, sir," John agreed, without quite understanding. If they took Siwa, as planned, tomorrow, they were still a full day ahead of the start of the offensive. They had to seize the oasis before any garrison that might be there could use their radios, and he thought they'd stand a better chance of that at night. But he was only the navigator.

They stood to just before dawn, as usual. "Now, then," Blanchard said. "We don't know if this place is held by Eyeties or not. We want it as intact as possible, together with any petrol that may be available. You say if we follow this track it will take us into the oasis, Warrey?"

"Yes, sir."

"Right. Can you find your way across the desert to the north of it?"

"I think so, sir."

"You need to be certain. Take seven tanks. Captain Plassey will be in tactical command. Sweep to the north and east of the oasis, and then launch your attack at . . . how long will you need?"

183

"Four hours."

"Hm. Make it ten ack emma. Synchronise, Plassey." The captain obliged. "We will move to within a strike distance by that time and at ten o'clock we will assault the oasis from the south. You will come in from the north. Questions?" He looked from face to face. "Very good. Gentlemen."

They finished their meal, drank the last of their tea and scurried to their machines. In the desert dawn the tank engines seemed to make an enormous noise and it was difficult to suppose anyone in Siwa would not be alerted once they were within certainly a mile. But hopefully they would not be expecting an attack from out of the sand sea.

"You stay up here with me," Plassey told John. That was a relief, even if the two men were crammed against each other in the small hatchway. It was still cool as the seven tanks rumbled away from the track to the north; John could only pray there were no patches of soft sand to trap them – now he was really out on his own.

He knew a peculiar mixture of exhilaration and apprehension. Although he had been in action more than once, and certainly more than any of the men he was leading, he had never been trained to go into battle, not as part of a team, or indeed a plan – his fights had always been unexpected and spontaneous. While the men he was with had spent their entire adult lives preparing for just this moment; Plassey studied his watch, and the men beneath him waited for their instructions with a seeming lack of emotion, their true feelings betrayed only by the odd fart that drifted up through the cupola. "Eight o'clock," Plassey said, and waved his hand. The tanks screamed to a halt in a flurry of dust. "Brew up." He swung his legs out of the cupola and dropped to the ground. John followed him and they studied the map while their men made tea. "Where do you suppose we are?"

"Two hours, steering north by west . . ." John prodded the stiff paper. "Here."

"I hope you're right." Plassey looked left and right at the

unchanging desert. "That makes Siwa eighteen miles away, south by west. And we have to be there at ten. Take fifteen," he told his commanders. They drank tea and ate biscuits, always keeping an eye on their watches. The sun rose behind them and the day grew very hot. At nine o'clock Plassey waved them back into their tanks, took his own position and grinned at John. "Lead on, MacWarrey," he said. "Into battle."

The tanks drove west of south. John levelled his binoculars, as did Plassey, shoulder to shoulder, both men desperate to locate the minarets above the town. But they had not gone more than a few miles when there was a loud crash behind them. Plassey held up his hand and the tanks slewed to a halt, while the fourth in the column circumnavigated the fifth, which had lost its right-hand track.

Plassey jumped down and stamped back, John at his shoulder. "Outcrop of rock," explained the commander. "Didn't see it until we were on the damned thing."

"Can you repair it?" Plassey had his hands on his hips as he gazed at the damage.

"I think so. But it'll take time."

"Then you're on your own," Plassey told him. "Can you make some kind of identification of this spot?" he asked John.

"It'll be pretty rough."

"Do it anyway. We'll send someone back to you after we take Siwa," he told the stricken commander. "But get yourself in proper working order as soon as possible." He strode back to his machine. "And keep a proper lookout," he told his men. "Are there liable to be many of those?" he asked John in an undertone.

"It's always possible."

Plassey muttered under his breath. Does he expect me to be a magician? John wondered. They proceeded more slowly now, while the seconds ticked away, but they had time in hand and it was a quarter to ten when they topped a rise and looked down on Siwa, a peaceful scene with people in the fields watered by the oasis, and . . . a column of trucks on the road to the

Libyan border, perhaps four miles beyond the town, coming towards them.

There was also an Italian flag flying from the town hall. Plassey waved his hand and the tanks withdrew out of sight. Plassey and John got down and lay on the ground to study the situation further through their binoculars. "You will remember the history," John suggested. "Alexander the Great and all that."

"Whether we blow the place apart or not depends on the Eyeties," Plassey said.

"You must expect them to return fire."

"In which case, goodbye history." It occurred to John that his commanding officer was actually looking forward to blowing the ancient town apart. "But we have to get that lot," he said, nodding towards the column, "intact. There are bowsers down there."

John was studying the apparently empty desert to the southeast, and now he could make out a cloud of dust. "Bingo," he said.

Plassey swung his glasses. "Spot on. But he goes first."

They rejoined the tank. "Five minutes," Plassey told his commanders.

They waited, an uncanny feeling, as the heat increased and sweat dribbled down their necks, while a faint wind stirred the sand, from the east, isolating all sound. "The people in the town," John ventured, "are Egyptians. That is, they are on our side."

"They're Egyptians," Plassey riposted. "They're on the side that wins, regardless." A huge noise erupted from beyond the ridge. "Let's go," Plassey shouted, waving his tanks forward.

They zoomed up the the ridge, soared over it and crashed down into another shallow valley beyond, which for the moment cut them off from both sight and sound of the action. Plassey cursed and swore, but then they were climbing up again and roaring down the far side, nothing now between them and the town. Plassey was now using his radio. "Hold your fire," he said.

Blanchard's attack was now in full swing, as his tanks had been much closer when they had opened fire. The Italians were attempting a resistance, but they had no anti-tanks guns as they had not expected such an attack out of the desert, and they were being smothered by the rapid fire from the tanks' two-pounders. Several of the houses were already in flames, although John saw to his relief that the old Mud Town seemed outside the general action. The radio crackled. "Take out that supply column," Blanchard commanded. "We can handle the town. But save as much petrol as you can."

"Roger," Plassey said. "You heard the man. Don't hit the tankers."

The six tanks swung to the right and raced at the road beyond the town. The Italians certainly saw them coming, and while several machine-guns were unloaded and opened a chattering fire, the rest began to attempt to turn the trucks and bowsers, an impossible task on the narrow road. "Down," Plassey commanded, and John dropped into the heated confines of the tank. Here the noise was tremendous as the two-pounder opened up as well as the machine-guns, to which was added the pings and clangs as the Italian bullets struck the tank and ricochetted into the morning.

Plassey had his eyes glued to the rangefinder. "Traverse right, up three, fire," he commanded, and the gun boomed, the recoiling barrel seeming to fill the confined space. "Steady, steady, traverse left three, down one, fire." And again and again. "Got the buggers," he said with satisfaction, and raised the hatch again.

John joined him in the cupola. The battle had been short, swift, and the victory total. Four of the Italian trucks were on fire, as, unfortunately, was one of the bowsers, sending a huge column of black smoke skywards. But the other three tankers were undamaged. In front of them men lay scattered, their blood soaking into the sand. Those who had survived stood with their hands above their heads, the faces registering total consternation.

"Nice going," Blanchard said over the radio. "My congratulations to everybody. I would say we have just won the first victory of the North African campaign."

Chapter Ten

The Conquerors

There were more than a hundred Italians in Siwa, but they seemed positively anxious to surrender. Another fifty or so surrendered with the destroyed supply column. But they had had radios. Blanchard summoned John. "Find out if they got a message off when we attacked," he said.

The senior officer was a major, who smoked a pipe and looked disturbingly urbane. His name was Caglione. "Were you surprised by our attack?" John asked.

"Absolutely," Caglione said. "We were told there would be no attack from the British. Certainly not out of the desert."

"And when you saw us coming, what did you do?"

"I did not see you coming. I heard the sound of shots, but when I went outside your tanks were already in the town."

"Meanwhile, you had summoned help."

Caglione puffed smoke. "There was no time."

"I assume, as an officer and a gentleman, you would not lie to me," John said.

Caglione smiled. "And I assume, as you are an officer and a gentleman, you will not insist that I give away military secrets."

John reported to Blanchard. "I suppose he's right," the English major said. "We must get on to this place Jabberwock as quickly as possible. Layton, have all the tanks refuelled. Plassey, what about this maverick of yours?"

"I promised we'd send back for him, sir."

"Oh, yes? I suppose we'll have to. One tank. And we'll leave

188

two here to guard the prisoners until relieved. We'll assault Jabberwock with the remainder."

"Fourteen tanks, sir?" John asked. "Al-Jaghbub is a fortified frontier post."

"We'll hope that friend of yours didn't manage to warn them we're about," Blanchard said. "Sergeant, make to HQ: ancient ruins intact but inhabited. We need walking back-up. Brew up, gentlemen, then let's be on our way."

John took a cup of tea to Caglione, who looked suspicious, but drank it anyway. "Do you know someone called Umberto?"

Caglione raised his eyebrows. "He is Chief of Police in Tobruk. Have you met him?"

"We're old friends. Now tell me, do you know someone named Renaldo? When last we met he was a lieutenant."

"Renaldo," Caglione said thoughtfully. "You have some odd acquaintances, Lieutenant. Captain Renaldo is in the Security Branch."

"I see. You mean he works for Umberto."

"No, no. He is Military Security. That is quite distinct from the Military Police. Military Security is a law unto itself."

"Ah," John said. "I'm glad of that."

It was mid-afternoon before the squadron was fuelled and ready to move off for the border. In the four hours since they had captured the town they had seen no enemy activity, either on the ground or in the air, so both Blanchard and John felt reasonably sure that Caglione had not had the time to get off a message, and that the chances of achieving surprise were good. On the other hand . . . "How many did you estimate are in the garrison?"

"A couple of hundred, the last time I was there," John said.

"Which is not to say they will not have been reinforced."

"Equally it's possible that the garrison might have been reduced, once they took Siwa. What about guns?"

189

"I didn't see any. They'll have machine-guns. And again, they may have enhanced the defence."

"Or not. Ah, well, someone once said that war is an option of difficulties."

"Napoleon?" John suggested.

"Do you know that?"

"Not for certain. But he seems to have uttered most of the military aphorisms we're familiar with. Incidentally, this place is of great importance to the Senussi. It contains the tomb of the founder of their order, Sidi Muhammad ibn Ali as-Sanussi al-Kabir. We really don't want to knock it about if we want these people to help us in any way."

"Soldiers, even officers," Blanchard said severely, "are not supposed to be intellectuals. Save that till you're a general." He summoned his commanders. "Let's go. We'll follow the road, to the border, then we spread out and charge. Shoot up everything that even looks like an Italian."

It seemed hotter than ever as the tanks raced along the road at a good twenty miles per hour. They were burning petrol as if it were water, but John had promised them there would be fuel in Al-Jaghbub – supposing they didn't destroy it in taking the town. The Italians would of course see the dust plume coming towards them, but if they did not know there was a British squadron in the vicinity they would have to suppose it was the supply column coming back; Blanchard had enjoined strict radio silence until he gave the order to attack.

John was now riding with the major in the command tank. "This is a bloody good road," Blanchard commented.

"It's been improved since last I drove along it," John agreed. "But the Italians always were good road makers."

And indeed, when they were still some ten miles short of the frontier, they came across a working gang, consisting of Senussi labourers under the supervision of half-a-dozen white men. Blanchard waved his hand, and the tanks did not stop or open fire, but rushed past, leaving the Italians enveloped in dust and bewilderment. John wondered if they had a radio.

But half an hour later they were at the frontier.

The customs post was manned by Italians, as expected. The lead tanks shot up the building and sent Italian soldiers scattering in every direction, but there was no time to stop and pick up prisoners. Al-Jaghbub was only a few miles further on and they kept on their way. Within minutes the walls came into view. "Remember the tomb," John begged.

"If it's occupied, we blast it," Blanchard insisted. But the walls came first. "Spread out," Blanchard commanded over his radio. "We want breaches."

The fourteen tanks formed a line, all opening fire together. The surprise was complete and within the town there was tremendous confusion; people could be seen running along the walls and one or two fired rifles with such inaccuracy that Blanchard did not even bother to shut the hatch. He was heading for the gate, where the road entered the town. This was made of wood, as the walls themselves were only made of sun-baked mud, and were not strong enough to withstand the rapid fire of the tanks' two-pounders. They crumbled in every direction, in many cases taking the defenders with them into a heap of rubble.

The tanks roared on, reaching the collapsed walls and lurching over them. John thought that to his dying day he would never forget the scream of terror that rose from one Italian soldier trapped and unable to move as the tank reared above him and then descended with a horrible crunch. Blanchard glanced at his white-faced junior. "That's war," he said. "Could happen to you, some day." John swallowed in a desperate attempt not to be sick.

Then they were rumbling through the narrow streets of the town itself, dislodging signs and even the front of buildings, scattering dogs and camels and goats, and people, men, women and children, who ran screaming in every direction.

Those members of the garrison who had not been on the walls

had withdrawn to the central square but they too were no match for the tanks, armed as they were only with rifles and a few machine-guns. A white flag was already fluttering above the hotel and Blanchard turned his guns on the barracks, sending the more solid stonework flying away in splinters and bringing the garrison running out, hands in the air. "Cease firing," Blanchard said into his radio. "Well, Warrey my lad, two victories before dinner. We're all going to get gongs for this."

They entertained a very shaken Italian colonel to dinner, together with his senior officers. "You have crossed the desert, in tanks?" He scratched his head. "But what will you do now? Go back? I have sent a message to Tobruk. There is a column marching to our relief at this moment."

"Now that is interesting," Blanchard said. "When do you expect it to get here?"

"It will be here tomorrow morning," Colonel Sarchi said. "Then, if you have not returned across the desert, you will have to surrender."

"I'm sure you're right," Blanchard agreed, and went off to call Cairo.

John remained with the Italians. "Do you know anything of a Captain Renaldo?" he asked the colonel. "Military Intelligence?"

"I know Captain Renaldo," Sarchi said, distastefully.

"Can you tell me where he is?"

"I would say he is in Tobruk. Is he a friend of yours?" The colonel's tone indicated that if he was, then *he* wasn't.

"Not a friend," John said. "We have some unfinished business."

"He is not a good man with whom to do business," Sarchi advised.

"I believe you. And what of Colonel Umberto? Is he too in Tobruk?"

"Yes. That is his headquarters." Sarchi grinned. "When you are taken prisoner, tomorrow, you will be taken to

Tobruk. No doubt there you will meet both Umberto and Renaldi."

"No doubt," John agreed.

Blanchard summoned his officers to a late night meeting. "Cairo sends its congratulations," he said. "Not least because we are diverting a sizeable Italian force, including tanks. Our orders are to leave here at dawn and make for the fuel dumps indicated on Warrey's map. There are four." He prodded the stiff paper. "That activity might draw off even more Italian armour, but in any event the offensive will have started by then."

"And the force coming after us?" Plassey asked.

"They'll just have to follow us about, if they don't get recalled." Tobruk, John thought regretfully, would have to wait.

Somewhat to his surprise, he slept heavily. But then, it had been an exhausting few days. He was awakened before dawn, by the sound of aircraft and the crump-crump of exploding bombs. The entire village turned out, but none of the bombs were actually dropped on Al-Jaghbub; the bombers were softening up Italian positions further north. "We're away," Plassey shouted.

Again, two tanks were left to oversee the prisoners, absurd odds to John's way of thinking, but the Italians had been disarmed and were showing no great ambition to escape, and the remaining twelve vehicles roared off into the desert, following the tracks to the west, as marked on John's map. They found the first dump easily enough, shot up the defenders, fuelled up, and then blasted it at close range, sending black smoke billowing into the air as the tanks exploded, before swinging up to the north to deal with the next. "Easy as shooting fish in a barrel," Blanchard commented. "The poor devils don't know what's hitting them."

Certainly the raiding party were not molested; the column sent south to destroy them, if it had ever existed, was hastily recalled to the defense of Sidi Barrani, to no avail, as the advanced position fell two days later, the general in command being killed and

193

his second-in-command, together with more than a thousand men, taken prisoner. The following week the British were at the border, storming Sollum and Fort Capuzzo, and capturing twenty thousand Italians in the process. Bardia followed on 5 January with another huge batch of prisoners, forty-five thousand. The Italians were collapsing all along the line.

During this period the desert force had remained centred on Al-Jaghbub, seeking and destroying any dumps that could be found, and making thrusts to the north to disrupt enemy movements. They had celebrated both Christmas and the New Year with the sniff of an amazing victory in their nostrils. Morale had never been higher. The offensive that had begun simply to get the Italians out of Egypt was turning out far more successful than anyone could have hoped. And now at last, on 21 January, the orders came for them to leave Al-Jaghbub and drive north, for Tobruk!

The Australians actually got there first, storming into the seaport and, unable to find a Union Jack to illustrate their triumph, instead hoisted one of their bush hats in the main square. Blanchard's tanks, racing up the road from the south, were held up by the thousands of Italian prisoners, shambling along with their arms in the air, seeking British or allied troops to whom they could surrender. Blanchard cleared them off the road and told them to keep going east, while he led his tanks into the town. John supposed that seldom before in all its glorious history had the British Army gained such a complete victory. Not only had they advanced a hundred and fifty miles in six weeks against an enemy five times their own strength – the British had attacked with only two divisions, and the Italians had had ten – but they had utterly destroyed the enemy army, with upwards of a hundred thousand prisoners for the loss of five hundred of their own. It was time for congratulations all round, and John had the great pleasure of being introduced to General O'Connor, a fiery little Irishman, commander-in-chief and creator of the plan that had brought such startling success. "My best congratulations," he told Blanchard and his officers. "You did a great job."

"What do we do now, sir?"

O'Connor grinned. "We keep hitting him while it's hurting. Have your machines checked out and get ready to move." He beckoned John to one side. "There's an MC waiting for you in Cairo, when this little show is over."

"Me, sir? What about the others?"

"This is for your earlier trip. I'm also going to recommend you for promotion and a permanent position with the Army as an intelligence officer. No more typewriters, eh?"

"Thank you, sir." But his head was spinning. Did that mean no more Cairo, no more Arsinoe, no more Shepheard's . . . and no more Margo? On the other hand, Captain Warrey! He would be able to get married. What a different world did England seem, compared with the desert, and people like Margo and Soroya.

Which reminded him that he had a great deal of unfinished business to attend to before the Army moved out again.

He went first of all to police headquarters, which, like most of the city, had been badly damaged by the RAF, and was now guarded by British MPs. "Where are all the policemen?" he asked the sergeant.

"Well, quite a few got strafed, sir; the wounded are in hospital. Most of the survivors are on the street. We've disarmed them, of course, but we need them to keep order."

"What about their colonel?"

"I don't know about him, sir."

Neither did anyone else. There was a chance Umberto had been killed, but no one could remember burying a senior officer. As for Renaldo, Italian Military Intelligence had pulled out of Tobruk some days before – it was most probable that Umberto would have gone with them. John went to see Roberto, whose office was bedecked with British flags.

"I would have supplied the Australians, if they had asked,"

he complained. "But you . . ." he embraced John. "To see you, fit and well and wearing uniform . . . The rumour has been that you were killed, or died in the desert."

"And who spread that rumour, do you suppose?"

"I have no idea. Now, Giovanni, as you are here, and victorious, I am hoping you will do me a favour. There is all manner of talk about requisitions and sequestrations, and that sort of thing. I wish you to make it plain to your commanding general that I am not to be interfered with, eh?"

John nodded. "Come along with me and we'll go see him now."

Quesmi shook his head. "I cannot do that, my friend. I cannot risk anyone knowing that I am actually working for the British."

"I do assure you that we are in total command of the town, Roberto, and that you are in no danger."

Roberto grinned. "But who can say for certain that you will always be here, Giovanni?"

In fact, before John could arrange a meeting between Roberto and O'Connor, he was on the move again. O'Connor meant what he said about hitting the enemy while he was hurting, and the British and Australian forces charged along the road out of Tobruk, the Italians always falling back before them, when they were not surrendering in droves. A week after the fall of Tobruk, Derna, some two hundred miles along the coast, fell. John, now a captain in Intelligence, travelled by truck behind the assault force, having to say goodbye to his comrades in the tanks; Blanchard's squadron had in any event been returned to its more normal position in the Seventh Armoured Division, nicknamed the Desert Rats. He had a staff of his own, now, an MP sergeant, by the name of Cooper, and a private, Wilmot, to act as orderly, together with a driver, Nye.

They travelled as fast as they could, trying to keep up with the armour, but of course were soon a day behind, and by the time they reached Derna all resistance had ceased. It had been an exhausting business. As everyone else was travelling as fast as they could, each unit was virtually self-contained, existing off what they could themselves carry. At least John and his squad had a truck, which could be loaded, but all they had was bully beef, marmalade, biscuits and tea. Water was again rationed to a gallon a day for drinking, shaving and washing. John felt it was necessary, to maintain their status as victorious troops, that he and his men shave every day; washing was left to individual inclinations. But washing was necessary, for the sand got everywhere, especially for the Intelligence Unit, travelling as they were in the wake of the armour and thus in a perpetual sandstorm.

Unfortunately, the sand also got into the engine and break-downs were frequent; John rapidly discovered why, when he was picking his team, it had been stressed that at least one of them should be a qualified mechanic.

Once Derna was reached and it was possible to have a bath and some decent, or at least different food – spaghetti – John went through his usual routine. It was his job to interrogate every prisoner he could and discover what the Italians were next up to. He gathered that they were relying on the immensely strong fortress of Benghazi, another two hundred miles away and at the north-eastern corner of the Gulf of Sirte, where they hoped to make a stand. But again he had missed both Umberto and Renaldo, always supposing they were still alive.

Generals O'Connor and Neame studied the map when he reported. Immediately to the south of Derna rose the Jebel Akhtar Mountains, not all that high, but sufficiently an obstacle to confine the British and Australians to advancing along the road, and the road would eventually be dominated by the fortifications at Benghazi. "Looks like being some show," commented one of the staff officers. "Do we have the strength, sir?"

"Or the back-up," remarked another. The advance had been

so tumultuous they were in danger of outrunning both reinforcements and fuel and ammunition supplies; not that there were a
great many reinforcements available, but they knew additional
units were on their way from England.

O'Connor had continued to study the map while his officers
discussed the situation. Now he prodded. "This track leading
south of the Jebel, is it any good?" He looked at John.

"I can find out, sir."

"Do that."

John duly interrogated one of the Italian officers and was able
to report that the surface was above average. "Right," O'Connor
said. "Now, gentlemen, it is essential that we keep the enemy on
the run. He is retreating to Benghazi, where he will hope to stop
us, because he knows as well as we do that we are outrunning our
supplies. He is also confident of his position, not only because of
the fortifications of Benghazi itself, but because the Jebel Akhtar
protects his right flank, and he has the sea on his left, so that he
can prepare to meet us on a narrow front. Well, gentlemen, we
are going to turn that position. I propose, that while the infantry
proceed along the road to launch a frontal attack upon Benghazi,
the armour will take the desert road south, below the Jebel, and
then swing west and cut the coast road below Benghazi. This
will not only enable us to attack him from two sides at once, it
will prevent him receiving any support, either in men or fuel and
ammo, from El Agheila in the gulf. If he does manage to stand
a siege, he will have to depend on what can be brought in from
the sea, and I am sure our navy and air force will interdict that.
Questions?"

"Fuel, sir," someone said. "It is damn near two hundred
miles, as the crow flies, from here to, say, Agedabia. We
can't send bowsers across the desert." He glanced at John.
"It's been tried."

"Agreed," O'Connor said. "The tanks will have to exist on
their own. They can carry sufficient fuel for about two hundred
and fifty miles; that is, just sufficient to make the crossing and

fight a battle at the end of it." He grinned at his officers. "It is a battle they will have to win, because there will be no question of their coming back."

He summoned John after the meeting was over. "I'm sending you with the armour, Warrey. Not just as an Intelligence Officer. You know the desert."

"Thank you, sir. Permission to ride with Major Blanchard."

The tanks were filled to the brim, and in addition were loaded with every can of petrol for which space could be found. Every man carried four days' iron rations in his haversack, and two water bottles; there would be no washing or shaving until the battle was over. Both guns and engines were cleaned and greased to the maximum. Then they moved out, driving south and then west at a steady fifteen miles an hour, stopping only to top up their tanks; obviously they could not go into battle with petrol cans strapped to their vehicles, so the excess had to be used up before they encountered the Italians.

They drove into a yellow and brown wilderness, upon which the sun glared down from a flawless blue sky. Presumably they could be seen for miles from the huge plume of sand that rose behind them, but they were relying on the probability that there was no one for miles to see them – save perhaps the odd Senussi. They stopped at dusk to eat and top up their tanks again, then drove on into the night, following the glow of the light on the rear of each squadron commander's tank; the commanders themselves were relying upon their compasses.

After the heat of the day, the chill of the night was a great relief, even if it was cold enough for the odd shiver. At two they stopped again to refill, eat, stretch their legs and have an hour's sleep. "We're on schedule," said the Brigadier.

They rolled up gentle slopes and down others. As the sun rose they saw the bulk of the Jebel Akhtar rising some thirty miles to their north, but they could also see the hills tailing off to the west;

they had passed round the mountains. And a few minutes later, topping another rise, they looked down on a sizeable village, from the guarding fortress of which there floated the red, white and green Italian tricolour. "That will be Beda Fomm," the Brigadier said over his radio.

In accordance with previously issued orders, the brigade now split into squadrons; it was not their duty to attempt to take Beda Fomm, only to seek and destroy any Italian armour that might be in the vicinity, and then cut the coast road. Blanchard's squadron turned more to the north and passed east of the town, which was waking up to the realisation that a large armoured force had suddenly appeared out of the desert; they could hear Italian being chattered over their radios, and the garrison artillery opened fire, but at too great a range to have any effect. Holding their course at just west of north, the squadron lost sight of the rest of the brigade, which was passing south and west of the town, but contact was maintained by relay tanks, detached for that purpose.

"Enemy tanks reported approaching from Benghazi," came the voice along the relay. "Charlie Squadron will maintain course and speed."

"You heard the man," Blanchard told his men.

They were still motoring over the desert at something under ten miles an hour, conserving fuel and maintaining their position as long as possible. The town of Beda Fomm was now out of sight behind them, but they heard the sound of gunfire from the west, and excited chatter over the radio. "There's one hell of a lot of the bastards," someone said. "And this time they seem to want to fight."

"With us where we are, this time they don't have anywhere to to run to," Blanchard remarked.

Still the squadron held its course and speed, until the order came from Brigade. "Charlie Squadron will swing due west and engage the enemy in its front."

"Hooray!" Blanchard shouted. The twenty tanks of the

squadron moved up the next slope and looked down on the coast road and the sea for the first time since leaving Derna. To their left a mass of British and Italian tanks were engaged in a fierce mêlée. To their right were masses of men and trucks on the road, but a good distance away. Directly in front of them was a squadron of Italian tanks, hurrying towards the battle. "Our object is to destroy those fellows," Blanchard said into his radio.

The tanks rumbled down the hill. For the moment the Italians seemed unaware that they were being approached from their flank. Then excited orders flew across the air and the tanks turned to meet this new threat. "Fire as you bear," Blanchard commanded.

The two-pounders barked, the tanks bucked and roared, and their interiors became hotter than ever, filled with nostril-blocking odours from cordite to humanity. Blanchard had closed the hatch and was staring into the rangefinder. "Line her up. Traverse right. Range three five oh yards. Fire!"

John couldn't see what was happening but Blanchard gave a shout of delight. "Brewed the bastard! Round, Sergeant. Round, for God's sake."

The driver swung the wheel and the tank slewed round, almost its own length, throwing the crew to and fro. "Near one," Blanchard said. "Load, God damn it. Fire! Got the blighter! Good shooting, Corporal. There's another . . . shit, that's one of ours."

John peered through the slit, saw the tank in flames, watched in horror as a body emerged from the cupola, its clothes on fire, and half rolled, half fell to the sand, where it kept on rolling, still burning. "Poor beggar," Blanchard commented. "Hard a-starboard. Here's another."

General O'Connor surveyed the officers gathered in what had been the Italian Officers' Club in Benghazi. "I am sure you would all like to know the final tally," he said. "Well, gentlemen, to speak in round figures, we have taken one hundred and thirty-three thousand Italian prisoners, four hundred tanks, and eight hundred and fifty guns. I think we may claim that the Italian Army has effectively been destroyed as a fighting force. This has been achieved at a loss to ourselves of five hundred and fifty men dead and missing, just over twice that number wounded, and ten tanks."

He paused to allow his words to sink in, and someone shouted, "Three cheers for General O'Connor."

They roared their approval and the general smiled; he knew that it had been his leadership, and especially his decision to send his armour across the desert to enclose the enemy in the jaws of a pincer, that had truly gained the enormous victory. "Thank you, gentlemen. I would only like to say that I am proud to have led you. And that we shall resume our advance immediately. Once we have captured El Agheila, all Cyrenaica is ours."

Once more, the mad rush forward, after another futile search. Renaldo had been in Benghazi, John learned from one of the prisoners, but had left before the road had been cut. Of Umberto no one had any news. John began to wonder if he had not, after all, been killed when Tobruk fell. Or perhaps had removed his insignia and merged into the general mob of surrendering soldiers, in which case he could be on his way to some Indian Ocean island as a prisoner for the rest of the war.

But it was Renaldo he really wanted.

El Agheila fell on 9 February. By now it had all become common-place, the burning enemy tanks, the terrified local population and the hordes of prisoners marching across the desert, arms held high, often in the care of a single British soldier. And once again, the abandoned military and police headquarters.

But at last, a glimmer of hope. "Colonel Umberto?" asked one of the officer prisoners to be interrogated. "He was here yesterday. I am certain of it."

"You saw him?" John asked.

"I spoke with him."

"And presumably he was making a run for it?"

"I do not believe so," the officer said. "We had no orders to evacuate the town. We were told to fight to the last man."

"And Captain Renaldo?"

"He was here too."

"Yesterday?"

"No, a couple of days ago. He could be in Tripoli by now."

John drove up to the front, just outside El Agheila, where British patrols were encamped. "Where are the enemy?" he asked the captain in command.

The officer waved his arm. "Somewhere over there."

"You're a bit thin on the ground, aren't you?"

"All that's necessary, old man. They really are shattered. As soon as we catch ourselves up, logistically, I imagine the old man will move on Tripoli. We want the Eyeties out of this entire country."

"Seems like a good idea," John said, using his binoculars to sweep the horizon, and frowning. "They're not all that far away."

"Eh?"

"There's a command car on that hill over there. Looking at us."

"Bloody cheek." The officer levelled his own binoculars. "Hm. But as I say, they're in no condition to mount a counter-attack."

"I hope you're right." John continued to study the command car. "Have you ever seen those uniforms before?"

The captain looked again. "Not Italian, are they?"

"No, by God," John snapped. "Those are Germans!"

Chapter Eleven

The Prisoners

"You're absolutely sure about this?" asked General Neame.

John stood to attention. "Yes, sir."

"And they were observing our position," Neame commented. "You saw no support forces?"

"No, sir."

Neame glanced at his superior.

"I suppose it had to happen," O'Connor said. "Even supposing Mussolini hasn't shouted for help, Hitler must be getting a little worried about the quality of his allies. They're being beaten out of sight in Albania, now they've been beaten out of sight here. Graziani has resigned. What we need to know is if the Germans are planning any aid other than observation. I would say the answer is probably yes. The question is, what? We're not going to be ready to advance again for a month or two. If there are going to be German units in front of us when we do resume our advance, we simply have to know." He looked at John. "We have already sent aircraft over on reconnaissance," O'Connor said. "But they have uncovered nothing, and several have been shot down. The Germans are too good at concealing their movements from the air. We do know that an enormous amount of equipment, and presumably men, has been put ashore in Tripoli. The question is, are those men Germans, and does the equipment include any Panzer elements? Are you with me?"

"Yes, sir."

"I hate to ask this of any man, Warrey," the general said. "But whatever you do, must be a military reconnaissance. I'm

204

not having you shot for spying. Let me put it to you straight. I want you to get as close to Tripoli as you can and discover if any German units have been put ashore, and if there are Gernman units, what they consist of. I do not believe that you can do this and get out again. If you can, you'll get the DSO. If you can't, well, maybe you'll still get the DSO. But you must get the information back. Harmon!"

"Sir!" The sergeant hurried into the room.

"I want you to equip Captain Warrey with one of your new machines."

"Sir!" Harmon bustled off and returned a moment later with a hand-held radio.

"Believe it or not," O'Connor said. "This has a range of two hundred miles. For a brief period, and providing the batteries are fully charged, which they are at the moment. It can of course be used for talking, but that is not its primary purpose. Harmon."

"Sir!" Harmon showed John the machine. "It's essentially a distress signal. But it can be concentrated to a very high frequency by using this button here. Once you have done that, sir, it will emit such a signal for a brief period. It has a sequence. One touch, and it will emit a single bleep. Two touches, two bleeps, three touches, three bleeps. Four touches, four bleeps. That is its limit."

John took the machine, gingerly.

"My people will be listening out constantly on this wavelength," O'Connor said. "Twenty-four hours a day. If you can talk to us, fine. If you are in a position where you cannot talk to us, you must signal us, as follows. One bleep, no significant German forces discovered. Two bleeps, German infantry have been landed. The number is irrelevant; we can contain any German infantry. Three bleeps. German armour has been landed, one division. This will probably have to be estimated. Four bleeps. Two armoured divisions have been landed. Here again this will have to be estimated, but better be safe than sorry, eh? I may say that it is highly unlikely the Germans will have sent two of their panzers, but you never can tell. Have you got that?"

"Yes, sir. One bleep, no Germans. Two, infantry only. Three, armour. Four, sufficient armour to indicate two divisions."

"Even if they take you as you send that message, they won't know what you have sent. Unless you tell them, of course."

"Yes, sir."

"Very good. Then I won't ask you how you are going to approach them. I know you are good at using the desert."

"Yes, sir. When do I leave?"

"Tomorrow morning. At least to return to El Agheila. You may prefer to begin your reconnaissance at night. That decision is yours. You will have orders for the commanding officer on the ground that you are to be given whatever you wish and whoever you wish."

"Thank you, sir."

"So, have a good night. By the way, there's someone here who you might like to see before you go. The Majestic Hotel, on the front."

John knew who it had to be before he even reached the door. The virtual wreck he had last seen had quite disappeared over the following weeks and Margo looked as trim and attractive as ever in the earlier days of their acquaintance. She was also wearing uniform, khaki tunic and skirt, Sam Browne belt, khaki stockings and flat-heeled brown shoes. Her hair was gathered in a tight bun.

"Well, hello," he said.

She kissed him on the cheek. "Now wait a moment. I'll put on my cap and you can salute me."

"Is that a fact."

She closed the door. "I simply had to come up and see all the success you chaps have had."

"Then you're not on duty."

"Well, yes and no. I am always on duty."

"But you'll have dinner? The boss virtually commanded it."

"I know. I'd love to have dinner. But up here, not in the dining room."

He raised his eyebrows. "Don't tell me you're coming over all feminine at last."

"You never know your luck. Shall we order?" She telephoned room service, and while they waited she produced a bottle of whiskey.

"So, how was it?"

"Exhilarating."

"And not a scratch?"

"I was born lucky."

Suddenly she was serious. "Are you going to be lucky the next time?"

He gazed at her. "What next time?"

"Who are you taking with you?"

"For Jesus' sake. That's top secret."

"So am I. I've been given permission to volunteer."

"It happens to be my show."

"I accept that. I'll come down a rank. Or more, if you want it."

"Why?"

"It's a very important job that needs doing."

"Why you?"

"You and I have worked together, well, in the desert. And maybe . . . well, I have a lot of memories too."

"Which are likely to get very real. Both Umberto and Renaldo are still out there, you know."

"I do know. I owe that bastard more than you do," she said.

"He killed Soroya."

"That too."

Their dinner arrived, and they waited for the waiter to leave. "I didn't think you cared for her that much." John poured wine.

"But you did."

"Yes. She was . . . difficult to sum up briefly. A kind of earth goddess."

"I sort of guessed that."

"But this mission I'm on isn't about revenge, Margo. It's gathering information. In addition, O'Connor doesn't reckon I'll get back. He figures I'll spend the rest of the War as a prisoner in Italy. That doesn't mean I won't have a run-in with Renaldo first, and that could be nasty. It could be even nastier for you."

"I'll be in uniform."

"You can still be searched."

"So what's new? I am volunteering, Captain Warrey." She chewed her roast chicken, slowly and thoughtfully. "I'd make it worth your while." Her cheeks were pink.

"This isn't Shepheard's," he reminded her.

"I owe you that, too."

John finished his meal. "I've an early start in the morning. It really has been great seeing you again."

She stared at him, disbelieving. "You mean you're not staying?"

"I said, I need an early night."

"And you won't take me?"

"Of course I won't take you, Margo. I'd need my head examined. This is one trip where I intend to worry about just me." He got up. "If you put your cap on, I'll salute you."

"You bastard," she said. "Oh, get out."

He put on his own cap, went to the door.

"Is it Soroya?" she asked. "You really loved that girl."

He considered. "You know, I think you're right."

Odd, he thought, as he lay on his bed at the barracks. He had never really thought about it before. Perhaps he had been afraid to. But Soroya haunted his dreams. Her death even haunted his waking hours. And Margo? Had he been a cad? Was it caddish to turn down a woman who had long since passed her sell-by date, as regards him? And where did that leave Aileen?

He was up at dawn, taking the road from Benghazi round the

east side of the Gulf of Sirte, the desert always on his left hand, the scene of the recent great victory gained by the Eighth Army, and the sea always on his right. He passed a considerable amount of troop movement, but none of it very urgent; the victory had been so complete it was difficult for anyone to envisage an Italian counter-attack. There was even a considerable volume of civilian traffic, as the locals endeavoured to get back to normal.

Outside El Agheila, the troops, British, Australian and Indian, continued to peer to the west. Back on duty were his old friends of the Seventh Armoured Brigade. "Some movement there, all right," Captain Plassey remarked. "I wish we had the petrol and the ammo; we could get to Tripoli, I'd bet."

John reported to Blanchard, handed over his orders. The major read them in silence with a slowly gathering frown. "Sounds pretty dicey to me," he commented when he had finished. "There's no way you can go along the coast road. Our last reconnaissance showed the Italians holding Sirte in force."

"I know that, sir. But . . ." John spread the map on the table. "There are all these tracks down here in the desert. I can get south to Hofra, and then across to Waddan, and then swing up north to Abu Nujaym and approach the coast from there. If there are any German units in Tripolitania, I should be able to spot them from there."

"And what do you suppose the enemy will be doing while you tour around their backside?"

"Well, sir, it's up to me to travel very fast. They won't expect it. I know it's a long shot, but I have the means of communicating with the general's headquarters, even if I'm about to be captured."

Blanchard scratched his head. "You'd do better with a squadron of tanks."

"A squadron of tanks would bring down everything they have. One fast-moving vehicle, manned by a couple of determined men, has a good chance of getting in far enough to find out what's going on."

"So who are you taking with you?"

"I'd like to ask for a volunteer, sir. He must be a top-class driver."

"Sir!" Layton stood to attention.

"You? You're my assistant."

"There's no better driver than me, sir."

This time Blanchard pulled his ear.

"At night?" John asked. "Without lights?"

"Day or night," Layton declared. "You know that's true, sir."

"One other."

"Sergeant Pope, sir."

"He has to volunteer," Blanchard pointed out.

Layton grinned. "He will, sir."

Pope did, and they were given the most serviceable of the command cars. "We can mount a machine-gun," Layton suggested.

"We have to think in terms of speed and evasion," John told them. "Now, here is the plan. And here is the secret."

He showed them the transmitter and how it worked. And told them the code. "If anything happens to me, one of you must use this. Equally, if we are taken, no one must know the code."

"Yes, sir," they answered in unison.

Then it was a matter of waiting for nightfall. It was still fairly early in the morning so the three men had a good rest period ahead of them. Perhaps the last rest period we will ever have, John thought. It was hard to accept there was a war on. The tanks were encamped some ten miles outside El Agheila, just off the road to Benghazi, but close enough to the sea to enjoy it. Utter peace, John thought. Utter . . . war!

A bugle was blowing and men were scurrying to their tanks. "What the hell is going on?" he demanded.

Layton had been at the command tent. Now he hurried up. "Chalmers has been attacked."

Major Chalmers commanded a flank guard, a further ten miles into the desert. "Eyeties?"

210

"Armour," Layton said. "German armour. I'm sorry, Warrey, but I have to join my unit."

"Of course." John watched him go, and turned to Sergeant Pope.

"I reckon I'm needed as well, sir." Pope hesitated. "I reckon our reconnaissance may not be necessary."

John watched him go, looked at the transmitter. Then he went to the command tent, where the Brigadier was surrounded by his anxious staff. "El Agheila is under heavy attack," someone told him.

"Are we in touch with Benghazi?"

"Contact is being made now."

They both turned to the Brigadier, who was reading the message from headquarters.

"El Agheila has been ordered to evacuate and fall back."

"Enemy tanks reported north-east, sir," the telegrapher said.

"Damnation!" the Brigadier snapped. "They've done exactly what we did, and sent armour across the desert. Well, that's it. We have to counter-attack, right away. Signal all formations."

"What about the people from El Agheila?" someone asked.

"They'll have to fight their way out. We cannot risk being encircled here. Take your people out." He looked at John. "You had a special mission, I believe."

"Yes, sir."

"Well, it seems pointless now. Get out of here while you can."

"Do we know how much armour the Germans have, sir?"

"Too bloody much."

"With respect, sir. I'll just go and have a look first," John said. "That was what I was told to do."

All around him the tanks were starting up and taking up their formations. Blanchard leaned out of his cupola as he rolled by. "What the hell are you doing? There are Germans just over that ridge."

211

"How many?"

Blanchard brought his tank to a halt. "A couple of dozen. But there's a lot of dust behind."

"And more over there." John pointed.

"So we've heard. We'll blast the buggers."

"Is there room for me?"

"You bet. Come aboard."

John abandoned the command car and climbed into the tank, while trying to calculate. Obviously there was at least one Panzer division out there. But from what Blanchard had said, there could be more. He thumbed the switch on the transmitter, and pressed the button four times; with the racket going on around them it would have been impossible to speak in any case. Anyway, the matter was going to be settled here and now, he thought, as the entire brigade was formed up and swinging to face the enemy, behind a screen of scouts. They advanced into the seemingly empty desert for several miles, before there came an urgent message from the recce commander. "Enemy armour beyond the next hill. Supported by artillery. One of our tanks has brewed."

"Artillery?" the Brigadier queried. "Out there in the desert?" That didn't make sense, and the brigade prepared to attack. They topped the next rise, the three regiments alongside each other in column of squadrons, and paused to take stock of the situation. In front of them, some five miles away across a shallow valley, there was at least a brigade of tanks; even at this distance they could be seen to be larger than the Italian machines the British had hitherto encountered. But they were presently motionless, behind a screen of rather small and obviously light guns, supported by infantry; the infantry were definitely German. "Those are anti-aircraft guns," the Brigadier commented over the radio to reassure his troops. "Not artillery."

No one commented; they could all see the British scout, which was still burning in the valley, surrounded by the sprawled dead bodies of its crew. "Brigade will attack."

"Follow me," Blanchard told his men, and the squadron rolled down the hillside. They reached the floor of the valley without mishap, within about three miles of the enemy, John estimated, and then the anti-aircraft guns, their muzzles brought down to aim horizontally, opened fire. John could see the flashes, but had no idea where the shells were going until there was a sharp expletive over the radio. "Brewed," Layton said.

"There's another one, sir," said the corporal driver.

John twisted his head left and right. It was difficult to see clearly, as the squadron was now enveloped in flying sand and the British tanks were returning fire. But what he could see was devastating. At least five of the attacking tanks were on fire, hit by the small but armour-piercing shells of the anti-aircraft guns, firing with deadly accuracy. In ten minutes they had lost half as many machines as in the entire earlier campaign, and they had not yet closed the enemy.

"Fall back," the Brigadier commanded.

"Fall back?" Blanchard looked at John in dismay.

Obviously they were risking unacceptable casualties – from anti-aircraft guns? The tanks turned and fled for the shelter of the hills, followed now by the German armour. The shooting was fierce, and several more British tanks were knocked out, for the loss of only one of the Germans. "We'll give the bastards a taste of their own medicine," the Brigadier said. "Prepare to receive enemy tanks," he told the support group.

"What might be called a tactical withdrawal," Blanchard commented.

The brigade raced over the undulating desert and came in sight of their assembly point, and reassuringly, a row of anti-tank guns waiting for the enemy to appear in pursuit. "Spread out, make your way behind the artillery, and regroup for counter-attack," the Brigadier said.

"Squadron will steer two-four-five," Blanchard said. All the squadrons opened up as they altered course, allowing the anti-tank guns a clear field of fire. "There they go," Blanchard shouted happily as the British guns exploded.

John stood beside him in the cupola. The Germans were coming over the rise in line abreast and the British shells were bursting amongst them. But none of them seemed to be knocked out, and they didn't stop their advance as they belched flame and smoke. John watched in dismay as two of the support lorries exploded, while one of the guns had also been hit. "Holy hell!" Blanchard commented. "Our guns can't stop them!"

"Pull out," the Brigadier commanded. "Fall back on Benghazi."

The tanks streamed for the coast road. No one spoke. Quite apart from the sudden overwhelming defeat, the morale-sapping understanding that they were out-gunned, was the suspicion that they were heading into a trap, if the Germans could cut the coast road at Derna, as the British had at Beda Fomm. "We will refuel in Benghazi," the Brigadier said, "then, unless the boss has decided to stand siege, we will have to shoot our way out to the west, along the coast road."

"You're welcome to come along with us," Blanchard told John. "In fact, I think you'd better."

"There's something I need to do in Benghazi," John said. "I'll find my own transport." He couldn't just abandon Margo, whatever their current non-relationship. His hope was that she had already got out.

But it didn't seem likely. Benghazi was in turmoil, roads jammed with vehicles, harrassed MPs shouting traffic orders and blowing whistles to no great purpose, people crowding the streets, obviously preparing to change sides yet again, tanks advancing menacingly to clear a way through the crowds, command cars blowing their horns . . .

"I'll get down here," John said.

"Be as quick as you can," Blanchard told him. "We're going to the fuel depot. We can't wait for you, but if we're still there when you get back to us, you're welcome to a ride."

John grinned. "I may be two."

Blanchard waggled his eyebrows. "I'm sure we can squeeze her in."

Once he left the security of the tank John was in a maelstrom of people and traffic through which he had to fight his way to reach the hotel. He did not presume it was necessary first to go to headquarters, as his information, such as it had been, and his projected reconnaissance, had been entirely overtaken by events.

The exterior of the hotel was crowded with waiters and sightseers, and again John had to push his way through them to reach reception. The counter was unattended, so he ran up the stairs and along the corridor to Margo's room. The door was unlocked, and he threw it open. There was evidence of a hasty departure, the bed still unmade, her breakfast still uncleared, but she had definitely left. Thus his responsibility was over.

He ran back down the stairs, and thrust his way back into the crowd, making for the fuel depot. But by the time he got there, the tanks had left.

There were a handful of MPs remaining, and he went over to them. "We're pulling out, sir," said the sergeant in command. "You coming with us?"

"You bet," John said, and scrambled into the cab of the truck, room being made for him.

"Quite a turn-up, ain't it, sir?" the sergeant asked. "Just when we thought we had it in the bag."

The driver was leaning out of the window and shouting at people who kept getting in front of him. They didn't pay much attention. It took them half an hour to reach the gates, and then there were the suburbs to be negotiated.

By now the RAF had been called into action, and planes were wheeling overhead. But they were of course trying to attack the Germans. The road outside the city was nearly as crowded as within the walls, and it was impossible to see what was happening

215

even a few hundred miles further down the coast. "Shit, shit, shit," growled the driver.

People kept trying to clamber aboard, and the MPs had to throw them off. Then there was an explosion and a tinkle of flying glass. John had no idea what had happened for a moment, until the truck slewed sideways, scattering people, and then plunged into the shallow ditch beside the road, turning over on to its side with another clatter of shattering glass. He clutched at the door as he was about to fall onto the sergeant, and gradually pulled himself up to the open window. Then he dragged himself out, stared at the faces that were staring at him. "You all right, Sergeant?" he asked into the cab, where the sergeant was also struggling up.

"Some bugger shot my driver," the sergeant complained. The remaining MPs had been tumbled out of the back. Now they assembled, uniforms dirty, several red caps missing, but looking sufficiently determined; they were all armed with revolvers. "What do you reckon, sir?" the sergeant asked.

"I'm afraid it looks as if we'll have to walk out," John said.

"I'd like to catch the bugger who fired that shot."

"I think we'll have to leave him," John said. Leave so much, he thought. There could be no doubt that the Eighth Army had suffered a crushing defeat. They had been taken entirely by surprise. Now it was all a matter of pulling out and regrouping, and hopefully counter-attacking. But how far away would the regrouping be?

They walked along the road, the crowds thinning now. The sun was directly overhead; it was very hot and they had very little water. They looked longingly at the gentle surf breaking on the sand to their left, but knew they hadn't the time to stop for a bathe. Now there were very few people to be seen. Those that had transport had fled, those that didn't had gone back to Benghazi to await the return of the Italian administration, who presumably were following the Germans.

"How far is it to Derna, sir?" the sergeant asked.

Stop Rommel!

"Something over a hundred and fifty miles," John told him.
"Jesus! Do you reckon we can make it?"
"Not without food and water." John looked up at the slopes of the jebel, rising on their right. "Think there might be some farms up there?"
"Would they sell us anything? Anyway, we're not that well off for cash."
"If we are going to survive, Sergeant," John said, "we are going to have to take what we need."
The sergeant gazed at him for several seconds, then grinned. "And us policemen. But you're right, sir. We'll follow you."
They left the road and climbed into the hills, suffering severely now from both hunger and thirst, as well as heat, so much so that when they found some shade from a grove of stunted trees, John made them rest for an hour while the sun began to droop to the west. "Listen, sir," said one of the policemen.
"That's a goat," said another.
"Easy, now," John said. "We don't want to frighten him off."
They crawled through the scrub and reached a low ridge, beyond which there was a valley – and a house. Or at least, John reckoned, a large hut. Around the hut there was a flock of goats, and tethered close to the building were two camels. "Now there's a sight for sore eyes," the sergeant said.
"Three, three and three," John said. "You to the left, you to the right. We'll approach the front. Supporting fire if necessary."
"Yes, *sir!*" the policemen said enthusiastically.
The two flanking groups moved off. John allowed them ten minutes each, then he and the sergeant and the remaining two MPs crawled forward. The goats commenced bleating even more loudly as they scented the intruders, and a dog began to bark. A man appeared in the doorway of the hut and John stood up, revolver levelled. "Out!" he bellowed.
The man gaped at him, then stepped back. John fired and the shot ploughed into the upright beside the door. The flankers

217

had arrived behind the hut, and now moved forward. The man reappeared, hands raised. "Any of your people speak Arabic, Sergeant?" John asked, advancing behind his levelled revolver.

"No, sir. But this character may speak Italian."

"Come out," John commanded, in that language. Which the man obviously understood, for he emerged completely. "Any others?" John asked.

"We are good people, effendi," the man protested. "We no make war."

"Then we won't make war on you," John promised. "At least, not more than we have to." He gestured the man to one side and stepped into the doorway. The dog growled, but did not attack him. He blinked into the gloom and saw two women, one old and one young, and three small children, huddled against the far wall. "Good evening," he said, and stepped back outside. "We need food and water," he told the man.

"Yes, yes, effendi. There is a well." He pointed, but the MPs had already spotted it.

"Think it's safe to drink, sir?" the sergeant asked.

"This chap drinks it. And what alternative do we have? Bring some up." The MPs were hauling on the bucket.

"And food?"

"Oh, yes, effendi. Food."

He bawled into the hut and his wife appeared – John reckoned the other woman was his mother. A pot of goat stew was provided, along with couscous. It had been around a while but was still very tasty to the hungry policemen. "Now what, sir?" asked the sergeant.

"It will take us at least a week to walk a hundred and fifty miles," John said. "What we have to find is some kind of vehicle. Something that can cope with the desert; the Germans will have cut the road by now, I should think."

"Do you know the desert, sir?"

"Yes," John said. "I know the desert."

"Thank God for that," the sergeant said,

"Oh, shit," remarked one of his men.

Their heads turned, to watch a line of German soldiers coming over the ridge.

The sergeant reached for his holster, but John grasped his wrist. There were at least twenty of the Germans and they were armed with rifles; the policemen did not stand a chance. "Are we prisoners, sir?" the sergeant asked.

"I'm afraid we are," John said, and stood up, raising his hands.

The policemen followed his example, but the Germans continued to advance cautiously, while now even more of them appeared over the ridge. "Throw down your weapons," came the command in English.

John and the policemen threw their revolvers on to the ground. "You are military police." The officer was young and a little nervous. "What are you doing here?"

"We were the last out of Benghazi," John said. "And our truck overturned."

The officer looked him up and down. "You will come with us."

They discovered, when they reached the coast, that they were not the only prisoners; several hundred Tommies and Australians were already on the road, marching west, looking as dejected as only those who have had the fruits of victory snatched from their grasp can. Also on the road was a considerable amount of armour, both German and Italian, making east as night fell. The enemy was certainly acting with an energy and decision that had been entirely lacking before.

John found himself in the company of several officers, some of whom he knew; he was relieved to discover that none of the Armoured Brigade were there, suggesting that perhaps the tanks had managed to get out. Or been wiped out.

"What the hell happened?" someone complained. "Just like that, boom."

"Panzers," said someone else. "They're unstoppable."

"Well, they'll have to be stopped some time, or we're going to lose this goddamed war."

"Brass," muttered someone else.

They were halted by the side of the road to allow several command cars to pass. The cars slowed at the sight of the British prisoners and the man in the back of the lead vehicle stood up. He was not a big man, but very compactly built. He wore the uniform of a German general, his high-peaked cap tilted slightly back on his head. His features were curious in that while they were softly rounded, the expression was granite-hard.

"I know that chap," said one of the officers. "Saw his photo in the papers. Name of Rommel. He was one of the chaps who duffed us up in France. With his Panzers."

"So he's had lots of practice," said someone else.

General Rommel gazed at the officers, then saluted them before driving on.

They were marched back into the city they had stormed so tumultuously only a few weeks earlier, and then evacuated so hurriedly only a few hours ago. Crowds lined the street, waving Italian and German flags, eager to prove their loyalty to the Fascist cause by shouting obscenities at the Tommies. Inside the city they were taken to the prison, where the officers were finally separated from the men. At least they were given something to eat and wine and water to drink; some of them were quite done up. And I never even had the opportunity to say goodbye to the sergeant and his policemen, John thought sadly.

"So what happens now?" asked Captain Rogers.

Major Reynolds, the senior officer present, replied. "I imagine we are going to be shipped across the Med to Italy," he said.

"Supposing we get there," someone commented, "and are not torpedoed by the Navy or blown up by the RAF?"

"Well, if that happens," Reynolds said, "we won't have anything more to worry about, right? Supposing it doesn't happen, we shall spend the rest of the War in an Italian prison camp. So, brace yourselves."

"It's pretty good in Italy in the spring," someone said.

"Yes, but then it'll be summer, and autumn and winter and spring all over again. Pretty damned tedious."

They were trying to keep their spirits up, John knew. He couldn't blame them. But what a foul-up. A prisoner all over again. And this time it looked like for keeps. The door opened and the officers instinctively stood to attention. There entered an Italian officer with four orderlies. The captain sat at the table, one of the orderlies on his left. "I am to take down your particulars," the captain said.

"Didn't know you were that sort, old boy," Reynolds said.

The British laughed, the Italians frowned. "Come along now. Name, rank and number, eh?"

The officers duly obliged. John was last. The Italian stroked his chin. "Warrey," he said. "Warrey. You were attached to the Seventh Armoured Brigade. But you are not a tank officer, Captain Warrey."

"I was learning," John explained.

The captain pointed with his pen. "You are an officer in British Intelligence. You will come with us."

"Captain Warrey is a British officer in uniform," Major Reynolds snapped. "He must be treated as such."

"I understand this," the Italian said. "Nevertheless, he will come with me." He stood up, and John looked at Reynolds.

"I suppose you'll have to go," Reynolds said, "but if there's any funny stuff we'll have this fellow's guts for garters when the War is over. Keep reminding him of that."

John left the room, escorted by four of the Italians. He was marched along a corridor, up some steps and into another room. "You told me to look out for this man's name, Colonel Umberto," the captain said.

Standing beside Umberto was Renaldo.

Chapter Twelve

The Victors

"Giovanni!" Umberto said. "You are like – what do they say in English? – it keeps turning up. . . ?"

"A bad penny," John said.

"Oh, yes, a bad penny. But in so many shapes and sizes, eh? First you are Miss Cartwright's navigator. Then you are a typewriter salesman. Now you are a soldier."

"There happens to be a war on."

"This man is a spy," Renaldo said. "He must be tried, convicted and shot."

"And you are a murdering bastard," John said, "who I am going personally to throttle one day."

Umberto was looking confused. "You two have met?"

"Don't try that one, old son," John said. "Wasn't it you sent him after us?"

"I am afraid I have no idea what you are speaking of," Umberto said.

"I will tell you," Renaldo said. "My superiors in our Military Intelligence were not happy with the way in which you let Warrey and Miss Cartwright go, after they had been caught red-handed, supplying arms to the Senussi. I was ordered to re-arrest them before they left Italian soil."

Umberto's face was cold. "Why was I not informed?"

Renaldo shrugged. "It was determined that you had developed a friendship for this man and might have interfered with the operation."

"And what happened?"

222

"We attempted to arrest them, as I have said, and they resisted. Seven of my men were killed. I was fortunate to escape."

Umberto stared at him. "How many were you arresting?"

"Well . . ." Renaldo looked embarrassed.

"There were three of us," John said. "Miss Cartright, myself, and my servant, Soroya. You met her, Umberto."

"But . . . one man and two women, killed seven of your people?" Umberto looked about to burst into laughter.

"These people are highly trained assassins," Renaldo declared.

"Oh, really, Renaldo," John said. "Would it interest you to know that when I fired at your people it was the first time in my life I had ever tried to kill somebody? And as you claim not to know about this, Umberto, I assume you do not know that both Miss Cartwright and Soroya were raped by this thug's men, and that Soroya was then murdered by them."

"That gorgeous creature is dead? My God! This is a very serious accusation."

"Those are all lies," Renaldo declared. "We ordered them to stop and without warning they opened fire. My men had not expected this. We returned fire as best we could, but taken by surprise as we were, as I have said, my people were all killed. I managed to get away. It is possible one of the women was hit. I cannot say for certain."

"You are a bloody liar," John said.

Umberto was looking from one to the other. "Can you prove what you say, Renaldo?" he asked.

"I am speaking the truth. He is the liar," Renaldo said.

"Can you prove what *you* say?" Umberto asked John.

"Not here."

"Ha," Renaldo commented.

"The only witness I have is Miss Cartwright, who escaped with me to Egypt," John said.

"Well, I intend to get to the bottom of this business," Umberto said. "Meanwhile . . ."

"Meanwhile, Warrey is to be held on charges of spying,"

223

Renaldo said. Umberto leaned back in his chair. "He was in plainclothes when he opened fire on my people," Renaldo said. "We know he had been on a spying mission here in Cyrenaica. I insist that he be tried."

"But you have no proof of this," Umberto argued. "You have just said that."

"I will obtain proof."

"How? Where?"

"When we take Tobruk. I will obtain proof there."

"Tobruk!"

"Do you suppose we shall not recapture Tobruk?" Renaldo demanded.

"Well. . ." Umberto was clearly in a difficult position, unwilling to be accused of defeatist talk. "I am sure we shall."

"At which time I will obtain proof of his spying. Meanwhile, he is to be placed under close arrest."

"He will go to Italy with the other prisoners."

"He will not," Renaldo insisted. "If necessary, I will appeal to General Graziani himself. This man will remain here in Cyrenaica under close arrest until his guilt it proven."

Umberto scratched his head. "It doesn't matter," John said, unwilling to make his friend's difficulties worse. "He will not be able to prove anything other than his own villainy."

John was locked in a cell in the police building. To his relief, the cell was high up rather than in some rat-infested dungeon; for this he supposed he could thank Umberto. From his eyrie he could watch the British and Australian and Indian prisoners marched down to the dock for embarkation for Italy. There were an awful lot of them. He was pleased to be where he was. He felt that once one was in Italy, one was there for the duration. But in North Africa . . . surely the British would be back.

The next couple of weeks were quite comfortable. He was well treated, had a bottle of wine every day with his meals, was exercised and allowed to shower every day. Nor was he lonely, as he was visited almost daily by Umberto, enquiring after his health, and by Renaldo, alternately threatening and mocking. John felt he could put up with this until the tables were turned. But every time he thought of Soroya, sprawled on the sand, he had to exert all his willpower to stop himself leaping on the Italian and strangling him there and then. Patience, until O'Connor counter-attacked, as surely he would. Until the day Renaldo came in, all smiles. "I have something to show you, Mr Warrey. Come with me, please."

John raised his eyebrows, then saw the four armed guards waiting in the corridor. He was escorted down the stairs, not to the ground floor, but to a window overlooking the courtyard. "There, you see," Renaldo said.

John frowned through the window and could not believe his eyes. Several command cars had just entered the yard and their occupants were disembarking. Two of them were general officers – O'Connor and Neame.

"There you have it," Renaldo said. "The entire British high command. Taken in Derna, totally surprised by our thrust across the desert. We are now driving for Tobruk and Egypt. Nothing can stop us."

"You?" John asked. "Surely you mean the Germans?"

Renaldo grinned. "The Germans are assisting us, to be sure. Now look over there. Is that another pleasant sight?"

John followed the direction indicated, and once again felt he had been kicked in the stomach. From another command car three uniformed women were being made to get down – and one of them was Margo. "She is wearing uniform," John said.

"What is a uniform?" Renaldo chuckled. "Merely an outer covering. It can easily be taken off. I intend to hang the pair of you, beside each other, in Tobruk. After we have . . . talked a little, eh?"

John didn't waste his time asking if he would be allowed to talk with Margo first. At least, from a distance, she did not look as if she had been roughed up in any way. And she was here in this same building with him. He didn't know what value that might turn out to be.

Umberto came to visit him the next day. "It has been a disaster for the British," he said. "Two generals, just like that. And O'Connor . . . a brilliant man. But then, one has to say it, this man Rommel is even more brilliant. You know that Graziani has resigned?"

"No, I didn't know that. Who is to be his replacement?"

"There are several names being bandied about. This is not good for us. Or you, my friend. Graziani was a soldier of the old school. Now we are liable to get some ferocious Fascist in his place. Someone to match the Germans, eh?"

"It'll all be academic," John suggested, "when General Wavell counter-attacks and drives you all back into Libya."

Umberto smiled. "That is not going to happen, Giovanni. Our troops are across the border into Egypt, and this time we are not going to be driven out."

"You mean Tobruk is in your hands?"

"No. Tobruk is holding out. But it is quite invested, except for the sea, of course. It will fall."

"I wouldn't count on it."

"I will tell you why it will fall, Giovanni. It will fall because you do not have the men, or the material, to relieve it. The Germans have invaded Greece and Wavell has been ordered to send as much of his command as he can spare to relieve the Greeks. You are simply overstretched. There will be no counter-attacks. General Rommel expects to be in Cairo by the autumn."

"At which time you will expect Tobruk to fall. Renaldo is rubbing his hands."

"Yes. It is difficult. There can be no doubt that you were in civilian clothes when you were in Tobruk last year. I may believe that you did not know the war had started between Italy and Great Britain, but you may have a difficult task persuading a military court of that. And then, if you did shoot up Renaldo's party . . . did you really kill seven men, Giovanni?"

"You haven't cautioned me," John grinned.

"Oh, I will only testify in your favour. But I do not know how much I will be able to do."

"Listen, Umberto, how is Miss Cartwright?"

"As well as can be expected."

"Just what do you mean by that?"

"As with all the people we captured in Derna, she is feeling dejected."

"But she has not been ill-treated?"

"Of course not. She is a soldier captured in uniform. This time."

"Will you give me your word that she will not be ill-treated?"

"Certainly. As long as I am in command, no prisoner-of-war will ever be ill-treated."

"Thank you. I don't suppose I could have a word with her?"

"That is not possible."

"Right. Then I wonder if you could let her know that I am alive and well?"

"I think I can do that."

"And the immediate future?"

"You will remain here, under guard, until Tobruk has fallen. Then you will be tried. I will do my best to help you and Miss Cartwright. But . . . we must hope for the best."

Or a miracle, John supposed. If Wavell had indeed been forced to send all his reserves to Greece, then there *was* no hope of a counter-attack. Nor, he supposed, was there much hope of Tobruk holding out. From his window he watched Generals O'Connor and Neame being embarked for Italy. Now he wished he could be going with them. With Margo, of course.

He did not see her again, as his window did not overlook the courtyard where the prisoners were exercised, and he was always exercised on his own. All other prisoners were only passing through. He watched the women captured with Margo being embarked, but she was not with them. Renaldo meant what he had said. The news he received, relayed by Renaldo with great glee, was all bad. The British had been thrown out of Greece, then out of Crete. Their attempts to relieve Tobruk had failed. Rommel was preparing for the final drive on Cairo. "Your people are done, eh?" Renaldo told him. "Why do they not just surrender?"

There was the odd letter from home, from both his mother and Aileen, but they were so heavily censored they were meaningless. Not, he supposed, that they would have been very meaningful in any event: England, Aileen, Sam Carson, old George Brand, Bullock, his mates at the training school, all seemed like creatures from another planet.

Renaldo visited him, as usual grinning from ear to ear. "Your Churchill has finally sacked Wavell," he announced.

"So who do we get now?" John asked.

"Some fellow with a quite unpronounceable name. Archangel or something like that."

"Auchinleck," John suggested. He knew that Sir Claude Auchinleck had been proving quite a success commanding the Empire forces in the Middle East.

"That is it," Renaldo said. "He will take command just in time to surrender Cairo."

John had to riposte. "Seems to me every time you visit me you say Cairo is about to fall. I've been here for two months. What's holding you up?"

"Logistics. Rommel wishes to have full stocks of petrol and ammunition before he launches the final attack. These all have to brought up from Tripoli, you know. It will happen, my friend."

The very next day the Germans launched their attack upon Russia.

Presumably Mussolini had been informed of the coming offensive; there were, apparently, Italian troops, as well as Rumanian, Hungarian and Finnish, taking part alongside the Germans.

Yet it had all been a closely guarded secret and the Italians in Benghazi were totally surprised. But equally totally confident. "Russia is in a mess," Umberto declared. "Well, look at what happened to them when they tried to invade Finland. It is because Stalin shot all his top generals back in 1937. Most of the Russian people hate Stalin and his henchmen anyway. The Soviet State will collapse like a punctured balloon."

It was difficult to know how much of what the Italians said was true and how much sheer propaganda. But even if the figures for Russian losses in men, tanks, aircraft and territory as related by Umberto and Renaldo were to be halved, it was still clear that the Soviets were suffering immense and perhaps unsustainable losses. It was galling to have such great events going on and be locked up in a prison cell, not knowing what was going to happen . . . and to be greeted by Renaldo one morning in the autumn with one of his offensive grins. "Don't tell me," John said. "Rommel is at last ready to advance into Egypt."

"Bah," Renaldo said. "He is already in Egypt."

"But not yet in Cairo, eh?"

"Bah," Renaldo said again. "It is Tobruk I wish to talk about."

John's heart gave a painful lurch. "You've captured it?"

"No, they are fighting like dogs to hold it. But you know, they have a system. They use their fast destroyers to replace whole regiments, and any important personages, when they feel it is necessary. You understand, Giovanni, that this is a very dangerous enterprise. Every time they lose one or two ships to our bombers and our submarines. Then most of the people being evacuated are drowned. This is very sad, eh? But some are rescued and captured." Icy fingers closing on John's heart. "One of their ships was sunk three nights ago," Renaldo explained, "and several of the men on board were captured. They have been brought to Benghazi. Amongst them is someone I am sure you would like to meet again. Come."

He gestured to the guards who always accompanied him and

the door of the cell was opened. John walked through various corridors, to arrive before the door of another cell. He dared not try to decide who it might be; it could only be one of two or three people. People who knew he had been a spy. And he was right. The door was opened for him.

"Roberto," Renaldo said. "Here is your old friend, John Warrey. Giovanni, you remember Roberto Quesmi, I am sure."

Roberto looked very much the worse for wear. It appeared that he had not been given a change of clothing since his shipwreck, and his shirt and pants were stiff with dried salt water, while he was shoeless. He also looked as if he might have been roughed up a little, but the bruises could have been suffered when the ship had gone down, or when he was being rescued afterwards. He retained his spirit, however, and his control of himself. "Who is this man?" he asked.

"Come now, Roberto," Renaldo said.

"I have never seen him before in my life," Roberto declared.

Renaldo looked at John. "Should I know him?" John asked.

"You are two very foolish men," Renaldo said. "Do you not know that I have witnesses to the fact that Signor Warrey came to Tobruk to see you, Roberto?"

"Ahem," John said. "Captain Warrey, if you please."

"Where are these witnesses?" Roberto asked.

"They are still in Tobruk," Renaldo admitted. "Or perhaps dead. But no matter, I have you. You need to listen to me very carefully, both of you. My superiors say that I cannot question Signor Warrey very closely, or Miss Cartwright, because they are British officers wearing uniform when they were captured. I can only question them closely if I can first prove that they have been spying, out of uniform, in Cyrenaica before or since the declaration of war. And I did not suppose I could do that until we retook Tobruk. But now you have fallen into my hands, and you, Roberto, have no rights at all. I can do whatever I wish with you. And then, you see, when you have confessed that Signor

Warrey and Miss Cartwright are spies, I can do what I like with them also. Are you listening?"

"I know nothing of Miss Cartwright," Roberto muttered.

"Ah, but you do know about Signor Warrey."

John found he was holding his breath. "I am an import–export agent," Roberto said. "Before the War I dealt with several firms in Cairo. One of them sold typewriters. This man came to me with samples of typewriters. I gave him the addresses of certain people I knew might be interested in buying his machines. I suppose he saw those people. Then he went back to Cairo, as far as I know."

"He was obviously not wearing uniform when he was selling typewriters," Renaldo said.

"I did not know he was in the Army."

"You see how easy it is?" Renaldo asked.

"I'm afraid I don't know what you're on about," John said. "What Signor Quesmi has told you is the truth. Before the War I was employed to sell typewriters. When the War started, I was recruited by the British Army. The two things are not related."

"But they are. Because you then returned to Sheikh Ali with arms and ammunition. You and Miss Cartwright." Renaldo grinned. "Still wearing civilian clothes."

"I know nothing about the guns," John insisted. "And as I told Colonel Umberto, when Miss Cartwright and I left Cairo, with the intention of employing guides from Sheikh Ali's tribe to lead us into the desert, war had not yet been declared."

"Lies," Renaldo said. "All lies. Admit it, Roberto. You introduced Signor Warrey to Sheikh Ali. You set the whole thing up."

"I do not know Sheikh Ali," Roberto said.

Renaldo regarded him for several moments, then shrugged. "As you wish. But you know, you are going to tell us everything, eventually. If you do so now, it would go far better for you."

Roberto hunched his shoulders.

"Bring the woman," Renaldo told one of his people.

"If you touch Miss Cartwright . . ." John said.

"You are such a knight in shining armour, Mr Warrey," Renaldo said. "I am very much looking forward to touching Miss Cartwright. But first, she will watch."

The door opened and Margo was pushed in; they had now been joined by three more of Renaldo's men. Margo was flushed and her uniform dishevelled. But she was more incredulous than outraged. "Johnnie?" she asked. "I thought you were dead."

"He may well wish he was," Renaldo said.

"You!" Margo snapped. "You bastard!"

Renaldo stepped up to her. "You are going to amuse me very much," he said.

Margo spat in his face.

"I don't think she's really into men," John said.

Renaldo wiped his face. "Ha," he said. "Ha, ha, ha. Then I shall introduce her, perhaps. But first, sit." His voice suddenly cracked like a whip and Margo sank into a chair. "And you," Renaldo told John.

John obeyed. The odds against him, seven to one, were again too great without a weapon – and he did not know how reliable Roberto would be in a punch-up – while overlaying the entire situation was the certainty that there was no way out of this building.

"Now, you see," Renaldo said, "This fellow Roberto is proving stubborn. We are now going to make life very difficult for him. You hear this, Roberto? Would you not like to tell us the truth?" Roberto licked his lips. "Feed him," Renaldo commanded.

Roberto's head jerked, but his arms were firmly gripped by two of the guards, pushing him downwards into the chair. Another guard gripped his jaws, forcing them open, and a fourth uncorked a bottle which gave off a noxious smell. "Castor oil," Renaldo explained. "It is good for the bowels in small doses. But unpleasant to take. And if one has too much of it . . ."

Roberto was making a a horrible noise as he tried to speak and could not; the top of the bottle had been pushed into his mouth.

A lot of the oil spilt on his shirt and thence the floor, but equally a lot went down his throat. "My God," Margo muttered.

"Do not worry, my pretty maid," Renaldo said. "You shall have some too. It is better than burning your sex with electrodes. Although maybe we shall do that as well, eh?"

The bottle was taken away, Roberto panted and vomited as the oil attacked his stomach, and he fell from his chair to groan and writhe on the floor. "Speak," Renaldo recommended. "While you can." Roberto panted and vomited some more. "Give him another dose," Renaldo commanded.

The guards knelt beside him and once again his jaws were grasped. "When we are finished with you, you will never wish to go to the john again," Renaldo said.

"Wait!" Roberto screamed. Renaldo nodded, and Roberto's jaws were released. "I am sorry, Giovanni," Roberto panted. "They will kill me."

John said nothing. There was nothing to say until he had heard what Roberto was going to confess.

"Well?" Renaldo said.

"I set Giovanni up with contacts in Cyrenaica," Roberto said. "This was done through a man named Carmichael, who managed a typewriter agency in Cairo. But his people were all military intelligence. They posed as commercial travellers to gain information about our dispositions in Libya and Somaliland."

"And Sheikh Ali?"

"I introduced Giovanni to Sheikh Ali. That is all. I know nothing of any guns, or any arrangements between Giovanni and the sheikh. And I never met Miss Cartwright before today. I swear these things on my mother's grave."

"And I am sure your mother would be heartily ashamed of you," Renaldo said. "You say you knew nothing of any guns, or any arrangements Sheikh Ali might have made with the British. But you knew he was opposed to Il Duce, to Italian rule in Cyrenaica."

Roberto sighed. "I knew this, yes."

233

"Yet you sent Giovanni to Ali. What did you suppose they were going to talk about? The next eclipse of the moon? You have confessed to spying against Il Duce. You are going to be hanged."

Roberto began to weep as he slowly pushed himself up. "I have told you what I know. You said it would go better for me."

"Well, it will. I will not feed you any more castor oil. But you will make a written statement of what you have just said and sign it. Now, Giovanni, you have been identified as a spy. Will you not tell us about it and name your contacts?"

"What you have just heard is a pack of lies," John said.

"This is very foolish of you," Renaldo said. "Would you like some castor oil? Or shall I feed Miss Cartwright?" Margo gasped. Renaldo stood above her. "I think you and I have a lot to speak about," he said. "But let us go somewhere where the air is not so foul." He jerked his head and Margo was pulled to her feet. "After all," Renaldo said. "Our last conversation was so rudely interrupted."

"Margo," John said. "Tell him what he wants to know."

Renaldo grinned. "And save her skin, eh? Well, it might save her something."

The door was opened and Margo thrust out, to be checked by the appearance of Umberto, who had several of his policemen with him.

"What has happened here?" Umberto demanded.

"I have been doing my job, Colonel," Renaldo said. "The man Quesmi has made a complete confession."

Umberto's nostrils twitched. "You have tortured him."

"I gave him a little drink, that is all."

"And now he intends to give Miss Cartwright a little drink as well," John said.

"I will take charge of these prisoners," Umberto said.

Renaldo glared at him. "They are my prisoners, Colonel."

"I have an order here, consigning them to my custody."

"An order? Signed by whom?"

"By General Rommel."

Renaldo snorted. "This is an Italian matter. It has nothing to do with the Germans."

"The Germans believe that it does, if these people have information regarding the dispositions of the Senussi in Cyrenaica."

"You told Rommel this?"

"You will obey this order, Major."

Renaldo hesitated, then clicked his heels and saluted. He waved at his men and they marched off.

"Well," John said. "I never thought I would be glad to be in the care of the Germans." Margo's legs gave way and she slid down the wall of the corridor to sit on the floor. Roberto was still groaning and twisting.

"Have that fellow attended to," Umberto said. "My God, the stench." He ushered John out of the cell, bent over Margo. "Are you all right, Miss Cartwright?"

"I'll recover," Margo muttered, and straightened her skirt.

"Come." Umberto led them to his own office on the floor below, closed the door. "Now listen very carefully," he said in a low tone. "I may have been able to save you from Renaldo, but I am not sure if I can save you from the Germans. To get this precious piece of paper," he tapped the order on his desk, "I had to convince General Rommel that you know a great deal about Senussi intentions and dispositions, and were, in fact, intended to lead a desert revolt, like Lawrence in the last war, eh?"

John and Margo exchanged glances; it was very close to the truth. "The general is concerned about this," Umberto went on, "because already there have been clashes between his patrols and the Arabs. So you see, he will wish to question you. I think General Rommel is an honourable man, but he has a war to win, and for all our propaganda it is not really going well. The men and tanks, and the aircraft he needs to conquer Egypt have been taken away from him and sent to Russia. If you do not answer his questions, he may well turn you over to the Gestapo, and that would not be nice at all. For you. Even if you do answer his questions, you may still be shot. So it is, how do you say, out of the stove and into the oven, eh?"

"Close," John said. "What you mean is, we're no further ahead."

"Listen," Umberto said. "I will help you."

"Help us to do what?"

"I am going to take you to General Rommel. He is presently close to the front line. Therefore to reach him we must pass Tobruk. This is invested, as you know, by our troops. But there are ways in and out, for one or two determined men." He grinned at Margo. "Or even women. If I were to halt for the night, it might be possible for you to escape and get into the city. Once you are there, you will be able to leave, by what they call the Tobruk Express, eh? You must realise this is very dangerous. You could be shot escaping, you could be shot by your own people trying to get into the town, or you could be torpedoed, like poor Roberto, when you try to leave."

"What about Roberto? We can't possibly leave him here to be duffed up by Renaldo's thugs."

"We can take him with us," Umberto agreed. "But that will increase the risk; he is not a reliable man when it comes to physical matters."

"Nonetheless, he has proved himself a brave one. Now tell me, Umberto, why are you going to help us again?"

Umberto shrugged. "Perhaps I do not believe that Great Britain and Italy have any business being at war. It is a madness, between two such people, with such a history of shared culture and co-operation." He gave one of his disarming grins. "Besides, I like you. Both of you. And I wish to atone, if I can, for the murder of that so beautiful Arab woman."

"For which kind thoughts I can forgive you anything," John said.

"You do realise that you have just spoken treason?" Margo pointed out.

"Of course, but you are the only two who can testify to it. I am placing my life in your hands, as your lives are in mine."

"And when you let us escape?"

"I am not going to *let* you escape, Margo. You are going to do it, even if I have to tell you how and when."

"I think we'd better get with it," John decided.

They had to submit to being handcuffed, along with Roberto, and placed in the back of Umberto's command car. This was not only to satisfy the onlookers in the prison compound, but also Umberto's driver.

"Where are we going?" Roberto asked. He looked terrible, as might any man after an overdose of castor oil, and shivered all the time, despite the heat. "To visit General Rommel," John told him.

Roberto gulped. "If we are handed over to the Germans, we will be tortured and then shot," he complained.

"At least they don't use castor oil," John pointed out.

There was no way they could let as depressed and at the same time excitable a character as Roberto into Umberto's plan. In any event, John was more interested in the whereabouts of Renaldo – or the lack of whereabouts. He would have supposed the military policeman would have wished to see them go . . . but Renaldo was not to be seen.

"He's probably sulking in his tent," Margo suggested. John hoped she was right.

It was getting on for three hundred miles from Benghazi to Tobruk, following the coast road. It was mid-morning when they left, and they lunched at Tolemaide, sitting in the car and gazing at the Roman ruins. "When this is over," Margo said, "I'd like to come back and have a closer look at those."

"I will show you them myself," Umberto said gallantly.

Progress continued to be slow, for the road had been badly damaged during the fighting, and there was a constant stream of traffic, both going and coming, while they were forced to shelter at the side of the road when in mid-afternoon they were attacked by a swarm of RAF bombers. "Now that would be a turn-up," John said, huddling in a ditch beside Margo, "if after all this we were to be blown up by the RAF."

"I'm glad you can joke about it," Margo said.

John was actually more worried about the car, without which all their plans would come to nothing, but it survived and soon they were on their way again, now further impeded by ambulances and wounded and dying men. "We will not reach the front line tonight, Signor Colonel," remarked the driver.

"We must go as far as we can," Umberto said.

His idea, of course, was to reach Tobruk during the middle of the night and then call a halt.

"Planes," Margo said.

But although, to their alarm, it swept low over them, it was only a single plane, an Italian one, flying east. "Now where would he be going?" John asked.

"It could be any one of several places," Umberto said. "The Germans have laid down airstrips all over the place."

John wriggled his fingers together to restore circulation and wondered why he suddenly felt uneasy.

At dusk they had reached Derna and the driver again raised the matter of resting for the night. Umberto agreed that they should dine in a restaurant, for which purpose the prisoners were released from their cuffs, although Umberto felt obliged to accompany them each in turn to the toilet, including Margo.

"He definitely fancies me," she told John when she returned, pink-cheeked, and speaking English. "What do we do if he requires some form of payment for all this?"

"We do what has to be done," John told her. "Don't we?" She glared at him. "Lie back and think of England."

* * *

It was nine o'clock when they finally left Derna and they had not driven very far when they saw flashes on the horizon. "They are bombarding Tobruk," Umberto said.

He had not handcuffed them after dinner, ostentatiously demanding a parole. The driver had made no comment. Now it was utterly dark on the road and they drove under dipped headlights. There were still people all about them and their progress was even slower, until it came to a full stop at a roadblock.

This was manned by German soldiers, who required to inspect Umberto's credentials. "You will have to take the subsidiary route," said the lieutenant in command, in passable Italian. "The main road is under fire."

"Of course," Umberto said. "Drive on."

John watched the German officer return to his caravan and through the open door saw him pick up the telephone. His uneasiness grew.

The new route, clearly a hastily laid roadway, was hardly better than a track, at once bumpy and pot-holed and, even late at night, crowded. As Umberto's driver was now very tired, their progress slowed almost to a walking pace. "All right," Umberto said, apparently grudgingly, studying his map with the light from his torch. "There is a command post another mile along the road. Pull in there and we will sleep until dawn."

"What's that noise?" Margo asked.

From away to the east there was an explosion of sound and once again the night sky was lit up by glaring discharges. "General Rommel must have commenced his final advance," Umberto suggested.

John and Margo squeezed hands; if that were true, and Rommel was to win again, getting into Tobruk would accomplish nothing, as if Egypt fell the town certainly would. "Here," Umberto said.

The car swung off the roadway and onto an even more bumpy track. But now there were lights, and several people, all Italians in this case. Umberto stepped down and was saluted by an anxious lieutenant. "I have prisoners here for General

Rommel to interrogate," Umberto said. "What is happening up there?"

"The British are counter-attacking, Colonel," the lieutenant said.

"Yippee," Margo commented.

"That is not possible, after their defeat," Umberto said.

"It is happening, Signor Colonel."

"Then where is the General?" Umberto inquired.

"I do not know, Colonel. The situation is very confused."

Umberto chewed his lip. "Well," he decided, again with apparent reluctance. "We must find him. But my driver is exhausted. We must rest for a few hours. We will look for the General at daybreak. It is most important that he see these prisoners. Now, we wish beds for the night."

"Beds, Colonel?"

"The floor will do. I meant accommodation."

"Yes, sir. And the prisoners?"

"My orders are not to let them out of my sight," Umberto said. "We will share the accommodation."

The lieutenant looked at Margo and rolled his eyes, then gave orders to his sergeant. They were led out of the command post and to another recently erected hut, empty of any furniture save for a table and chairs, but there were some blankets in the corner. "This will have to do," Umberto said. "Send my driver to me."

The sergeant saluted and hurried off. "Now you know what to do," Umberto said. "But please do not hurt either my man or me more than is necessary. You understand this?"

"Yes. And we will always be grateful to you, Umberto." John grinned. "Again. Give me your revolver." Umberto obeyed, and John stood by the door. Margo was already tearing the blankets into strips.

Roberto was looking from one to the other, eyes rolling. "What is happening?" he asked.

"Just do what you're told," John advised.

"Anything you're told," Margo added.

240

The door opened, the driver stepped inside. John pushed the door shut and held his revolver to the nape of the man's neck. "Utter a sound, and you are a dead man."

The driver gasped, and before he had time to take in his surroundings, Margo was strapping a strip of blanket round his eyes; if he had seen anything, it would have been Umberto standing against the wall with his hands up. By now Roberto had got into the act, and between them he and Margo bound and gagged the driver and laid him on the floor. The driver also had a revolver and Margo thrust this into her waistband; John had an idea she did not intend to be captured again – alive.

"Take off your jacket and cap," John told Umberto, who again obeyed. John tried them on. They didn't fit very well, but in the darkness he did not suppose anyone would notice. He nodded to Margo and Roberto, and Umberto was also bound and gagged and blindfolded. John was testing the single window at the rear of the room. He doused the lantern, plunging them into utter darkness, and opened the window.

The noise outside was tremendous; a siren was wailing and the sound of gunfire seemed very close. Could Auchinleck really have recovered sufficiently to mount a successful counter-attack? That actually cut both ways. If they could survive long enough they stood a good chance of being rescued. But if the attack was really being successful the Italians might wish to pull back, in which case Umberto and his driver would be discovered far more quickly than they had anticipated. "Let's go," he said, and climbed out of the window to drop to the sandy soil. Margo followed and Roberto came last.

As Roberto dropped to the ground, the door was thrown open and the room flooded with flashlight beams. "Colonel Umberto!" It was Renaldo.

"Run like hell!" John hissed, grasping Margo's arm and hurrying her into the night. But it was no longer dark, with car and truck headlamps shining in every direction.

"Halt!" someone bellowed. John straightened his cap and stood straight. "Sir!" The sentry came to attention as he recognised John's rank.

"I must take these prisoners to safety," John said. "Find me a vehicle."

"Over there, sir." The sentry pointed to several trucks and cars, close together, all with their engines running, awaiting orders to move off.

"Eureka," John muttered.

"Stop those people!" The shout came from behind them. Renaldo! John swung his fist and sent the sentry tumbling. He dropped beside him, snatched his rifle and threw it to Roberto, who without hesitation swung round, fell to one knee and sent several shots winging back towards the command post. Someone screamed and fell; John hoped it was Renaldo.

But they weren't going to make the motor pool now. People were yelling and several more shots were fired; the Italians seemed to be shooting at each other. John seized Margo's arm and jumped into a ditch which led to a half underground bunker. Roberto was behind them and they ran along, bending double, while the shouts and the firing came closer. Four men were in the bunker, manning a machine-gun and looking utterly confused. They blinked at the apparent colonel in alarm. "Out," John commanded. "The British are here."

"But the gun, Signor Colonel!"

"Abandon it. There is no time to dismantle it. Do you wish to be taken prisoner?" The men exchanged glances, and John suspected that they thought that might not be a bad option. But they would not dare confess that to a colonel, and instead clambered out of the concrete shelter. "Guard the back," John told Roberto, and peered through the slit through which the machine-gun protruded. This overlooked the roadway and to his amazement he saw a whole mass of armour rolling down it. German armour, in full retreat! Maybe the British *were* coming.

"Do we shoot?" Margo asked.

"Not on your nelly. They're going in the right direction for a change."

"Trouble," Roberto whispered.

There were voices very close. "They cannot just have disappeared," Renaldo said. "They are here somewhere. English spies."

"The order is to retreat, Signor Major," someone protested.

"We must find these people first," Renaldo said. "Do you think I flew all this way to let them get away?"

"So it was him in that plane," John muttered. "He's a persevering cuss."

"Spread out," Renaldo was commanding. "You down there," he bellowed into the bunker. "We are looking for three escaped spies, two men and a woman. Have you seen them?"

John knew Renaldo would recognise his voice if he replied, and probably Roberto's as well. And the machine-gun was facing the wrong way. In the darkness it was difficult to determine how many men the policeman had with him. "Wait," he whispered.

"You in there," Renaldo shouted again. "Are you struck dumb?"

"Perhaps they have left," someone said.

"Without orders? I will have them shot for desertion. I am coming in," he shouted.

Roberto fired at the first man who dropped into the ditch, and he fell with a shout. But it was not Renaldo. Margo flattened herself against the wall, firing as she did so, and John also fired along the ditch and was then struck a savage blow in the thigh. There was no pain, only a tremendous feeling of breathlessness. My God, he thought. After all that, I've been hit.

"Got the bastards," Renaldo said, standing above John and shining his flashlight down. By thus limiting his visibility he overlooked Margo, crouching in the dark corner, and she shot him at close range. He gave a gurgling gasp and fell, half across John.

243

Roberto kept firing, again and again, until he ran out of bullets. But the rest of the Italians had retreated following the fall of their commander. Margo dragged Renaldo off John, knelt beside him. "Is it bad?"

"I have no idea. I don't feel a thing."

"You're losing a lot of blood." She tore open his pants to look at the wound, took off her jacket and then her shirt to tear into strips.

"I never knew you cared that much!" he muttered.

"Silly boy."

"Help me," Renaldo groaned. "Help me."

Margo turned her head to look at him.

"I am wounded," he said. "Badly wounded."

Cut off his balls, Arsinoe had said, John remembered. Now the pain was starting as the shock wore off.

"Listen," Renaldo said. "When my people come back, and you are again taken prisoner, I will not harm you, if you help me now."

"And suppose your people do not come back?" Margo asked. "And ours do?" The noise continued to be tremendous, and was coming closer.

Renaldo forced a grin. "Then I am your prisoner. I am an officer in uniform and must be treated accordingly."

"You are a filthy, raping bastard," Margo said. "I ought to shoot you again, in the gut. But I'll let you lie there and bleed."

"Help me, for the love of God," Renaldo moaned.

John shrugged. "Help him. We're supposed to be fighting for the preservation of civilisation."

"I have no more clothes to spare," Margo said coldly.

"I will help him," Roberto volunteered.

"Men!" Margo remarked.

Then they waited for several hours, while it became light and all hell was let loose above and around them. John felt weak from blood loss, and the pain was now considerable. They heard cheering.

"Do we go up?" Margo asked.

"Wait," John told her. "Better wake him up."

Roberto, who had bandaged Renaldo and was sitting beside him, shook the policeman's shoulder, and again, then bent over him. "He is dead."

"Civilised behaviour," Margo commented.

"We tried," John said.

They listened to a voice, which came down the far end of the tunnel. "Anyone in there?" It was speaking English.

"We thought you were dead," Blanchard confessed. "The Italians didn't list you amongst their prisoners."

"They had other plans for me, and Margo. Where is she, by the way?"

"Haven't a clue, old man. But your friend Quesmi is doing well."

"And Umberto?"

"Don't know him."

"He was Chief of Police in Tobruk. He was the man who really got us out."

"You'll have to check the POW lists. If you have time. You're down for a spot of leave, whenever you get out of this hospital. And that medal, of course."

"You go?" Arsinoe looked utterly shattered. "Always you go. This time, you come back?"

"I really have no idea."

"And we never have sex," Arsinoe pointed out. "Maybe this the last time."

"Ah, yes. What a splendid idea. But I really have to rush. Listen, I'll be in touch."

"You go," she said sadly, and sat on the bed, hands dangling between her knees.

*   *   *

245

The party due for leave assembled in the lobby of Shepheard's Hotel. Everyone was in the best of humours, not only at the thought of actually going home, but because the British and Allied counter-attack had been so successful. Tobruk had been relieved, and the Allies were almost back at El Agheila.

"Can we hold it this time?" John asked Carmichael, who had come to see him off.

"I don't see any reason why not. The Germans are pouring every man they have into Russia. Rommel has to make do with what he has. Oh, we'll hold our ground." He grinned. "So we won't need you any more, eh?"

"I wonder where they'll send me next."

"Probably India or somewhere your Italian will be invaluable."

John grinned in turn and watched Margo coming towards him. She was as soignée as he ever remembered her, had had her hair done, was made up . . . and might never have spent a night in the desert. "Don't tell me you're coming home with us?"

"No," she said. "I'm staying here, at least for a while. I was thinking, we still have some unfinished business."

"I think we're due to go up to Alexandria and board this afternoon."

She wrinkled her nose. "Ships that pass in the night."

"It's been some night." He kissed her.

"We will get together, one day," she said.

"I wouldn't bet on it. The first thing I am going to do when I get back to England is get married."

John was home just after Christmas, to the news that the Americans were in the War. "So I would say we should win," George Brand said. "Although it will still take some time, as we have to fight the Japanese as well. However . . . how's the leg?"

"Recovering, sir. I'm told I should be able to throw away the stick in a week or two."

"That's good. You want to be able to stand to attention at the investiture, eh?"

"And at my wedding, sir."

"Oh, quite. Absolutely. No regrets, there?"

Just how much does the old beggar know, John wondered. "Should I have, sir?" he asked, innocently.

Should I have, he wondered? No man could go to war and not have regrets, as well as might-have-beens. And an awareness that he was really nothing more than a chance of fate, that he was alive where so many were dead. Had Soroya lived, could he have held Aileen in his arms and given a passable imitation of being totally in love? He did not suppose Soroya had actually loved him, but she had given a very passable imitation of being his wife, with all the immense, concentrated passion that she had possessed. Life with Soroya would have had its pits as well as its peaks, but it would never have been dull.

Had Margo . . . but Margo was an eternal enigma, pursuing her own way through life. He had no doubt she was grateful to him for saving her life, and would have expressed that gratitude in any way he chose . . . but that was most certainly not love.

As for Sam Conway . . . He yielded sufficiently to temptation to telephone Blitton Hall. He thought it might be a good idea for her to see how he had turned out, resplendent with the ribbon of the MC pinned to his tunic, with a wound to show for his experiences . . . nothing more than that. "I'm sorry, sir," said the voice on the end of the phone. "We have no one by that name here."

Either he was firmly in the past, or she had achieved her ambition and been posted in the field. He wondered where? As would he be, eventually, when he had honeymooned and been pronounced fully fit. Aileen in fact was moving on sooner, as she had had only a week's leave. "Do you know that you have never once talked about the war in the desert," she remarked, as she packed. "Was it that bad?"

"Sand, flies and corpses," he said. "Not a good subject for a honeymoon."

She closed her suitcase and he took her in his arms. They were married, she wore his ring and she had done everything he could possibly ask of a wife during the past week. Yet they remained utter strangers and presumably would stay strangers, until the War was over and they could set up house somewhere. On another planet, perhaps. "Happy?" he asked.

"Oh, yes. Or I will be, when I feel I have all of you and am no longer sharing with the Army."

"It'll happen," he assured her.

The phone rang. "John Warrey? War Office here. You've been posted."

"Well, thanks for waiting until the end of my honeymoon. Where am I going?"

"It's back to Egypt, I'm afraid, old man. Rommel has sprung a counter-attack, and there's a spot of bother. You leave tomorrow. Embarkation orders will be delivered tonight."

"Egypt," John breathed.

"Egypt?" Aileen asked. "Again?"

"Seems there's a spot of bother," John said.

But oh, how he wanted to go.   ▪